T0349451

# TRINITY

A NOVEL FROM THE IMAGINATION OF
# TOM DELONGE
# TRINITY
WITH NEW YORK TIMES BESTSELLING AUTHOR
## A.J. HARTLEY

# TRINITY

BY TOM DELONGE AND A.J. HARTLEY

BASED ON THE ORIGINAL SCREENPLAY BY NICK NEVADA

Copyright © 2024 To The Stars Media Inc.

All rights reserved. No portion of this book may be reproduced in any fashion, print, facsimile, or electronic, or by any method yet to be developed, without express written permission of the publisher. This is a work of fiction. Names, characters, places and incidents are the product of the author's imagination or are used fictitiously. Any resemblance to actual persons, living or dead, or to actual events, are unintended and entirely coincidental.

To The Stars Media Inc.
1150 Garden View Road, Box #230393, Encinitas, CA 92024
ToTheStars.Media
*To The Stars… and Sekret Machines is a trademark of To the Stars, Inc.*

Cover Design by Joe Brisbois
Book Design by Lamp Post
Managing Editor: Kari DeLonge

Manufactured in the United States of America

ISBN 978-1-943272-43-3 (Hard Cover trade)
ISBN 978-1-943272-44-0 (eBook)
ISBN 978-1-943272-47-1 (Hard Cover Limited Edition)

Distributed worldwide by Simon & Schuster

## ACKNOWLEDGMENTS

Thanks to Vernon Goode and Gerald Coleman.

# PROLOGUE

It's a tricky thing, memory. Some things it locks in tight like a bug in amber, perfectly preserved so you can take them out years, even decades, later and find them just as they were, perfect in every detail. This kind of memory is rare. Precious. Others get changed, expanded with things that never happened. Details borrowed from other events, other times, get tacked on till the memories themselves are only partly true, and it's not clear which parts those are. And, of course, other parts get dropped entirely, like stones in the ocean that sink without a trace, vanishing into the dark. It's said that you can train your memory to hold on to the things you want and discard the rest. And I've also heard that all your memories are really still there, fully intact, but over time we lose the maps and keys that would find them and open them up.

I guess that could be true. I don't know.

What I do know, is that it's not always good to remember, that you're better moving on, shedding the past like snakeskin and never looking back. But sometimes you don't get that lucky. Sometimes you get branded by a memory, your past burned hard and indelibly into your heart, your soul, no matter how much you want it to be otherwise. I'm old now, but I carry these things with me still, for better and worse, and it's like my bones have grown around them, so that I can no longer tell where I end and they begin.

This is a story about memory: the things you hold on to, and the things you'd rather drop into that ocean darkness, are the things that make you who you are whether you want them to or not, and it begins before most of you were born. When it all *really* began is, I guess, debatable, but I'm going to start on a warm March morning in 1962 because that was when it started for me. I've thought about it all a lot over the years—a hell of a lot—and though memory has, no doubt, played some of its usual tricks on me, I remember most of it like it was yesterday. Some of it, the parts that happened to other people, I've had to piece together from what I learned after it was all over, but I think I have it pretty much.

Pretty much.

I won't tell the story as if it was all about me, though: I don't want to do all that "suddenly I knew" *Wonder Years* shit. In fact, I won't even put myself in the story, not directly. I'll just be one of the characters. You'll probably figure out which one, but that doesn't matter so much. Because even though I'm telling you what I saw, it's not about me. It was never about me.

It's so much bigger than that.

# TRINITY

TRINITY, NEVADA. 1962

# CHAPTER ONE

Van Lopez was having the dream again. He wouldn't remember it, but it would eventually wake him and hold on to the edges of his consciousness for a few minutes afterwards, tugging at him like a dog that wanted feeding. He was riding a horse through the desert, or rather he was sitting on the horse while someone else controlled it. Someone much larger than he was. There was a curious scent in the air which made him inexplicably anxious and the sky was strange. In the valley something was hot and smoking, something as strange as the sky from which it had come.

*We shouldn't be here . . . .*

Van came out of sleep with a start, heart hammering and breathing ragged, his mind filled with a kaleidoscope of light and sound that meant nothing to him but managed to raise the hairs on the back of his neck sure as if he'd gotten a shock from the ragged cloth-wrapped cable on the lamp beside his bed.

He sat up, staring around his bedroom as if he might see something that would make sense of it all, but it did what it always did: the familiarity of the place—the shaded window, the heap of yesterday's clothes, the record player with the uneven stack of singles—all served to remind him of what was real and push the dream away till he could forget it. Or very nearly.

He checked the luminous dial on the alarm clock. Six a.m. He forced his brain to figure out how long he had before he needed to go to school and whether he had time to get under the truck first and look over the transmission. A month ago Van had managed to convince his father to replace their ancient Chevy pickup with a six-year-old Ford F100 that had appeared in Don Hendricks's showroom over on 2nd Street. His dad—Danny—hadn't been convinced by the F100, which hadn't had much TLC in its short life, but Van had sworn up and down that, if they bought it, he'd do all the necessary work himself.

Danny had given him his skeptical look, often a prelude to rigid denials and the kind of dour forbidding Van had learned to avoid, but—unable to stop himself—Van had babbled about what that Y-block V8 engine could do with a little attention. No, the body work wasn't up to much, several light bulbs were busted, the fuel pump needed looking at, and the spark plugs would have to be replaced, but that was nothing, and when it was done, the thing would *haul* . . . . He'd gone on about the truck's *potential*, one of Van's favorite words, staring at its battered cherry red exterior like he'd struck gold. "Waxing lyrical," his brother Andy would say. When he'd remembered his dad and looked quickly back at him, half ready to step out of range and drop into an apologetic and respectful silence, Van caught a different look, rare and momentary, part amused, part sad and sort of far off. Wistful.

Danny, rugged and silent, had glanced away, looking down the street as if trying to track something that had just gone by, then shrugged and nodded.

"Ok," he said. "Your call."

*Your call.*

Van had never heard anything like that from his dad before, and he knew what it meant. He was old enough to be treated as a man, just about, and was being allowed to make a man's decision. Van had stared, his chest full and his eyes wide at the enormity of the thing, and for a moment said nothing. At last he managed a nod which matched his father's.

"All right then," Van heard himself say. "Let's do it."

And then he was grinning broad and happy, and it wasn't till they got the sputtering, lurching vehicle home that he realized that his father had given him just enough rope that he might accidentally hang himself with it.

This, after all, was to be a family vehicle, the only one—other than Danny's old Norton motorcycle—for the three of them. It would have to be able to survive the rough tracks and dirt roads that skirted the fence lines his father tended for the local ranchers. That was what put food on their table, so it needed to be reliable. Southern Nye County's major resource was space, miles and miles of it, much of it sun-blasted and desert-dry. Water and food troughs had to be kept filled, and if Danny's transport crapped out between jobs, cattle got stressed. Miss a few feeds and the steers might start dropping right there, and that was Danny's job up in smoke.

Van knew he couldn't risk that happening. It wasn't as if his father had a lot of employment options.

He dressed quickly and went downstairs. The radio was on as usual: Stevie Fly, KTNT deejay, local celebrity, and the unofficial voice of Trinity. He seemed to be on the air around the clock, playing records in the afternoon, reading news bulletins and editorializing in his lounge-cat drawl, then hosting late-night call-in shows, which gave a platform to every wacko in town. Bigfoot sightings, secret agents spying on the local florist, UFO fantasists: Stevie got them all. And Van's dad lapped that shit up. He'd sit there for hours unmoving, eyes on the radio speaker like it was a TV set, saying nothing, nodding occasionally.

Van hated it. He knew some of the kids at school called in for a joke, talked about flying saucers or the Lake Mead Monster, but they usually got called out or couldn't keep from busting up. But a lot of folks around Trinity took it all pretty seriously. Maybe it was just a way of connecting the town and it didn't really matter, but the way people referenced all that hogwash like it was straight from the mouth of Walter Cronkite annoyed him.

Van's brother Andy was still sacked out in his room, but his dad was up and at his usual spot, leaning against the frame of the kitchen window, looking out into the predawn darkness, the fingers of one hand spreading the slats of the blind so he could peer out without being seen. He had a mug of coffee in the other hand, half raised to his lips, but seemingly forgotten. He wasn't moving. On the radio, Stevie Fly's molasses and cigarette ash voice was talking to some flake who had gotten all coy about whether she would sound crazy if she said what she'd obviously called in to say.

"That's OK, hon," said Stevie, like he was her shrink or something, "I'm here for you. Lay it on me."

The flake hesitated a second then hesitantly began to tell her story. "I guess it started last week. There were these lights over my house, just like sitting there. Three of them . . ."

Van sighed, then opted for casual.

"Morning," he said.

His father didn't move, but his eyes flicked across the room for a moment before returning to the street outside. He said nothing.

"Everything OK?" Van tried, busying himself with the cornflake packet so it wouldn't look like he was staring.

"Not sure."

Van's heart sank.

"Yeah?" he said. More forced casualness. "What do you see?"

For a moment his father said nothing, but his eyes narrowed, as if trying to make sense of something baffling.

7

When he spoke, the word was barely audible, a baffled murmur delivered like he was talking to himself.

"A van," he said.

Van set the cornflakes down, took a breath, and joined his father at the window. He peered out, trying to make sense of the shadows.

"The blue Econoline?" he said. There wasn't a vehicle on the road Van couldn't identify. "Last year's model. Inline 6. Nice split grill."

He leaned in and spread the slats wider to get a better look, but his father spun around and slapped his hand away.

"What are you, stupid?" his father demanded.

Van backed away, hands raised in surrender, all casualness gone.

"It's just a van, Pops. No big deal."

His father ignored the remark and went back to gazing out. Red-faced, Van returned to his cereal, careful to make sure his annoyance didn't attract further attention. On the radio, the flake had come right out with it and said she was being visited by aliens or some damn thing, and Stevie Fly—instead of telling her to get out in the fresh air and make some friends—was making soothing, encouraging noises and calling her "sister." Van glared at the radio. He was eating in resentful silence when his brother entered the room.

Andy was 16, two years younger than Van. They were both paler-skinned than their Latino father but had his black hair and dark eyes. Andy was slim and rangy, with high cheekbones that gave him a hard, angular look. He took in the scene quickly and his mouth went thin as a pencil line. He looked at his brother and something unspoken passed between them, something cautious and weary, something they had shared many times before.

Van made a shrug so small it barely reached his shoulders, and focused on his cereal. He looked older than his brother by more than the two years that actually separated them, as if he'd seen more, done more, than was possible in a Nevada high school.

"Hurry up," he said. "Time for school."

It wasn't, but he wanted to be somewhere else.

"You using the truck today, Pops?" Andy asked, his eyes still on his brother.

Their father kept on looking out, then blinked as if the question had only just reached him, and grunted, "What?"

"I asked if you were using the truck today," said Andy, as careful as someone defusing a bomb. "Wondered if we might borrow it. Run some errands before school."

Van shot him a questioning glance, but Andy gave his head a fractional shake to silence him. He waited for his father to speak, then licked his lips and added, "Whaddya think?"

There was another loaded pause and then, still gazing out at the blue van parked across the street, their father muttered, "Sure," and added, "If I need to, I'll take the bike." Then he paused, eyes still on the van. "But I ain't going nowhere."

That was said with resolution, even defiance.

The two brothers exchanged another look, weary this time, resigned.

"Fetch me my carbine before you go," he added, still not looking at them.

Van opened his mouth to say something but changed his mind. Sometimes it felt like nothing would ever change.

○      ○

The truck started on the third attempt, its rattling cough turning to an uneven rumble punctuated with sputters and pops.

"Can't believe you got him to buy this piece of junk," said Andy, lacing up his Chuck Taylors.

"Give it time."

"Time is what it's already had. It's old and getting older and crappier by the minute. Give it any more time and the thing will collapse into dust and scrap."

"What do you know about it?" Van shot back, stung. He had already bonded with the F100.

"Woah, there, Mister Mechanic," Andy crooned, amused. "Touched a nerve? What is this, your first love? You need a girl in your life, big brother."

"And you need to shut up."

"Oh yeah," said Andy, grinning. "Definitely touched a nerve."

Van backed the truck out of the hard earth driveway and into the deserted street. He could feel Andy's challenging stare, but he was still thinking vaguely about his father, still standing at the window, still watching the innocuous blue van. He was getting worse.

The sun was up now, but only barely, and the distant mountains were painted an improbable gold. The last of the snow lay on their crags and high reaches as if layered on by an artist. Van frowned at them, wondering how you would capture that look with a brush without it looking like the lid of a chocolate box. He caught Andy watching him and gunned the engine, filling the dawn with animal snarl.

"Where to?" he said.

"What?"

"You said you had errands."

"Right," said Andy, looking away. "One errand. Head northeast toward the army base. I'll direct you."

The army base was one of Trinity's open secrets. Everyone knew it was there, but no one talked about it. Trinity was that kind of place: a town which had sort of happened, individual plots spilling into each other and turning isolated individuals into a taciturn, accidental community.

"Where we going?" Van pressed.

"I said I'll direct you," said Andy.

Van was used to his brother's petulance and his need to be in control, but something in his manner struck him as furtive.

"You wanna tell me where we're going, or you wanna walk?" he said.

"Just over onto Gamebird. Corner of Sagebrush."

Andy still wasn't looking at him. Van drove along the baked dirt road, thinking. At last he said, "There's nothing there. Fields. A construction site. Where we going?"

"I'll show you, OK? Jeez." Andy sighed. "What's with the third degree?"

He shifted on the seat, trying to get comfortable with his head against the passenger door, and closed his eyes. "It's too early for this shit," he muttered.

"Your idea," said Van.

It was no more than three miles on largely empty roads through open country: fields of alfalfa, cotton, and cattle pasture, all enjoying a blessed respite from the heat that would arrive like a Biblical plague over the next few months. Even in March, though the days started cold—only a few degrees above freezing—it would be in the upper sixties by mid afternoon and would go up another eight to 10 degrees per month through the end of July, when hundred-degree temperatures were routine, and bad days could push as high as 112, 114. Sometimes more. It was unforgiving country. The Paiute who had lived there before the region was colonized had only survived because of the artesian wells tapping the aquifer beneath the mountains.

It was still new to Van and Andy, who had only been there three years, having moved from the dazzling gypsum sand flats of New Mexico when the ranch their father had worked on closed down, its cattle victims of drought and sickness. They felt like outsiders here—the little town was almost as white as the New Mexico desert they had left behind—and were still finding their feet in the intermittently hot and cold war that was high school. People were harder to navigate than the desert or, for that matter, engines. Van was silent as he drove, taking it all in, slowing and smiling silently as he caught the blur of a coyote loping across the road. It flashed him a look and its eyes glowed bright and otherworldly in the Ford's headlights, then it slunk into the scrub brush and was gone.

In time most of this land would be consumed by housing and commercial development as Las Vegas sprawled, flexing belligerently to the southeast, but in '62 this was still mostly open country, its unincorporated towns small and scattered. Trinity had only the minuscule beginnings of a telephone system since the previous year, and few of the roads were paved. Van and Andy didn't know it, but they were among the last to grow up with the view they had that morning, the wide, hard ground turned into fields by brutal labor, the clear vantage on the rugged peaks of the Spring Mountains to the east and the Nopah mountains to the west, and all around the hard, blank grip of the Mojave desert. It was a vast, humbling space, which—for all its ground features—was mostly sky. Even with his brother half asleep beside him, Van felt alone.

He liked it, and for a moment he stopped worrying about whatever nonsense Andy was up to this time, and watched the sunrise bring the desert to vibrant life, gold and pink and turquoise.

The construction site appeared almost out of nowhere: a billboard proclaiming "Homes of the Future!" and a chain link fence, inside which they could just make out the shapes of graders, a crane, and other building equipment, sitting silently like sleeping mastodons. Posts had been driven into the ground at regular intervals and small, regular lots taped out, with poured concrete foundation slabs laid over what had once been the vast wildness of the desert. If this was the future, Van didn't think much of it. His mind flashed back to the coyote, and he wondered if the animal had been driven from a den around here. Maybe he could paint that, the coyote looking out over the desert toward those gilded mountains, maybe with the ugly sprawl of tract housing filling the valley.

*Too on the nose? Maybe.*

"Pull over there," said Andy, breaking into his reverie. "And turn your lights off."

"Why? What are we doing?

"For once, just do as I say, OK? And keep your voice down."

Van frowned and turned the engine off. "I don't like . . ." he began, but Andy was already out and closing the door softly.

*God damn it.*

Andy was walking softly along the fence. He tried the gate and found it latched but unlocked.

"Andy!" Van hissed, clambering out of the truck.

Andy spun around, forefinger on his lips and eyes wide with exasperation. He pushed the gate wide and pointed, mouthing, "Wait."

Van hesitated as his brother slipped inside the perimeter, breaking into an easy run.

14

*Like the coyote*, Van thought.

There was a prefabricated cabin with a light on in the window, and great, regular stacks of building materials, mostly bound with cable as if only recently unloaded. Andy vanished among them, and for a moment Van truly was alone in the dawn silence. He marveled at the efficient ugliness of the building site, and hugged his arms around himself against the chill of the morning. He listened, but barely heard his brother before he saw him. Andy looked excited and, for all his careful stealth, could barely contain a giggle. It made him look young as few things seemed to these days.

"Roll the truck in through the gate," he said. "Quietly. Park it over there next to that sign, then come give me a hand.

"Andy, what the hell—?"

"Just do it, OK? It's for a good cause."

"Someone will see!"

"Contractors don't get here till seven or later. There's a watchman, but he'll have been stewing in Jack Daniels overnight, so . . . don't sweat it, big brother."

And then he was gone again, scampering off like a jack rabbit.

Van sputtered his frustration but put the truck in neutral and struggled to push it slowly forward and in through the gate, taking care not to catch the already battered body work on the aluminum posts. Once it got rolling, he hopped in and guided the F100 over the hard, uneven ground. Then he brought it to a gentle stop and got out, closing the door softly. Something of his brother's secretive glee had infected him, and Van felt a spike of wild joy at the idea that—in a way he didn't understand—he and his brother were going to stick it to the people who made those faceless boxes for people where there should be only snakes and the ancient stones they had plowed under. Even as he thought it, he knew it was dumb, but then Andy was back and whispering, "Help me with this."

It was a girder, bright and new-looking, about eight feet long: some kind of steel stud used for framing houses. Van stared at him.

"What? Help you how?"

"Get it in the truck, man!" said Andy, as if it was obvious.

"What?" Van replied.

"You know what we can get for a couple of these? Come on. Quick!"

"You're not serious," said Van. He watched as Andy tried to get his fingers under one end of the girder.

"Come on," said Andy. "Won't take but a minute."

"No way," said Van.

"I won't scrape up the bed," Andy said. "Promise."

Van frowned, momentarily confused, then realized his brother was talking about the varnished oak lining the back of the F100.

"That's not . . ." he began, then shook his head. "Get in the truck. We're leaving."

But Andy was still carefully lifting one end of the girder, looking around with a shifty intensity.

"I said *get in the truck*," he repeated, his voice lower now, cooler.

"I'm telling you," said Andy, pretending not to hear the shift in Van's tone. "This is good stuff. Serious cash right here."

"And I said no," said Van, stiffening.

Andy looked at him, gauging how far Van was prepared to go.

"Are you kidding me?" he said. "It's just some rich guy's metal scraps. What do you care?"

"I care that it will come back on me, on dad," said Van, "and I'm done talking about it. Get in the damn truck."

Andy let the steel beam drop but he came out of his crouch fired up, lurching toward Van.

"What are you, the goddamned sheriff?" Andy spat. "You're taking their side?"

"What side?" Van demanded, his voice rising. "Don't play the . . ."

But he didn't get to finish the sentence. There was the clang of a metal door flung wide and a flurry of movement from the cabin.

"What the hell you think you're doin'?" bellowed a voice.

"Nice going, Lone Ranger," snapped Andy, as if this was Van's fault.

Van hesitated, but only for a moment. On the steps of the cabin was a big, bearded man. He was cradling what looked, even at this distance, like a shotgun. Van dove for the driver's side and leapt in. Andy was still out at the back, but he roared "GO!" as he shimmied into the passenger seat.

Van turned the ignition key and the engine puttered into unimpressive life. At the same moment, there was a blast of sound, flat and hollow, and the passenger side mirror tore right off. Van cursed, shrinking in place, then checked the rear view in time to catch the watchman reloading his shotgun.

The F100 rocketed backwards, sliding on the dusty ground as Van yanked the steering wheel hard, sending the truck slewing around. Then it was surging forward in great uneven bounds as the old engine fought for rhythm. Van aimed the hood at the gate and put the truck in gear as another shotgun blast slammed into its tail. Van checked the mirror again, but his brother just screamed, "The fuck you waiting for? *Go!*"

Van floored it. As he sped through the gate and onto the highway, he caught sight of the watchman running for a vehicle of his own. He was giving chase.

*Great. Just great.*

He turned to shoot Andy a menacing glare and was amazed to see his brother howling with laughter, leaning out of the window and flipping his middle fingers back toward the construction site.

The V8 was still warming up, but as it did so, the uneven, sputtering flash and roll settled into a long purr, and there they were, all 170 horses straining to get loose. Most of them, anyway. There was more work to do on that engine. Still, it would take something special to catch them once they hit their stride.

Van was still thinking that when he saw a yellow pickup blast out of the compound and onto the road. It clipped the gate, sending it crashing back against the chain link, but the truck didn't hesitate. It slid around in a pall of dust and exhaust fumes, and came barreling after them.

Van gripped the wheel and pushed the accelerator. The pitch of the engine rose a tone or two and the door panels began to shake. A couple of hundred yards further and the passenger door flapped open. For a half second, Andy was half out of the vehicle, leaning on the open door. Then he was back in and dragging the door shut.

"You really picked a winner with this thing," said Andy, covering his panic.

"Works better when it ain't getting shot at," said Van. He rode the accelerator to the floor.

The yellow truck—maybe a Chevy Apache?—was still coming, but it slewed from side to side on the road, and Van thought his brother's remark about the driver having been marinating in whiskey overnight might not be far off. He thought fast. In a flat-out road race he couldn't be sure the F100 in its current state would be able to hold off the Chevy. But if the driver wasn't entirely on the ball . . .

*It was worth a shot.*

At the next intersection, Van hung a hard right by the Four Spot horse stables, speeding toward the center of town. Andy was screaming at him, demanding to know what the hell he was doing, but he didn't look back. They needed some cover, and they weren't going to find it out here on the desert road. Another right took them briefly onto the newly paved Veterans Memorial highway but that only proved Van's suspicions correct: all things being equal, he couldn't outrun the Chevy. At the first exit, he took a left, tires squealing on the asphalt. Andy shot him a nervous look.

"Just let me out and I'll run," he said. "This is my fault, it's me he wants."

Van kept his eyes on the road. "Does he know who you are?" he asked, his mouth barely opening.

He felt Andy's shrug more than he saw it. "Don't see why he would," said Andy. "'Course, if he gets our license plate . . ."

Van sucked in a long breath, then—with grim resolve—said simply, "He won't."

He cut hard to the right onto Alamogordo, swerving hard around a parked semi, close enough to clip the Ford's wing mirror if it hadn't already been blown off. They shot past a lonely gas station with two ancient pumps, and a dusty liquor store, then turned west. The engine was straining now, and there was a new sputtering cough every few seconds that Van didn't like.

*Fuel pump?*

He checked the rearview mirror, and there was the yellow truck, sliding slightly as it made the turn, but still right on them. Van thought fast and made another turn so quickly he could feel the truck rock alarmingly toward the passenger side. Any faster and they'd have rolled.

Another quick look from Andy, and a forced grin which didn't hide the concern in his eyes.

Over the uneven roar of the V8 Van heard a distant hooting, owlish but long, sustained and desolate. He sat up and turned to the side window, calculating.

The Chevy was at least 50 yards closer than it had been.

They were on Verdant now, a long, roughly surfaced street of single-story ranch houses, hastily built after the war and already dilapidated. They sped, bouncing from pothole to pothole, past pipe rails and chain link fence, till the houses gave way to trailers, some lived in, some not.

"Dude," said Andy warningly. "There's nothing down here. It dead ends in the wash."

Van said nothing. He kept his foot down and checked his mirror. The yellow truck had matched him turn for turn, inching closer all the time. He checked his window, listening, and caught it again, the plaintive hooting wail.

The Ford kept going, picking up speed as the road dipped. Now the houses and trailers were gone and the way ahead was clear but shortening fast. Five hundred yards ahead the road dead-ended in a ragged screen of blasted shrubs and two clumps of sturdy looking trees. Their truck was speeding right at them.

"Van?" said Andy, shifting in his seat. "Man, what the hell?"

The panic was clearer in his brother's voice now. It had gone up a full octave.

"Hold on," said Van.

The pickup hadn't been fitted with seat belts.

He checked the rear view one last time and eased off the accelerator just a fraction. As the Ford slowed, he could see their pursuer get closer. Van tweaked the steering wheel, aiming between the two stands of water birch.

"Van!" said Andy. He started to reach across for the wheel, but Van elbowed his hand away.

With a hard jolt which rocked them forward and back the truck leapt through the trees and its front wheels were momentarily airborne before crashing down the embankment and into the dry creek bed. The pickup landed heavily with a crash, but it kept moving, sliding into the turn as Van angled the truck along what his father would call an arroyo. In fact, the creek wasn't completely dry, and water sprayed up onto the windshield.

Andy whooped with delight and relief, but a moment later Van saw the yellow Chevy nose down the bank, cautious but still coming. He listened again, and peered up and to the right. Two hundred yards ahead was a dirt ramp up the right hand bank of the creek bed, the only crossing point for a mile and a half. Beside that ramp ran the old freight line.

Van could just about see it, the dusty blue and occasional gleaming steel of the train flashing through the trees, heading toward them down the right-hand bank of the wash and blowing its desolate horn. If they hit the ramp clean and shot through the crossing just right . . .

Van floored it, swinging the truck left to get a better run at the ramp.

"What—?" Andy began, then realization dawned and he gasped. "No! Van—"

But they were committed. The train blew its horn again, louder now, like a siren from hell, and in that same instant Van wrenched the wheel around and sent the truck shooting up the ramp through the brush. He felt the wheels spin, felt the sudden darkness of the scrub bushes of the embankment as they were rocked back in their seats, and then they were out into the light again. The tires bounced hard on the railroad crossing and Van turned to see the front of the train bearing down on them, roaring its implacable steel warning.

And then they were across, the long line of freight cars shunting past the F100's tail gate. The chasing Chevy might as well have been 50 miles away.

"Oh man!" Andy shrieked. "That was wild, man! Holy shit. I thought we were . . ."

Van turned on him.

"Don't you ever pull shit like that on me again!" he said, eyes blazing.

"What?" Andy replied, genuinely surprised. "It was just a bit of scrap metal. What's the big deal?"

"The big deal is that we got shot at, Andy. And if he's able to ID us, the cops'll be waiting for us when we got home. And you know how Pops would react to *that*."

Andy had been about to laugh, shrug it off, say his big brother was being lame or something, but he looked sharply away, knowing full well what Van was implying. Cops showing up at their place, where their father kept a permanent stake out, eyes always on the road, rifle in hand? Things could only go badly.

For a moment there was nothing but the rattle of the long train behind them, then Van was focused on the road again and driving away.

Andy shifted, then opted for lightness.

"Hey, who knew this old rust bucket could move like that?" he said. "I thought it was no better than scrap."

"And you'd know all about scrap," Van replied.

Andy winced. "OK. Poor choice of words."

"How long has this been going on?"

"What? No time. Just today," Andy lied.

It was obvious.

"I saw you," Van said. "Two weeks ago. Down behind the drive-in on Fourth, with Vince Reed. He gave you something. Money, I figured."

Van waited, but Andy said nothing.

"He's what, eight years older than you?" Van pressed.

"Six," snapped Andy before realizing he had given himself away. "He's 22."

"And a full-on loser," Van added. "He and his idiot gang buddies."

"The Tunnel Snakes," said Andy.

Something in the way he said it made Van turn to look at him again, the truck slowing as he took his foot off the gas.

"Come on, Van!" Andy protested, "We have places to be."

"You stay the hell away from those guys, you hear me," said Van. "They're trouble."

Andy shrugged and looked away. "Trouble's what we got."

"You ain't one of them," said Van. "Never will be. You hear me? Andy. Look at me."

Reluctantly, his younger brother turned to face him, jaw set, eyes staring, but a flush of pink in his cheeks. "You sound like Mom."

Van winced, taken aback. They didn't talk about their mother.

There was a loaded silence, then Andy reached out and snapped the radio on. Immediately the cab was flooded with a man's crooning voice, all attitude and swagger, with some peppy female backing and a little honkytonk band backing him up. "*Sweet dreams, baby . . .*"

"Roy Orbison," said Andy, satisfied. "Good song."

Van gave him a swift look and nodded. The two brothers grinned at each other, then Andy turned the volume up and sang along, loud and unabashed, elbowing Van till he joined in. The sun was properly up now, and the crummy little town on the edge of the desert was suddenly luminous, gold as honey and improbably beautiful.

*Sweet dreams, baby . . .*

Van punched it, and the Ford sprang back to life. Thinking of the train, his hellion brother, and his damaged, frightening father, he sang, laughing till the tears ran.

# CHAPTER TWO

As Van and Andy sang along to the radio, Trinity was slowly coming to life, emerging into that glorious Nevada light and the widest, bluest of skies. You could almost smell the optimism, the certainty of rightness and promise in the air. It was 1962. JFK was in the White House, the U.S. economy was surging, and the nation was charged with the surety of even better days to come. The thrill of the space race was everywhere, touching the humblest of appliances with futuristic dials, lights, and chrome. Van's beat-up pickup notwithstanding, the bright, shining cars heading out into the morning sported jet nacelle taillights, and rocket-ship fins. A month earlier, John Glenn had become the first American to orbit the earth, and by the end of the year, the period's cheery, tech-heavy imaginings of the future would be celebrated weekly in shows like *The Jetsons*, whose whimsically absurd view of how the world might one day be would air in syndication for another two decades. The only clouds on the horizon came from a Soviet Union flexing its muscles and funneling supplies to what was beginning to look like a proxy war in Vietnam. In 1962 that still seemed like a long way from Trinity, Nevada, but Russian influence in Cuba had spawned the disastrous Bay of Pigs invasion the previous year, and by the end of this one, the United States and the USSR would be in total nuclear standoff, playing out the world's most deadly game of chicken.

Far away though that might all seem, and out of step with Trinity's glossy aspirations, it was also hard-wired into the little town's sudden boom. Because on the northeast side of town was a long, straight road, wider and better kept than any highway out here in the middle of nowhere had a right to be. It ran like an arrow for six miles before dead-ending in a series of fences, gates, and sentry watch towers. Beyond those were barracks and offices, runways and helipads. Trinity folks just called it The Base, and if they knew anything about what went on there, they knew not to discuss it.

But there's a point at which no amount of restriction, no cloak-and-dagger subterfuge, no "careless talk costs lives" propaganda can keep things under wraps, and one of those points is when everyone from miles around is exposed to the breathtaking spectacle of a nuclear explosion. Trinity had sat on the edge of what had been variously—and innocuously—termed the Nevada Proving

Ground and the Nevada Test Site, and would eventually become the Nevada National Security Site. Over the decade or so since the first one-kiloton bomb was dropped at Frenchman Flats in 1951, there had been a dozen separately code-named operations at the Test Site, totaling over 150 separate nuclear detonations. Those triggered on or above the ground created massive flashes, shock waves, and towering mushroom clouds that could be seen all the way to the hotels of Las Vegas, creating what had come to be called "Nuclear Tourism."

Trinity sat at the heart of it, proud, awestruck, and just a little uneasy.

"The Trinity East and the McAllister Motel are already sold out," said Monty, proprietor of the diner named after him. He was a big man, broad-shouldered and with a belly that overhung his waist band, but he moved easily and with an air of purpose, deliberation. His iron gray hair was razored respectably short, and even in an apron he wore authority like a general directing troops, speaking with measured, uncontradictable surety. "That new hotel off Main, the Marlborough, has only three rooms left. Place has only been there a couple of months and they are already at capacity."

He laid his copy of the *Trinity Bugle* on the Formica tabletop as proof, not that anyone would dare to contradict Monty in his own place. Sheriff Robert—Bobby—Watts, and his deputy, Jim Reynolds, nodded respectfully and considered the headlines.

*April Brings More A-Bomb Tests—And Visitors—To Trinity!*

"See?" Monty pronounced, as if they had argued the point. "Right there in black and white."

"Sure is," said the deputy. Reynolds was 25, and—in Watts's frequently offered assessment—keen as mustard but green as grass.

"The world we live in," Watts remarked with a shake of his head. His smile was both impressed and baffled.

"Another blast or two will give them *sputniks* something to see," Monty added, pronouncing the Russian word with distaste. "They say, when the ground shakes, it's the nuclear blast," he added, with a knowing grin that announced that he was wheeling out a joke, "but I reckon it's the Russkies shaking in their boots."

Reynolds laughed obligingly, pointing a finger at Monty in that "got me" way he did. Watts just smiled and bumped his chin up, but he noted the way Monty's bravado faltered a little bit on that remark about *sputniks*. For all his patriotic confidence in American know-how and righteousness, Monty had a long-standing worry about what the Soviets were up to and—more to the point—what, in every sense, they were capable of. The swagger was a way of compensating for his anxiety. In this, at least. Monty swaggered about everything.

On cue the diner's proprietor turned on Tommy—Red—Hauser, who was bustling inefficiently at the counter with a plate of pancakes.

"You not got table four served yet?" he barked. "He's been there 20 minutes!"

Red glanced over to where George Singer sat: a 75-year-old former pipe fitter who, even by his own admission, was not the sharpest knife in the drawer. He hadn't been there anything like 20 minutes, but Monty's word was law.

The Negro boy—as he was known in the parlance of the day—grimaced. For a moment, Sheriff Watts thought that Monty would correct the kid for using his first name or something, but in the end he just looked back to his law-enforcement customers and gave them a knowing eye roll.

"Filling in for Delores," he said.

"She OK?"

"She is, her mom's not," Monty answered. "So, I have no waitress. Might be out weeks. You know anyone?"

Watts shook his head ruefully.

"Any other time I'd get some nice high school senior, looking to make a little extra before college or whatever, but at this time of year, everyone's busy. So my bus boy and dish washer gets promoted. You'd think he'd be glad to get out of the kitchen . . ."

"You'd think," Watts agreed.

"Lots of folks wouldn't let a guy like him work at a place like this, but . . ." He gave an expansive shrug and opened his hands, like a martyr showing his wounds. "What are you gonna do?"

"He was a heck of a wide receiver in high school," Deputy Reynolds volunteered.

The two older men turned to look at him as if he had just offered up a fragment of Buddhist philosophy. Monty frowned. "Yeah," he snapped. "Till he decked a referee!"

Reynolds hung his head, chastened.

"Damnedest thing I ever saw," Monty continued, lowering his voice a fraction, but not so much that Red couldn't hear. "Worst game I'd ever seen him play. Got called for hold after hold. Backed the team up 80 yards on a single drive. Jawing at the refs the whole time. Then he makes this one-handed catch and tears off for the end zone, only to have the play called dead for a false start. Didn't like that. Comes tearing back to the ref, face black as thunder. Out of control, you know? He'd been raging half the game, but you could just tell that this time was different. That something had snapped. Anyway, he comes roaring up to the ref—Scott Baylard, it was—"

"Good ref," said Reynolds.

Monty gave him a baleful glare. "You wanna let me finish?" he snarled.

Reynolds framed an apologetic smile. "Sure, Monty," he said, a little stiff.

"So yeah," Monty went on, leaning in, "Scotty Baylard. Good guy and—as you say," he added graciously, "a good ref. Hell, truth be told, the guy hadn't even wanted to be there. He'd made his feelings about *integrated* high school sports very clear, but when it happened anyway, he agreed to keep working in spite of his principles. Putting the kids first, you know? And then here comes Red Hauser, screaming like something out of darkest Africa. Well, Scotty stands his ground, has a word or two with him. Lets him know who's in charge, right? I mean, he's the ref. Does that do the trick?"

"Nope," Reynolds inserted. Monty gave him a disbelieving glare, and Reynolds added quickly. "Should have done."

"That's right," said Monty, rewarding the good student. "It should have done. But then Red just flat out decks him. Out of nowhere. Pow. Straight right hook, knocks the guy about six feet."

"Hell of a punch," Reynolds remarked, coffee cup suspended in the air like he was seeing it all again in his head.

"My point," said Monty, raising his voice and giving the deputy a level stare, "is that he could have been arrested for what he did that day, not just sent off. Like, I wouldn't have been surprised if you"—this to Sheriff Watts—"hadn't come walking out of the stands and put him in cuffs right there and then. Assault, is what it was."

"Sure enough," Reynolds agreed.

"You should have heard the crowd!" Watts recalled, chuckling at the memory. "Boy, did they let him know how they felt! When he was marched off the field, the whole place sang "Dixie" at the top of their lungs. Only time I ever heard such a thing in Nevada."

"Killed his football career, didn't it," said Watts, noncommittal.

"Actions have consequences," said Monty sagely. "Ain't that what high school is supposed to teach?"

"No college scholarships," Watts mused aloud, "no shot at going pro. Not even a proper job."

Monty gave him his saintly shrug again. "Me, I don't judge," he said. "If a man can do the job and I need someone, I'll pay him."

"Sixty five cents on the dollar!" Reynolds inserted, laughing.

Monty pointed his finger like it was a pistol. "If a man don't like what he's paid," he snarled, "he's free to hang up his apron and walk out the door any time he likes."

"Except that you know he can't get a better deal anywhere else," said Watts, amused, but in a thoughtful way that was hard to read.

"There is that," said Monty, beaming, as if he had been complimented on his business savvy. "Course," he added, raising his voice so that Red couldn't miss it, "if he can't do the job, we may have to rethink his wages."

Red took a load of empty plates from the next table and moved back into the kitchen with his head down. Sheriff Watts, watched him go, sipped his coffee, and said, "You might want to cut the kid a break. He hasn't had many."

"I just calls 'em as I sees 'em," said Monty.

"Like a ref," said Reynolds, seriously.

Monty nodded thoughtfully, letting the light of his beneficence fall on Reynolds. "Like a ref," he repeated thoughtfully. "That is exactly right. Let me warm that coffee up for you there, deputy."

Watts watched him, wondering—not for the first time—if Reynolds could really be as green and guileless as he seemed, or if all that off-the-cob stuff was an act to stay in people's good graces. Monty topped up his coffee, gave the deputy an avuncular pat on the shoulder, and moved off to the counter where Matt Sawyer was inhaling sausage and eggs like there was a shortage. Soon he was holding court on how the weather might affect the upcoming atomic tests, and whether the explosion would be more impressive than what they had seen the previous December, a subject on which he had no more information than anyone else in the room, though that didn't stop him from adopting an almost professorial authority. Watts was still watching him over his coffee cup when Reynolds redirected his thoughts.

"Saw Vince Reed and his lowlife pals up on the ridge last night," he said.

"Doing what?" asked Watts.

Reynolds shrugged. "Just hanging, supposedly, listening to the radio. Stevie Fly had some guy on his show talking about how he had been abducted by aliens like that farmer from Brazil, and when they brought him back he kept getting these headaches. He went to a doctor and they found these hard little implant-things embedded just under his ears . . ."

"Is this relevant?" said Watts, losing patience.

"Guess not," said Reynolds, unabashed. "It was pretty interesting though. Anyway, Vince and the rest were listening to it. I know because they all got tats afterwards at Rick Worfram's place, and he said they were arguing about whether or not it was true. He also said they were waving a lot of cash around."

Watts's eyebrows went up, interested and impressed by the deputy's resourcefulness.

"Yeah?" he said. "Tats of what . . . ? No, let me guess. Some kind of snake."

"Got it in one, Sheriff!" said Reynolds, unreasonably impressed. "Right there on the biceps. A snake emerging from a tunnel mouth. Mouth open, like . . ." He modeled the look, eyes narrowed and hissing like a cat.

"I think I get it," said Watts. "All of them? Vince, plus Larry, Moe and Curly?"

Reynolds smiled indulgently to show he got the joke then corrected him gently, drawing his notebook from his breast pocket and checking it fastidiously. "Billy, Moe and Len, plus Vince, of course," he said. "Two till five in the afternoon. After which they got sodas and burgers at Harper's then drove up to the ridge. Rick said they were flashing a lot of bills and didn't even ask the price before getting inked. Vince paid for them all. Twenty bucks, if you can believe that!"

"So they've come into some money," said Watts. "That's good work, deputy."

"Just doing my job, sir," Reynolds replied with that improbable 'Just the facts, Ma'am,' version of police professionalism he'd gotten mostly off the TV. "Twenty dollars!" Reynolds repeated in wonder.

Though Reynold's gosh shucks amazement was over selling the matter, it *was* a lot of cash. Monty's fried chicken in a basket, served with a hot roll and fries—one of the diner's signature dishes—cost only a buck fifty.

"So, where's their money coming from?" Watts mused.

"Nowhere good," said Reynolds.

"We ask around," said Watts. "And I want to know where they are spending whatever they make, too. I have my eye on Nick's Liquors and the place by the Texaco station."

"Sandrino's," Reynolds prompted.

"Right," said Watts. "Though now the Snakes are all of age, we can't rattle the liquor stores like we used to."

"Don't worry, Sheriff," said Reynolds brightly. "We'll get 'em for something. Lowlifes."

Watts gave him an uncertain look, then inclined his head. He wasn't wrong. And then, as if summoned like demons, there they were. The diner was a low-slung rectangle, architecturally not that much different from the double-wide trailer which had preceded it, though this version was bigger and had been tricked out with chrome, vivid red seat backs, and a gleaming new juke box. A neon sign on the roof proclaimed it "Monty's!" in disingenuously friendly red cursive, and last spring, in a rush of economic optimism, the building's namesake had had the walls almost entirely replaced with plate glass. They made the place feel vast as the desert outside, a great, Space Age fish tank, bright as the future and shiny as money. It was through those windows that Sheriff Watts saw the Tunnel Snakes.

He'd been dimly aware of the swelling roar of their bike engines, turning to see them pulling in like the four horseman of a very American apocalypse. They rode slow, the Harleys pushing out a wall of sound flat as brick, and to their flanks great plumes of dust fantailed like smoke, a toxic Red Sea parting before them. Vince Reed was their unholy Moses, a 22-year-old delinquent who had embraced his many failures and bad habits and made a career of them. A few years earlier he had been a runty kid, wiry and snaggle toothed, trying to look cool with a pack of smokes rolled into the sleeve of his T-shirt. But something had happened to him just as he was finishing high school, as if his lack of prospects and talents had done something to his body, forcing it to evolve into something that could fend for itself without the assistance of good grades, aptitude, or charm. What emerged was suddenly long limbed and rugged, pale as milk no matter the weather, his hair black as raven wings, with matching mutton chop sideburns. His eyes were a hard ice blue, and his lip was permanently fixed in a mocking sneer. He hadn't become handsome as he shed his adolescence—far from it—but he had transformed, and the kid everyone had ignored, the screw-up loser Watts dimly remembered, had become a figure of wildness, of menace. It wasn't just that he had gotten bigger and stronger, though he had. It was that, no matter who he was talking to or what he was looking at, you sensed that he just didn't care. At all. The man had no anchor, nothing to ground him, so he rode around the desert on his oversized Harley like an unleashed bolt of electricity.

He hadn't killed anyone yet, but Watts was in no doubt that one day he would, and when he did, he would do it like a man stubbing out a cigarette, immediately forgetting about it and getting on with his day.

The other three, the ones Watts thought of as the stooges, were little more than Vince's shadows. One day, if they lived long enough, they'd be henchmen, or if they were lucky they'd somehow escape his orbit and have regular, uneventful and nondescript lives, but Watts thought the odds of that weren't good. Vince was a comet with just enough gravitational pull to drag them all along, and probably take them down with him. The one upside was that they'd almost certainly not be living in Trinity by then. They'd drift out west to California, or they'd be pulled into the drain that was Las Vegas.

Vince came in first, his horse-riding swagger like some movie gun-slinger, and just human enough to be amused by the uneasy looks he attracted from the diner's patrons. His blank eyes alighted on the sheriff and his deputy, and he grinned knowingly, flicking a one fingered salute from his temple in mock deference as he sauntered by. He led the way to a table in the corner and sprawled into it, long legs stuck out, torso folding into a studied slouch. As his fellow Tunnel Snakes took their places—greasy-handed acolytes all—he carelessly scanned the menu and then pushed it aside.

"Cheese burgers," he said, just loud enough to be heard all around the room. "You got that, Hauser?"

Red Hauser, the Negro boy in the apron, paused in the act of wiping down the counter, braced himself and turned to the group.

"Sure did," he said mildly. "How many?"

Vince did a slow circuit of his buddies with his eyes.

"Well, there's four of us," he drawled. "Why don't you take a guess?"

Billy, Moe, and Len snickered to themselves, and Watts was reminded of some nature show he'd seen on TV: hyenas chittering around a carcass while a lion fed, waiting for their turn, and skipping out of the way every time the big cat menaced them.

"Got it," said Red, turning quickly away.

"And don't overdo 'em, boy," said Vince to his back. "I like to see my meat bleed."

More hyena giggles from the gang. Watts didn't know the others as well as Vince. Billy Sands lived with his father who spent most days drunk and had probably taken some of his many disappointments out on his kid; Moe Taylor had repeated at least one grade, maybe two, and was, by all accounts, even dumber than he was mean; and Len Stiverson had all the makings of a fledgling psychopath. A few years ago a number of pets had gone missing: cats and small dogs. Most of the town had assumed it was coyotes, but then some of the remains had been found at the town dump, all methodically cut up. One set of parts was in a box marked with Len Stiverson's home address. Watts had investigated, but the Stiverson's had money and lawyers, and there hadn't been enough evidence to pursue safely. But Watts had looked into the little shit's vacant eyes and been as sure as he could be that the soulless little toe rag was as guilty as sin. He had tried to say something to the kid's platinum blond mom, but she had avoided his gaze and shut the conversation down with a fluttery gesture of her hand. Watts would have bet money that she at least suspected her darling boy of this and other things but was, frankly, scared of him. When Len had been picked up, first for shop lifting, then for peering into the bedrooms of his neighbors, she had made a show of protesting his innocence, but even then it had been half-hearted. Now, though the kid was only a year out of high school, they barely had any dealings with him, and Watts got the feeling that when darling Len saddled up and followed Vince Reed into whatever nightmare life awaited them far from Trinity, the family would breathe a sigh of relief.

Right now, Len was sitting at the table across from Vince absently cleaning his fingernails with a switchblade. Deputy Reynolds's eyes narrowed as he watched them. He had grown more alert as soon as they had come in, and he was now clearly getting ready to go over there and say something. Watts shifted just enough to get his attention and shook his head fractionally.

"Leave 'em be," he said. "Being assholes is not, I'm afraid to say, a crime."

"Let me just . . ." Reynolds began, getting to his feet.

Watts gave him a mini shrug.

*Your funeral.*

The deputy drew himself up to his full height and moved over to them in his own version of the saunter the gang had employed moments earlier. Watts kept his attention on his coffee, refusing to turn around, but he listened hard.

"Morning, boys," said Reynolds, doing his best Officer Krupke.

"Good morning to you, Officer," said Vince, bland and pleasant as the snake newly tattooed on his arm. "What can we do for you?"

"I'm just ensuring there are no disruptions to Monty's customers as they eat their breakfast this fine morning."

Watts rolled his eyes. He could hear the snorts of undisguised amusement from the lesser Snakes. Vince responded easily. "Can't imagine why we might be causing any kind of disruption, officer. Just in for a bite. Maybe play a few tunes on the box here before getting along."

"I heard you'd come into some money," said Reynolds, digging in.

"Yeah?" said Vince. "Well, the boys here have been mowing lawns for some of the local elders, and I just picked up a paper route, so we pulled in a few extra dollars this week."

"Is that right?"

"Good honest toil."

"You expect me to believe that?" said Reynolds, needled by the outrageousness of the lie.

"A man can believe in all kinds of things," Vince replied. "Right now, I just believe I'll feel better for some grub and a little music."

"Just make sure there's no trouble, you hear me?"

"Trouble?" Vince said innocently. "Why would there be any trouble?"

"Right," said Reynolds, already out of ideas. "Well, you just see it stays that way."

"Absolutely, officer," said Vince, with a grin Watts could hear.

"OK, then," Reynolds finished lamely. "You fellas enjoy your meal."

"We absolutely will, deputy. I appreciate you checking in on us."

And then Reynolds was back at Watts's table looking pink and flustered, knowing it hadn't gone well but not entirely sure why. The Tunnel Snakes were doing their hyena routine again. Watts sighed.

"Time we hit the road," he said.

Reynolds nodded hurriedly, his eyes flashing back to the Tunnel Snakes, but—for once—saying nothing. Watts paid their check, tipping Red Hauser more than he had truly merited to make a point to himself if no one else, and listening as Monty tried his blustering welcome on the Tunnel Snakes. They indulged him, pretending to be laughing with him rather than at him as he rehearsed a Bob Hope gag or two tenuously applied to the upcoming nuclear test, and then Moe Taylor, the slowest of the four, was asking if Andy Lopez had been in yet today.

Monty shook his head. "Nah. The Lopez boys don't usually come by till after school. Why do you ask?"

The question sounded guarded, even protective.

"No reason," said Vince bland as before, but quick, before Moe could respond. "Just like to check in on our pals."

*Andy Lopez and the tunnel snakes?* thought Sheriff Watts. *What would that be about?*

He pictured the two Lopez boys and their paranoid father, frowning as he headed out into the stiff light of the dusty parking lot, where Deputy Reynolds was already leaning on the police cruiser looking sourly back at the vast windows of the diner, though the glare made it impossible to see anything inside.

# CHAPTER THREE

Van was no worse at math than the other kids in his class, had been good at it once, when he saw the value of it. He had enjoyed basic arithmetic—addition, subtraction, multiplication and division—because he used it. Likewise he had got a kick out of geometry, because at its heart it was all shapes, and he could see enough of the truth of the thing in his head. Anything with a spatial dimension made sense to him, and he had even seen some practical uses for what he learned in algebra. But then they had run into calculus, and it was like a show he had been watching on TV had finished and whatever came on next was just . . . not for him. So he shut it off, confident that he would never miss it.

His math teacher felt otherwise. As Mr. Fleischman—a short, plump man who wore horn-rimmed glasses, sweater vests, and short sleeves no matter the weather—chalked up formulas on the blackboard, Van found himself rearranging the images in his head till they resembled Mayan glyphs. The thought conjured images of Mexican step pyramids shrouded in jungle and patrolled by jaguar. Van began to sketch absently in his notebook, framing ancient ruins and the half-occluded head of a watchful cat.

He had seen a mountain lion once out on the ridge over Flatbush when he was about 12. He'd had his dad's old Kodak Pony with him and had fired off a few quick snaps before the animal spotted him and bounded quickly away into the underbrush. It had been a magical moment, so he had been devastated when he developed the film and the whole roll had spoiled. The guy at the store where they did the processing had just shaken his head and said that Van wasn't alone.

"Whole boxes of film sold all over the area came in already exposed," he said, shaking his head. "I can give you your money back—both for the roll and the processing— since I can get that refunded by the manufacturer, but that's all I can do. Sorry."

Van had been crushed. That night he had sketched the puma six or seven times, trying to nail down his memory before it evaporated, but he didn't have the skill to do it justice.

Now he shaded the cat in the drawing with a pattern of dots and hatching, framing it with tendrils of vine. Beside him, Carol Bracewell craned her neck to look, peering through butterfly-wing glasses and twisting her face into a parody of bafflement and awe. Van ignored her, feathering the traces of erosion onto the temple stone, eying the composition critically for balance, but he was not really looking any more than a man stepping into water studies the surface of the pool. He was merely finding a way in.

In seconds he was effectively gone from the classroom, immersed in the steaming atmosphere of the waxy, vivid vegetation in his head, his ballpoint scribbling away almost forgotten. He could smell the faint hint of decay on the moist air, feel the centuries-old lure of the mysterious temples. The teacher's droning voice was long gone, but he could hear drums and an ancient, rhythmic chanting, words of awe and worship in a language he didn't know. And then somehow the rain forest in his head gave way to mountains, to a pale, familiar desert, to darkness and a new aroma, smokey, metallic and hot in his nostrils. In his mind he shifted around a boulder and saw where the darkness was slashed open with a strange light, fire-like but flickering with unearthly color. The sky was burning.

*We shouldn't be here . . .*

"Which gives us what?"

There was a heavy silence, and Van felt the eyes of the class suddenly on him. The teacher was speaking. Van's frantic pen went still and he looked up into Mr. Fleischman's implacable face.

"Well, Mr. Lopez?" he asked.

Van hesitated.

"What?" he said.

"I am asking you to volunteer your solution to the problem," said the teacher, unmoving.

"The problem?" Van echoed. Around him the class shifted with interest and relief: so long as Fleischman was picking on him, the rest of them were in the clear.

"On the board, boy," Fleischman snapped. "The problem the rest of us have been working on for the last 10 minutes. I wonder what you have been working on . . ." He held out his hand commandingly. "Exercise book," he demanded.

Van hesitated, eyes flashing to the board, processing hurriedly what he had been ignoring. He just needed a second . . . .

"Book, I said," demanded Fleischman with a mean flash in his piggy eyes, which said quite plainly that the teacher knew all too well what Van had been doing. He must have already seen. "Give it to me. Now."

Van sighed and offered the book.

Fleischman took it and made a show of consulting it as if expecting a viable answer to his question. "So," he said. "We are trying to calculate the parabolic arc depicted on the board by identifying the derivative to identify the maximum value of M, and Mr. Lopez thinks the answer is . . ." He paused to hold up the scribbled illustration to the class. "Jungle."

There was a ripple of amusement from around him, but Fleischman wasn't popular and the drawing was actually pretty good.

"A word with you after class seems in order, Mr. Lopez," said Fleischman with ill-concealed triumph. "And if you

46

can hitch a ride on the *African Queen* back to the classroom, we will return our attention—*turn*, in your case—to math."

He slapped the exercise book on Van's desk and turned back to the board. Forcing himself not to point out that the pictures were clearly Mexican—or maybe New Mexican, he thought vaguely—rather than African, Van scowled. From somewhere at the back, someone flung a screwed up ball of paper which hit him on the back of his neck. He turned. Dylan Sweet was striking a pose of what he clearly took to be some fancy painter doing a portrait of the girl next to him, Cindy Kaspak, who was pouting at him like a *Playboy* model. Van gave him a long, hard look till Kaspak wilted and Sweet dropped the pose, then he turned back to the blackboard. It made no more sense now than it had the last time he looked.

*Another quality educational moment to go down in the annals of Trinity High.* Another reason why he wanted to get out of this Podunk town, and further proof of why he probably never would.

As soon as Van got his books together and got out of the classroom, he was confronted by Dylan Sweet, who had apparently hung around while Fleischman gave Van the promised scolding.

"Nice work Pic-ass-hole," said Dylan.

"You waited for me so you could use that?" snapped Van.

Sweet smirked. "You think we're impressed by your Beatnik too-cool-for-school bullshit?"

"I really don't care what you're impressed by. I'd kind of hate it to be me."

Sweet hesitated, not entirely sure he understood, then fell back on the line he had prepared. "*Pic-ass-hole*," he said again. "Get it?"

Van said, "Sweet, there are things I got before you were born."

He walked slowly away, and Dylan hesitated. "What does that even mean?" he called after Van.

Van didn't look back, but as he rounded the corner he saw Stacy Nicholson. She looked like she was waiting for him. Any other day, he would have been glad to see her, but he wasn't in the mood. He avoided her eyes and made to walk on by.

"That was quite the image," she said.

Stacy was one of the cool kids, together as gravity and popular as ice cream. A looker too—tall, brunette—but carelessly so, and wicked smart. She was known to read medical textbooks at recess. Van didn't give a shit about what most of his classmates thought of him, but he didn't want Stacy Nicholson thinking he was some pantywaist loser.

"Yeah?" he growled. "What do you care?"

Stacy looked a little crestfallen, stung even, and she shook her head as if trying to clear it. "I just thought it was a cool picture," she said. "Especially since you were working with just a ball point. I couldn't do that. I mean, the technique. And it looked . . . lush. The jungle, I mean. Like—"

But here she broke off, self-conscious.

"Anyway," she concluded. "I thought it was cool. You should check out our after-school club. For art. That's all. See ya."

And with that she was heading off down the hallway. For a moment Van just stood there in stunned silence, and then the scale of his idiocy descended upon him like the anvil falling on Wile E. Coyote.

"Good job, Pic-ass-hole," Van muttered miserably, watching her go. "Very smooth. *Very* smooth."

O     O

At the end of the school day, Van loitered in the hallway, ostensibly waiting for Andy, but rather closer to Miss Vanleash's classroom than usual. Miss Vanleash, widely considered Trinity High's best teacher, taught art and ran the after-school painting club. Van had never considered joining, even though he spent as much time sketching and painting as he did under the hood of the F100. It was a girls club. Not officially, but in fact.

Now he leaned on the wall, checking first for any sign of Andy by the main entrance, and peered through the wire-reinforced glass of the classroom door. The light was on, but though he could only see the back of the room from this angle, it didn't look like there was anyone in there. It was also quiet.

Van sighed. Not being the kind of kid who joined things, he didn't know what days the clubs met, though he had a dim idea that today was when the baseball team practiced, and Stacy was probably there with all the other girls, sitting in their long skirts up in the bleachers. It was kind of hard to imagine her there, but that was what

Trinity girls did. It wasn't like they had teams of their own to play on. He wondered why it seemed weird to think of her there with the others, sipping bottled soda pop through a straw and giggling about the boys on the team. It wasn't like she wouldn't fit in, and he knew several of those players were interested in her. But she had a way about her, a look he caught sometimes that felt like . . . what? Wit? A way of seeing through the bullshit. Something like that.

*What the hell do you know*, Pic-ass-hole? he demanded of himself. "You barely know her."

"Barely know who?"

It was Andy.

"What?" said Van, startled. "Nothing. Just talking to myself, I guess."

"They put you away for that shit."

"Funny. You ready?"

"Actually, I gotta run an errand," said Andy. "I'll see you at home."

"What kind of errand? I can wait."

"Nah, man," said Andy looking quickly away. "I'm good."

Van leaned in. "What is this, Andy? You out stealing again? Hanging with Vince and the snakes?"

"That sounds like a really bad doo-wop band," Andy scoffed. "Vince Reed and the Snakes."

"Not funny," said Van, sensing the dodge. "What's going on?"

"I told you, I'm done with those guys," Andy protested.

"So what's this errand?"

"A favor for a friend." Van opened his mouth to ask the obvious question but Andy cut him off. "No one you know. It's not a big deal. Really."

"Since when did you get all secretive? I don't like it."

"You don't have to like it," said Andy, turning belligerent. "I'm not a kid. I'm 16, and I'm capable of looking after myself. Maybe you should do the same."

"What the hell does that mean?"

"You graduate in three months."

"So?" Van fired back, though he knew where this was going.

"So you gonna work on the truck and haul bales of wire and feed for Pops for the rest of your life? Maybe get a part time job at Monty's like Red? Quite the career!"

"Since when did you care about my career?" Van replied, genuinely surprised and a little uncomfortable.

"You could be someone," said Andy suddenly, the switch of direction hard and fast as when they had shot the railroad tracks that morning. Van stared at him open mouthed. "You think I don't know? You could be going to college. Hell, you got in. Why did you apply if you weren't going to go?"

"To keep people like you off my back."

"I'm serious, Van. I can't believe it's even a question. You have to go to college."

"With what money?" Van replied, glad of something he could swat easily.

"So go in-state."

"Still costs."

"So you carry some debt for a while, big deal," said Andy. "But if you don't . . . !"

The truth of the thing pained him like a shot to the jaw. "I couldn't leave Pops."

"Pops ain't your responsibility," said Andy. "And I'll still be here."

"Not if you wind up in jail."

"I told you, it's cool."

"Oh yeah. Stealing from building sites is super cool."

"Let it go, Van," said Andy. "Trust me."

Van gave him a long, perplexed look. It seemed his brother had gotten older without his noticing. The thought calmed him.

"Where did this concern for my future come from?" he asked.

"It came from the calendar, man. Can't you feel it? The winter is behind us. It's getting warmer all the time. The days are getting longer and hotter . . ."

"And?"

"And soon it'll be summer, and you'll be out of school and then . . . nothing. Not a student anymore. So what then?" Van said nothing, but Andy held his eyes, then prodded him in the sternum with one finger. "You're smart, Van. You could get out of here. Go somewhere cool. Get a real job. Make something of your life."

"You wouldn't think I was smart if you'd seen me get thrown on my ass in math class," said Van with a smirk. It was designed to lighten and redirect the conversation but Andy held course.

"Like you wanted to be a mathematician," he said, shrugging it off like that was dumb anyway. "That's not what you care about."

"Oh yeah?" Van replied, grinning. "And what do I care about?"

"Engines," said Andy, matching his smile for a moment, then turning more serious. "Words. Pictures. You have . . ." he fumbled for the word and lighted on one which felt big and rich in his mouth: "Talent."

"I could be a mechanic," Van said, embarrassed by the compliment. "Pretty sure Stamos would give me a full-time position."

"Making a buck, maybe a buck and a quarter an hour?" Andy fired back. "Up to your armpits in grease and working till dark every night into your 60s when your back gives out, like Joey Flintoff, or till some Buick slides off the jack and crushes your arm, like Ray McGovern. What was he, 26, 27? No, man. You could be something, but to do that, you gotta leave, and don't use us as an excuse to hold you back." Van shook his head, but he couldn't meet his brother's eyes. "I gotta go," Andy said.

"Errands to run," said Van, darkly.

"Yeah. I'll see you at home."

He turned on his heel and headed for the main doors at a jog.

"OK," said Van, barely audibly. "I'll see ya."

Van drove home alone, listening to the pickup's engine all the way, and stopping at Jimmy's auto parts for a replacement mirror and a fresh set of spark plugs. He'd try to get some of the work done before dark, and hopefully before his dad saw the broken mirror and started asking questions. At least the buckshot hadn't punctured the body work. That would have taken some explaining, and Van's dad could easily leap to the wrong conclusion.

*Hell, he could add two plus two and get about 15,000,* thought Van, bleakly. *Especially where guns were involved.*

Despite the detour to the store, Andy wouldn't have beaten him home, whatever his errands were, so Van sat for a moment in the truck with the engine off, wondering what sort of shape his dad would be in. It would depend on whether he'd been out today, and whether he'd started drinking.

He got out of the truck, closed the door quietly and wandered over to the garbage can, careful to make sure he had a paper bag from the store to toss. His dad would almost certainly be watching. It was what he did.

Van lifted the trash can lid and dropped the bag in, scanning the contents quickly. No empties. If his dad had gone on a bender, there'd be beer cans, and he'd have finished the tequila which had been sitting on the dresser. No matter how drunk his dad got, he was weirdly meticulous about disposing of his trash, so much so that he would sometimes take single cans outside before opening the next. It was almost a ritual, and another mark of his sometimes obsessive nature.

But today there was nothing, which was good. Danny Lopez wasn't a mean drunk and never lashed out at his kids, but he would go on endless, unintelligible rants about the government and secret agencies spying on him. All you could do was agree and offer him water and see that he got to be ok when his fury had burned out, but other times were far worse: then he'd just get sad and confused, would spend hours staring at pictures of the family before his wife—Van and Andy's mom—left. Mostly he said nothing. Sometimes he cried, long, noiseless sobs that shook his shoulders, though the rest of him sat hunched and rigid. It was a lot to take.

Van moved to the front door, considering his options, but it opened before he could try the latch. Danny snatched it open and stood there, watching him.

Van tried not to look guilty. "Hey, Pops."

"What're you sneaking about for?" asked Danny, unsmiling.

"Sneaking?" said Van, squeezing past him. "Just being quiet. Case you were resting."

"Where's your brother?"

"He had some things to do. I'm going to do a little work on the truck before dinner. I'll do my homework later if . . ."

"No," Danny cut in. "We need to take a little practice before the light goes."

Van shook his head. "No, Pops. We practiced on Sunday. I have stuff to do."

"Got to keep your eye in," said his father in a voice that allowed for no debate. "You have to be ready."

Standing behind him, Van squeezed his eyes shut and balled his fists, but he knew it wasn't worth protesting.

55

"OK," he said. "But I'm doing it in Andy's place too, yeah? He has homework and I don't want him getting behind."

Danny considered this seriously, then touched his shoulder affectionately and smiled. "Sure, son," he said. He moved off. "Get the 88 and the .45 from the safe. I have my Browning."

Van took a breath, and did as he was told, opening the safe with quick, practiced fingers and removed the Winchester rifle, the Colt pistol, and two boxes of ammunition like other kids pick out the silverware for dinner. He felt no thrill at handling the firearms, only the weary, leaden familiarity of indulging his father's insatiable need to be ready to fight for his life, though what he thought might be coming for them was never entirely clear.

They walked back up the dirt road that ran along the ranch fence, then cut up by the canyon track and into the old marble quarry. The quarry had been part of what put Trinity on the map in the years before the First World War, but the marble—though it had been mined in a promising variety of colors—had proved inferior, fracturing too easily to be of real use. By the mid-'20s, the part of the town that had grown up around the quarry was entirely gone. Apparently there had been buildings there for a while, but eventually they all burned. Now there was just rock, and a huge hole in the ground where cloudy water sat after rainstorms.

Danny set up bottles, cans, and a few paper targets mounted on wooden frames, and they shot, mostly without speaking, for half an hour, following a dogged routine. A pair of crows flew off squawking when the shooting started, and a buzzard circled lazily for a while, but otherwise nothing moved around the pale, shattered cliffs of the quarry. Danny nodded approvingly at a good shot, and cursed in Spanish when he missed. Throughout, he kept a watchful eye on Van, assessing his progress. For his part, and in spite of his unease around his father's inexplicable and relentless paranoia, Van found the shooting oddly calming, the focus, the precision of the thing. He could feel his heart slowing as he breathed, sighted, and squeezed the trigger. Even the kick of the rifle into his shoulder, the recoil, and the plink of the can backwards off its rock perch, brought a kind of satisfaction.

"Dinner time," Danny pronounced at last, considering the sky. He never liked to be out after sunset. "I'll make tamales."

Van grinned at that and proceeded to walk alongside his father, both men silent and as close to contentment as they were likely to get, but after a few steps, Van hesitated.

"You mind if I join you in an hour?" he said. "Kind of want to just sit out here for a spell."

Danny pursed his lips and his eyes went to the horizon where the sun was setting in gold and red fire beyond the mountains.

"Don't stay out too late," he said. "It's not safe."

Van wasn't sure what he meant by that, wasn't sure even his dad really knew, but he had heard it many times before and nodded.

"Of course," he said, adding with a smile, "Tamales."

Danny turned and walked away, the Browning over his shoulder. Van sat on a flat-topped stone overlooking the quarry, his eyes across the cavernous hollow to the rocky peaks, which gleamed improbably in the last light of the sun. He had sat here before. Once he had seen a coyote picking its way along the ridge. It had vanished and then, some 10 minutes later, had emerged out of the brush no more than 12 yards from where he was sitting. It had frozen, startled by his presence, and given him a long, thoughtful look. Their eyes had locked, and Van had kept very still, like they were connecting. Eventually it had moved along, slowly, and without a backward glance, as if it had determined that Van was a kindred spirit.

*Stupid*, thought Van, grinning at himself, but remembering what it had been like to look into the animal's dark, glassy eyes: the blank wildness and calculation, the frankness of the creature's thoughts. There was no pretense there, no social awkwardness. The coyote lived in honesty, and Van had envied it.

*Also stupid*, he thought, and actually chuckled aloud.

It was funny. The kids at school thought him strange, a loner, but cool in his way. Van didn't think of himself like that at all. In many ways he felt young, still in love with the wonders of the world. Some of his classmates wanted— actually *wanted*—to be accountants and lawyers and such, embracing an adulthood as gray as the suits that came with it. Van dreaded that, not because he was a rebel, but because it seemed as dull as concrete, and just as confining.

It was dark now, the moonless sky filling with stars. Van took a last long breath of the dry canyon air, tasting the notes of sage, and then stood up. As he did so, a light skipped across the night sky. A shooting star, he thought, pleased.

And then it stopped.

It hung in the blackness over the canyon, a motionless speck of white. Van frowned. The light was still, suspended like a helicopter, but he had seen it move into its current position and it had been fast. Really fast. And it had stopped on a dime.

*What the hell?*

He stared, shifting his balance slightly in case changing the angle gave him new data on the light, but it stayed where it was, until Van started to wonder if he had imagined its initial movement. Maybe it was just a star that had winked into view just as a shooting star had passed the same spot . . . ?

And then it divided. The light broke evenly into two, then into four forming a line like some rudimentary constellation. For a moment they held their position, then the two on the ends moved with lightning speed in opposite directions, still level with the other two, but coming to rest at the extreme edges of the quarry. Van gasped. He tried to gauge how high they were, what kind of distance they were covering, but there was no way of knowing. They might be small as dinner plates and only a few hundred yards up, or much larger, and considerably further away. Neither possibility explained the way they moved.

As he gazed upwards, he saw that the hundreds of true stars which were the background to this strange display were being blotted out as if something was moving across the sky toward him. It was no cloud. This had a precise, crisply-defined form, its leading edge a great disk-like curve. It made no sound at all, seeming to drift. It felt lower than the other lights, though Van wasn't sure why he thought that, and it seemed to be slowing.

It came to rest directly overhead. Van looked up, and where there had been only blackness he thought he could make out the smallest flickers of energy moving unevenly across the belly of the thing. It stopped and hung in space, utterly silent, but somehow watchful as the coyote had been, and—as with the coyote—Van felt its eyes on him.

A moment passed, though it could have been an hour, and Van could only stand there, frozen, baffled and amazed, until—without warning—the object—if that was what it was—seemed to pull steadily up, getting smaller and smaller until he lost it in the stars.

The four lights regrouped and became one as quickly and efficiently as they had separated, and then they too were gone, streaking away over the mountains, leaving Van alone and stunned in the dark.

# CHAPTER FOUR

While Van and Danny were shooting in the quarry, Andy was emerging from Si's Pawn Shop on Haybrook Lane, shoving his wallet into the back pocket of his jeans. He didn't see the stand of motorbikes till one of them revved hard, sucking his attention as clearly as if it had called his name.

Vince Reed in white T-shirt, black leather bomber jacket, ragged jeans, and cowboy boots was sitting astride his hog, watching Andy through cheap plastic shades. It wasn't his bike that was running. That was Moe's, a half rusted junkyard reclaim, bolted together out of so many spare parts that the original model wasn't easy to identify. Moe was the Tunnel Snakes' errand boy, and he had clearly been ordered to send a message. Other messages would follow, Andy knew, if he didn't respond.

He sauntered over, trying to look casual, thinking about the bills in his wallet.

"Vince," he said, managing to sound more nonchalant than he felt.

"Andy Lopez," said Vince, slow and reflective. He took a long drag on his cigarette, blew the smoke over his upper lip, and turned thoughtfully away. "What are you doing at Si's?"

"Just closing out some business from before," said Andy.

"That right?"

"Yep," said Andy, avoiding Vince's level stare.

"Seems to me you should have had some new business today."

"Yeah, I couldn't get to it," said Andy.

Vince smiled thoughtfully, nodding, then, like he was reflecting on one of the great mysteries of the world, said, "What are we gonna do with you?"

The question sounded real, as if a decision had not been made, but it was redolent with Vince's trademark menace.

"What do you mean?" Andy tried.

"Seems we had a deal," said Vince, his eyes unreadable behind his shades. "You do a little hunting and gathering for us, and we let you keep part of the cut."

"Hunting and gathering," Moe echoed, grinning like the idiot he was. "Like a cave man."

"And you were supposed to do some of that this morning," Vince concluded. "Or am I not remembering our agreement?"

"Yeah," said Andy, "I ain't doing that anymore. Sorry boys. Gotta get on the straight and narrow."

"Hear that, Vince?" said Billy. "He's sorry."

Vince nodded somberly.

"He's gonna be," said Len, his blank eyes showing no emotion at all. He said it without glee or threat. It was a statement of something certain and interesting, as one might observe the approach of a storm.

"Hold on now, boys," said Vince, playing the amiable negotiator, though the flicker of a smile around his shaded eyes held little promise of reprieve. "I'm sure Mr. Lopez has an explanation that will satisfy us."

"Yeah, like I said," Andy repeated, looking at the road beyond the store's empty lot, conscious of the silence. He hadn't seen a car pass since he came outside. "I'm not doing that stuff anymore. Wish I could help, but I got to keep my head down. School, you know. And family."

"Thought we were your family," said Billy, a preposterous remark, but one Andy didn't know how to counter. "But flakin' on your end of the deal? That's cruisin' for a bruisin' all right."

"Want to know what I think?" said Vince. He slid easily off his bike and spat into the dirt, but didn't wait for Andy to respond. "I think Andy here is more of a Lopez than he let on."

Andy had felt the prickle of fear since he realized they had been waiting for him. It had grown every second since, and now his mouth was dry. He felt very young and very small next to these guys, but that remark about his name struck a spark of defiance somewhere in his heart.

"What's that supposed to mean?" he demanded.

"Ooh," cooed Moe. "Feisty."

"It means," said Vince, taking a long, lazy stride toward him, followed by another until he loomed over the younger boy, "that you're a fuck up, just like your old man. A wacko. You boys just don't know what's good for you. You come to our nice little town . . ."

"With your beans," inserted Moe.

"And your *tortillas*," added Billy, pronouncing the l's so that Moe laughed.

"And you make promises to the people who live here," Vince went on, oblivious. "Good folks. Upstanding folks who know what a deal is and expect other people to abide by their word."

"Yeah," said Andy, shrugging off the slur as if he was pushing aside the point of a spear. "Circumstances change. No hard feelings."

"But see, that's where we have the problem," said Vince, making a pained face, as if wounded to his soul. "You come to our town, you play by our rules. You break those rules and we're . . . *offended*. Right, boys?"

"Hell, yes," said Moe.

"Damn straight" said Billy.

"You break the rules," Vince repeated, "and we own your ass. And if you don't do as you're told, you get pulled apart. You hearing me?"

Andy opened his mouth but nothing came out. His legs had begun to tremble very slightly beneath him. He licked his lips.

"I'm sorry," he managed, looking down at his Chuck Taylors. They were dustier than they had been, and he wiped the toe of the left one against the back of his right shin to clean it. "I just can't. My brother said that . . ."

"The brother who drove you to the construction site this morning?" Vince cut in, his lazy drawl gone. Andy took a breath. "Didn't think we knew about that, did you? You say you're done with all our little plans and operations, you being such a fine, upstanding citizen and all. But from where I stand, all I see is a punk who's not holding up his end. We need our cut."

"Yeah," said Moe. "Our cut."

In his mouth the word seemed to change, and fear spiked in Andy again. He glanced back toward the pawn-shop, but the lights inside had gone off. He was alone.

"Your cut of what?" he sputtered, not sure what else to say. "I didn't take shit this morning."

"And that's the problem," said Vince, tapping Andy on the chest with a stiff forefinger, "because you were supposed to. That was the deal. And so when you don't deliver . . . . Well, that takes us back to your being pulled apart."

"I'll go back," Andy gasped. "I can take the truck . . ."

But Vince shook his head.

"Too late, my friend," he said. "You gotta be taught a lesson about crossing the Tunnel Snakes. It needs to be something you'll remember. A lesson, like in school, you know. When I was in school, I read about this time in some ancient place . . ."

"Rome?" offered Moe stupidly.

"Might have been Rome, Moe, yeah," said Vince, "when they had all kinds of cool ideas for dealing with criminals and people who had welched on their friends. Like, this one thing they did was, they'd tie a guy's wrists and ankles to four horses, then they'd lash 'em . . ."

"Yeehah!" whooped Moe with the wave of an imaginary whip.

"And those horses would shoot off in four different directions."

"Nice," said Len.

"Sometimes it would be slow—a long, straining pull, you know?" said Vince. "Sometimes is would be fast—a quick snap that pulled your criminal or whatever he was into bits just like that. Which you think is worse?"

Andy swallowed. He had tears in his eyes, but he couldn't think of anything to say.

"Now we don't have horses," said Vince. "Not here. But we do have . . ."

"Our bikes!" Billy crowed.

"Yeah!" Moe agreed, just getting it. "Bikes are like horses. Cooler, of course. But they can still pull."

"And one bike is like 50 horses, right?" said Billy enthusiastically.

"It is?" said Moe.

"Yeah, dummy," said Billy with infinite disdain. "Horsepower. Says it right on it."

"Like, the bike has the power of 50 horses?" said Moe, comprehension dawning.

"Yeah," said Billy. "What did you think it meant?"

"That's cool," Moe mused.

"The point," snapped Vince, his composure buckling for just a moment, "is that we could strap you to the tails of our bikes right now, and your evening would go downhill in a hurry."

"Kind of flat around here, Vince," Moe suggested.

"You wanna shut up?" Vince snapped. "His evening would go downhill because we were pulling him to pieces. Get it? Doesn't mean we are actually going down a hill. Jesus."

"I said I'd go back!" Andy protested.

"I know, and I'm glad to hear it," said Vince. "But even if we don't actually leave you in separate piles, we gotta make sure you remember the deal. You understand. It's a business thing. Protocol."

Andy babbled, but Vince waved him quiet and nodded to Len, who got down from his bike hefting what looked to be a length of steel pipe.

"This is just a taste," said Vince, as Len sidled over considering where he would put the first blow. "You won't like it much. But you'll remember. And next time it'll be the horses."

Andy took a step back, but Moe rushed him, catching him around the middle and hurling him to the ground.

Then they were on him. At least then the terror subsided, drowned out as it was by pain.

Stacy Nicholson gathered up her books, zipped her bag shut, and left the baseball field without looking back. She didn't feel like sticking around with her friends, watching the boys practice, though she wasn't sure why. Most of the time she had had her head in a book, looking up vaguely when the girls cheered a hit or a catch, smiling at everyone, but feeling oddly out of it, apart, like she had wandered into a party where she didn't know anyone. It had been a relief to leave. It wasn't like the season had even started yet. There'd be many evenings ahead when she'd have to be out here or be thought weird or rude. It wasn't like there was much else to do.

"You OK, Stace?" called someone from behind her.

It was Candace—Candy—Green, Stacy's best friend since elementary school. Stacy flashed her a smile but didn't slow down.

"Fine thanks," she said. "Just want to get home."

"I'll walk with you," said Candy, unselfconscious.

Stacy's smile was a fraction late, but Candy didn't notice.

"Sure," said Stacy. "Great."

"You making plans for the test?" asked Candy.

"Test?" Stacy replied, feeling a stab of panic. "What test?"

"The A-bomb test, silly!"

"Oh. Right. I thought you meant . . ."

"Some school thing," Candy concluded for her. "There's more to life than classes, Stace."

"Like nuclear devastation," said Stacy dryly.

"I was thinking more like Dylan Sweet," said Candy with a furtive, sidelong grin.

"The guy who was just pitching?" she said, to show she'd paid attention. "What about him?"

"He was watching you. I'm sure of it. And Beryl Thompson said he had asked about you."

"Asked about me how?"

"I don't know. What difference does it make? *He asked about you.*"

"Asked what? Where I want to go to med school? Whether I think President Kennedy is going to send more troops to Vietnam? My favorite Shakespeare play?"

"Oh, Stace," said Candy, giggling and waving the questions away. "He asked if you were dating anyone."

"Oh, good," said Stacy, deadpan.

"You don't think he's dreamy?"

"I don't think about him at all."

"Football MVP last fall, probably the same for baseball this season, a lock for homecoming king, and have you seen his *so* ginchy car?! That powder blue Plymouth? Oh my gosh."

"His *daddy's* car," said Stacy, unimpressed.

"So you *have* noticed," said Candy delighted.

"I noticed that he's kind of a jerk. What are your plans for the test?".

"You're changing the subject."

"Yes, I am. Take the hint."

"Fine," said Candy with a theatrical pout. "*But* the two could be related."

"Meaning what?"

"A bunch of us were going to head up to Baldy Lookout. Great view of the test site right across the valley."

"I still don't understand why they are related."

"Because, the bunch of us . . ."

"Includes Dylan Sweet," Stacy concluded for her.

"It will if you come," said Candy with a wink. "Atomic test, maybe a little back seat bingo . . ."

"Oh, please."

"Come on, Stace. Get with the program! It'll be a gas!"

"Why do you even care?"

"Because I hate to see you alone all the time."

"I'm not alone, and even when I am I'm not lonely."

"Because you have your books," said Candy with a theatrical yawn.

"Yes, actually," Stacy shot back, defiant. "And my records, and my painting. I have lots of things to keep me occupied and entertained."

"Just not a boy."

"I don't need a boy. I don't have time for a boy."

"So you say. But what's the point of records if you can't dance?"

"I can dance just fine."

"Not by yourself. With someone. With a guy."

"I refer you back to my original question: why do you care?"

"Because!"

"Because a woman without a man is like a horse without tap shoes?"

Candy frowned. "Why would a horse need tap shoes?" she asked.

"Exactly."

"Boy, Stace. You really know how to make life hard. The team back there? You could have your pick."

"Maybe I don't want to pick," she snapped. "Maybe I'm not interested in being a housewife for one of those Neanderthals."

"Some of 'em are sweet," said Candy, petulant now.

"Yeah," Stacy conceded. "They probably are. But if I'm going to spend time with a boy it won't be because he can hit a baseball."

"What then?"

Stacy opened her mouth to shoot back something pithy but the words failed her. "I don't know," she said finally. "Maybe I'll meet someone in college."

"Oh," said Candy with an extravagant eye roll. "*College.* Fine. Go away to college and leave us all behind."

"You could go too."

"Nah," said Candy. "I'm fine here."

"Maybe you should look around before deciding to stay in the only place you've ever lived."

"And maybe you should mind your own beeswax."

"Ditto," said Stacy.

For a moment the two walked in silence on past the pharmacy on Broom Street. Stacy considered saying she was sorry, but Candy was already past it.

"Might not be so bad, I guess, for you. College, I mean. Become a nurse and land a rich doctor."

"I plan on being the rich doctor."

Candy laughed at that, then caught her friend's eye. "You're serious!" she said.

"Why not?" Stacy replied. "It's 1962. The world is changing."

"Trinity ain't."

"Give it time."

They walked on, past the hardware shop with the display of non-stick "Happy Pans" in the window.

"You think they work?" asked Candy.

"Got me."

"*Teflon*," Candy read. "Sounds like another planet. So come on, Stace. Wanna go up to Baldy to watch the test? It'll be fun. If there are Neanderthals, I'll beat 'em off with a Happy Pan."

Stacy laughed, then give her a quick look. "Wait a minute," she said. "This Dylan Sweet hangs out with Johnny Regis, doesn't he?"

Candy made a face and adopted a "so what" tone. "Him and a few other guys. So?"

"So you've been giving him puppy dog eyes since the Christmas dance!"

Candy looked away with a dismissive snort but her heart wasn't in it. "He *is* pretty dreamy," she admitted.

"Candy!" Stacy exclaimed. "So your wanting me to go watch the test with you is so that Dylan will bring Johnny for you!"

"Maybe. So what? It'll be fun."

"You canker blossom," said Stacy in her best Shakespearean voice. "You have betrayed our sex!"

"Stacy!" Candy shirked, giving her a mock slap. "I never did any such thing."

Stacy considered explaining the joke, but shrugged the moment off with a smile, and took her friend's arm. They were clear of the town center now, and the road was long and straight with hardly any buildings between them and the mountains, which were gold in the early evening light.

"If I painted that," she mused aloud, "it would look unbelievable."

"Yeah," Candy agreed happily.

"I mean it would look bad," said Stacy. "Cheesy. Too pretty."

"How can something be too pretty?"

Stacy shrugged. "Just can."

She felt the hitch in Candy's stride before she saw what she was looking at.

"Stace? Is that . . . ?"

On the edge of the parking lot by the liquor store, the body of a young man lay bleeding in the dirt.

O      O

Van and Danny had cleaned up the dinner things. On KTNT Stevie Fly had taken off his DJ hat and moved into talk show mode, and though Van would usually go to his room to avoid the crazy talk, tonight the languid radio voice had all his attention. If anyone else had noticed the lights he had seen over the quarry, this was where he would hear about it.

"You ever noticed how sometimes your film gets messed up for no reason, cats and kittens?" Stevie was saying. "You take pictures with your trusty camera, take it down to the drug store to get the film processed, all excited to see what you got, and then the envelope comes back and guess what? You got diddly squat. The whole roll is blank."

Van turned to the radio speaker and frowned. *Come on, man. We have genuine strangeness happening right here in Trinity and you give me film processing?*

"Now, it so happens that I have a pal over at one of the Kodak processing plants. I won't say which because, as you know, the walls have ears. Anyhoo, it turns out that the film for cameras gets packed and shipped in corn husks. OK? Stops the canisters getting broken in transit. But here's the part you're not gonna believe. Sometimes the corn is radioactive. That's what fries the film. And guess where the radiation comes from? You guessed it, right here in good old Nevada, from the A-bomb tests we all know and love. What's even wilder is the corn comes from hundreds of miles away, but it's *still* getting contaminated from right here in Trinity. And they *know*, man! The government started issuing warnings to Kodak warehouses whenever there was a test down here because there would be exposure. So what else is that radiation doing, huh? And what else are they not telling us?"

*Well, there are some weird-ass lights over the quarry pretty much now*, Van thought, fuming. *Maybe someone should be telling us about that?*

He shifted in his chair, wondering what kind of madness could make him take Stevie Fly seriously, when there was a knock on the door. Van looked up, a quizzical expression on his face, but his father became very still, his can of

Schlitz, still sweating from the fridge—the only one he'd opened so far—momentarily frozen in the air.

"It's OK," said Van, quickly. "Probably just Andy. Lost his key or something."

He got up, making a calming motion to his father as if he had set something fragile on a stand and didn't want it to fall, then made for the front door.

He flicked the porch light on and peered through the screen. It took him a moment to realize that the person outside was Stacy Nicholson. His heart leapt, but he knew the moment he saw her that something was wrong. He stared, baffled, slowly processing her hurried, anxious movement, her disheveled hair. Out on the road was a car with its lights on. Two other people were standing by it.

Van opened the door.

"Stacy," he said. "What—?"

"It's your brother," she said, her eyes red-rimmed, her voice catching. "He's hurt."

Van didn't need to hear anything else. He blundered out into the gathering night, making for the car. There was another girl—Candace Green, he thought—and a man he didn't know. Stacy's father, he guessed, the owner of the car. And in its back seat, crumpled like a discarded wrapper, his face bloody . . .

"Andy!"

The figure stirred slowly and carefully.

"I'm OK," he said.

"He's really not," said Stacy. "He says he got clipped by a truck out on the highway, but I think . . ."

Van didn't want her to say anything else. "I'll get him inside," he said, reaching in trying to hook his brother under his arm.

"Let me give you a hand with that, son," said the older man. "He's pretty beat up."

They gathered Andy up. He felt leaden, barely responsive, and he winced when they touched him.

"I think he's got a couple of broken ribs," said Stacy.

"Let me just get him inside," said Van.

"I can drive down to the phone booth and call an ambulance," said Stacy's father. "Or we can drive him to the hospital ourselves."

"No," Andy managed. His face was smeared with dirt and rivulets of dried blood which ran from his nose and mouth. One eye was swollen shut. In the porch light it looked rubbery and purple. Unreal.

"He should get looked over by a doctor," said Stacy's dad again.

Stacy was watching breathlessly, her face tear-streaked. Candace hung back, pale and silent. Van didn't think he'd ever heard her go so long without speaking. He elbowed the screen door open and half dragged Andy in, turned sideways so that Stacy's dad would squeeze through behind him. They blundered awkwardly into the living room, knocking an ashtray off the coffee table. It didn't break, but it sounded unnaturally loud in the tense silence. They eased Andy onto the couch, and then everyone but Van pulled back as if he had something contagious, though Van guessed they were just embarrassed and unsure of what to do. It was only then that they saw Danny, standing silent in the kitchen doorway, his Winchester rifle cradled in the crook of one arm like a sleeping infant.

There was a moment of stunned silence, and then Van was up off his knees, and shepherding his father back into the kitchen. "It's OK, Pops. It's just Andy. These folks have brought him home for us."

"They did this to him?" his father said, peering past Van to where his younger son lay bloody and unmoving on the couch.

"No, Pops. No," Van whispered, as if he were soothing a wounded animal. "They helped. They're good people."

Behind him Van heard a faintly indignant grunt, but Stacy grasped her father's arm before he could voice his outrage. He gave her a look, read hers in return, and relaxed.

"The government did this?" said Danny. "They came at me through my boy?"

"No, Pops," Van said, his voice rising, his eyes stinging. "It's nothing like that."

He put a steadying hand on his father's shoulder. He looked upset, disoriented.

"Is your mother around?" Stacy's dad asked Van. "Maybe she could . . ."

"It's just us," said Van.

"Oh," said Stacy's dad, suddenly awkward. "Right. Sure."

"We should go," said Stacy.

Van turned and gave her a quick, grateful look. He felt unaccountably embarrassed, even ashamed.

"Thank you," he said.

*For bringing him, and for leaving.*

"I'll see you in school," she said. And then she touched him: once, with the flat of her hand on his bare forearm, and he wanted to say something but didn't know what.

"Thanks," Van managed. "Thanks, Mr. Nicholson. Candy."

And then they were gone.

Van watched them drive off, then returned to the living room, where his father was sitting beside the couch, staring, bewildered, at his boy.

"It's OK, Pops," he said. "It will be OK."

He went to the kitchen for a basin of warm water and a cloth. There were iodine and band aids under the sink. He brought them in and sponged his brother's face, wiping away the dust and dried blood. Andy was bruising, great violet blotches spreading across his chest like storm clouds, and his face had ripened like a poisonous fruit, but beyond the ribs Van didn't think anything was broken. He tried to wind a bandage around Andy's midriff, but the effort seemed to cause more pain than it was worth, so he abandoned it, and just sat with him.

His father took the chair beside them, saying nothing, the rifle still in his grasp, and after a couple of hours, with the room in total darkness, he fell asleep. Very gently, Van lifted the gun from his hands and laid it by the chair. Van sat still, thinking in spite of himself about the lights in the quarry. Some time later he felt Andy shift and then heard him whisper,

"Sorry."

Van took his hand and squeezed it and then, because he couldn't let it go, murmured, "Tunnel Snakes?"

For a moment Andy just lay there, then—so small and silent that Van had to be watching carefully to see it—he nodded once.

"They done with you?" he asked.

Andy said nothing but he shifted one leg. Van looked down and frowned.

"Shoe," Andy mouthed.

He was working his foot against the arm of the couch. Van reached over and pulled the sneaker free. As it came off, a wad of dollar bills fell free, the money Andy had known better than to keep in his wallet. In spite of his bruised and bleeding face, he managed a smile.

"From before," he breathed. "I'm done now."

# CHAPTER FIVE

Van dreamed of the jungle he had sketched in math class, though he saw it from the saddle of an ambling horse, which picked its way through the vegetation on a trail of white sand. He was looking for something, though he wasn't sure what, studying the ground for traces, knowing he would recognize the clues when he saw them. There was no sign of the ancient Mayan ruins from his drawing, and the landscape, now that he looked at it, was actually quite barren: bare rock and distant mountains. As he looked, one of the last jungle vines withered before his eyes, burst into sudden flame, then turned to ash and smoke. Overhead, a point of light divided into four.

He sat up in the saddle, smelling the air, catching . . . what? Heat that threatened to scorch the inside of his nostrils, and a faint metallic tang. It reminded him of something. Then the heat was on his face as well, and he quickly looked up. The sky, which had been blue as turquoise, was ablaze. And suddenly he realized that the thing he had been looking for wasn't on the ground, it was up there, roaring through the burning sky, descending in a long, terrible arc bringing fire and death.

*We shouldn't be here . . .*

Van woke with a start.

He was slouched by the couch in the living room. Andy was still there, still sleeping, breathing evenly, but his father had gone. Van sat up, blinking, shrugging off the dream, feeling the awkwardness of the way he had slept cramping in his back and sides. He stretched, holding it till the ache subsided, and then, with one last look at Andy, stood up and went into the kitchen. Danny was there, coffee in hand, standing by the window, peering through the blind as he had done the day before.

"Hey, Pops," said Van. For a moment he wanted to talk about the lights he had seen over the quarry the night before, but his father's manner made him hesitate.

Danny glanced at him, then looked back out. "That van is back."

Van took a breath, but said nothing. After what had happened to Andy, he was in no mood to indulge his father's paranoia.

"We should get your brother into the basement in case they come. We can't protect him where he is."

"They're not going to come, Pops."

"If he can't stand, we can carry him down. Lock the doors behind us. Leave him the .45."

"He's fine where he is," Van replied through gritted teeth.

"We should move him before the sun comes up," said Danny, not hearing him. "They always come before dawn . . ."

"No, Dad!" Van shouted suddenly. "They don't. They never come. It's all in your head, and for once you should put it all aside and focus on Andy. You hear me? Someone beat the living shit out of him last night, and it wasn't the goddamned government. OK?"

Danny's face clouded, first with anger, then confusion. At last his eyes slid back to the living room door and he nodded.

"I'm sorry," said Van. "I'm just . . . I didn't sleep well."

His father tilted his head, as if hearing something far off, and again he looked bewildered, unsure of himself. It made him look strangely and, alarmingly, young.

"Pops?" said Van, knowing he had gone too far. "You OK?"

Danny seemed to consider this and then nodded fractionally. "I'll sit with Andy," he said, moving back to the living room. He hesitated in the doorway and without turning around said, "You're a good boy, Van."

Van squeezed his eyes shut, hardly daring to breathe, then said, "Thanks."

"Dinner at your mom's tonight," said Danny. "I'll drive you both over."

Van turned to him.

"Maybe next week, yeah, Pops?" he said. "Andy won't be up to it, and I have homework and—"

"It's what we agreed," said Danny. "Even if Andy can't, you should go."

Van tipped his head back as if ready to shout into the sky. "OK," he said at last.

"OK," said his father, moving into the living room to sit with Andy. "And you keep an eye on that van."

Van breathed out. It came out as something between a laugh and a sob. "Will do," he muttered.

○    ○

At the phone booth on the corner of High Bluff and Main in the predawn silence of the sleeping town, a figure wearing a quilted trench coat stood against the morning cold, picked up the receiver, and dialed a long series of numbers. The line crackled, and a hollow silence followed. It echoed faintly, eerily, as if the call were connecting somewhere deep under water, or across vast reaches of space. The figure listened, watching the shadows, alert but calm, cover story at the ready should someone blunder into view. There were four pulsing beeps on the line, and the figure in the phone booth dialed four more numbers. For a moment nothing happened, then came three pairs of clicks. At last there was a voice, but what it said was not in English.

The figure pressed the receiver closer to their ear, scanned the empty street and spoke in a low voice. "Jasmine. Winter. Maven. Hero."

There was another resounding silence, another series of clicks, and then a new voice came on the line. "Greetings, Skylark."

The figure smiled faintly in response and continued the conversation in fluent Russian.

O          O

Twenty miles across desert highways that stretched like jet trails through the rugged Nevada landscape, what the residents of Trinity knew simply as "the base" was bustling in spite of the early hour, and while this was customary in the lead-up to a nuclear test, it was even more crowded than usual. A convoy of 150 troops in trucks with supply vehicles had shown up in the dead of night, and when the sun rose the soldiers who were resident at the base were surprised to see that their visitors had arrived with M41 Walker Bulldog and M48 Patton tanks. At breakfast, some said they'd seen M60s.

"Main battle tanks in an inland desert?" sneered private Emil Washington. "To fight who? What? It's not like we're gonna look up and find a battalion of T34-85s rolling in from Los Angeles!"

"The Soviets might have shipped 'em across from North Korea," said his buddy, Mike—Sourface—Sourstein. "Pass the coffee. Got to have something to take away the taste of these eggs."

"Yeah?" Washington shoved the pot toward him. "And what's gonna take away the taste of the coffee? The eggs?"

"Funny."

"So the enemy are crossing the Pacific—unseen, mind you—*with armor*, and we're gonna fight them *here*?" Washington snorted. "You're daffy."

"You got a better idea?"

"Sure. Anything is better than an armored assault on a hundred square miles of Nevada nothingness."

"Let's hear it, then," said Sourface.

"Maneuvers," said Washington, laying the word out like a plate of caviar.

Sourface waved him off. "That's what they always say when they're doing something they don't want nobody to know about."

"War games, then," Washington countered. "Tactical training or something. It's not like there's anyone here to see."

"Heads up," said Sourface, with a warning nod. A group of uniformed men had entered the mess, though it was immediately clear that most of them were subordinate to the tall, lean guy in the middle. He carried himself with the kind of familiar authority that spoke of years of command. "Who's the brass?" Sourface kept his voice low.

Washington eyed the group as they took in their surroundings and the officer—if that's what he was—snapped to one of his attachés, who scribbled notes on a clipboard.

"Not regular army," Washington whispered.

"Air Force? Atomic energy?" Sourface speculated. The group, their business apparently concluded, was already leaving.

Washington shook his head. "I think lunch will be alphabet soup," he said pointedly.

"CIA?" said Sourface.

"That would be my bet."

Sourface blew out a long thoughtful breath, then shrugged. "Well, I know one thing," he said.

"Don't undersell yourself," Washington said with a smirk. "I'm sure you know several things. Some of 'em may even be right."

"You're a regular Mort Sahl today," said Sourface, deadpan. "What I know is that whatever is going on here is so far above my pay grade that I couldn't reach it with a long stick, and you know what means?"

"Not our problem."

The two soldiers clinked coffee cups.

○          ○

Having determined that Andy was in no further danger, and after Andy told him in no uncertain terms to leave him the hell alone, Van spent a couple of hours working on the truck. He fixed the mirror, switched out the spark plugs and adjusted the gap with his pocket gauge, then tinkered with the fuel pump. It was therapy for him, working with his hands, functioning on a kind of autopilot while his mind slept. That was crucial. If he thought too much about his family he wouldn't be able to sit still, and then he would go out looking for some serious trouble. He could feel it singing in his ears, a shrill, pulsing rage, rich and hot as blood. So he worked his wrenches and his screw drivers as if they were the only things in the universe, and gradually the impulse to punch someone, to kick and bite and bellow till some kind of cosmic justice had been done, subsided.

In place of his rage, he replayed in his head what he had seen in the quarry: the lights, and then the great dark thing that had—the phrase came unbidden into his head—looked at him. What was he to make of that? It was close to the military base, so maybe it was all some kind of prototype aircraft. The lightless thing, which had been lower and slower, might have been some kind of balloon—like one of those old zeppelins? It didn't feel plausible, but then the alternatives were even less plausible. He wouldn't give them room in his head.

Since Andy would spend the day resting up, Van washed his hands and spent half an hour rereading favorite pages from his dog-eared copy of Kerouac's *On the Road* as a way of grounding himself in the here and now, getting his head out of the quarry. Then he headed into school on foot. When he passed Monty's diner, he looked in through the plate glass windows, in case Vince Reed and his goons had stopped by, but he found himself staring into the faces of Dylan Sweet and his jock Sweaters. They made faces, and pretended to offer him money, like he was begging, and Van felt some of that shrill singing in his ears again, so he walked away, pausing only to nod to a put-upon Red Hauser, who raised a hand to stop him. Moments later, Red was outside.

"Hey man," said Van.

"I heard about Andy," said Red. "He OK?

"Be out of action for a few days, but yeah, I think so. Thanks for asking."

"And you?"

Van shrugged and grinned self-deprecatingly. "About the same. How are things in the palace of Monty? Waiting tables now, I see. Quite the heady promotion."

"My joy is unconfined," said Red, darkly.

"I'll bet."

"You coming in after school? I'll slip you some free fries when the comandante isn't looking."

"Can't tonight, man. Family dinner night."

"With your mom?"

Van bobbed his head.

"And . . . ?" Red turned back to the window and looked pointedly to where Dylan Sweet was yucking it up and holding forth like he was running for office.

"Yeah," said Van. "Afraid so."

"Tell me you won't make Andy sit through that," said Red, shaking his head.

"Not if it's up to me," said Van.

"Will it be?"

"Nah."

"Nah," Red agreed. "Nothing ever is."

They slapped palms and Van turned to go on his way, when Red stopped him.

"Hold up," he said. "Sam wants to walk with you."

Sam Jenkins was a scrawny white misfit who had been the first person to truly befriend Van after they moved from New Mexico in the summer of 1958. Sam's family were military, several generations strong, and his father had been awarded a Purple Heart in Korea after being stabbed by an enemy bayonet. His father had then killed the enemy in question with his own weapon, a piece of family lore that was rolled out every time Sam expressed doubt about joining the army. The Jenkinses were heroes, and Sam was expected to join their ranks the moment he got out of high school.

Sam patted Red on the shoulder as he headed back into the diner, then came down the steps to join Van.

"I heard about Andy . . ." Sam began, but Van headed that conversation off quickly.

"He's OK."

"Was it . . . ?"

"Vince, yeah," said Van. "Can we just walk?"

"You gonna do something about it?" asked Sam, ignoring him. "Puncture his tires or something."

"What am I, a cartoon character? No, I'm not going to puncture his tires. Jesus, Sam."

"You're not going to fight him, are you? He'll kill you. I mean, literally, *kill* you. I don't mean, like, beat you up. I mean he'd actually . . ."

"I know what you mean. Right now, I'm not going to do anything."

"Call the cops."

"And have Sheriff Watts pull the Snakes in so they can lie their asses off and then come kick my ass, too? It's not like there were witnesses. No," said Van, making a decision. "I can't afford to make things worse."

"Really? Huh. OK. Your call, I guess."

Sam sounded disappointed.

"It's not a movie, Sam," said Van. "It's not *Gunfight at the OK Corral*, you know? I'm not looking to get killed, or get Andy killed for that matter. And it could be that my brother may just have learned something I haven't been able to teach him, about who you make friends with. So just leave it, OK?"

"OK," said Sam, suddenly contrite. He walked alongside Van, taking little skipping strides as if he had to jog to keep up.

As the buildings around them fell away and the town opened up, the ground developed a weaving of grass and spring flowers.

"You still planning on joining up?" Van asked.

"It's what the Jenkinses do," he said with mock solemnity. "We're a family of heroes. *Get yourself in the army and make a man of yourself, son.*"

He grinned, but it looked wooden and when it faded there was a hollowness to his face.

"They'll send you to Vietnam," said Van.

"Really?" said Sam with mock surprise. "That hadn't occurred to me at all."

"Maybe by the time you're enlisted it will be over, and you can go somewhere tropical for a couple of years."

"Coconuts and girls in grass skirts," said Sam wistfully.

"Something like that," said Van. "You gonna watch the test?"

"Do I have a choice?" Sam replied. "It will be visible for, like, a hundred miles. I hope they know what they're doing."

"What do you mean?"

"Nothing," said Sam. "Just . . . All the power. You ever read about Japan? Hiroshima and the other place."

"Nagasaki."

"Right. People melted, Van. Ordinary people like me and you and Andy and our families. They fucking *melted*. God knows what else. I don't think they tell us what they're doing most of the time. I don't think they even know."

"This is the *they* that you are planning to join as soon as you graduate?"

"At least I'll be inside the secrets," said Sam. "See? Upside."

"And if you are with them, you'll be less likely to get melted."

Sam nodded, grinning, then rethought the thing. "Or maybe if I'm one of them I'm *more* likely to get melted," he said, doubtful.

"No one's gonna get melted," said Van.

"Tell the Russkies. The Cubans. The Koreans and Vietnamese. I don't know, man. We've got this test, and everyone will cheer and eat burgers and drink beer, like it's Fourth of July or something, when in fact . . . I don't even know. Everyone acts like it's normal, like it's a party, when what's actually happening is that we're ripping matter apart. You know? Stevie Fly says we're unraveling the universe, and the town thinks it's an excuse to sell hotdogs."

"Stevie Fly's just a DJ," said Van, pushing away possibilities he wasn't ready to deal with.

"Doesn't mean he's not right."

Van didn't know what to say to that, and for a long moment they walked on in a silence loaded with things unsaid, ideas that were too big to speak.

*Lights in the sky. A dark shape moving silently over the quarry . . .*

"They do make one hell of a show," Sam said.

"What do?"

"A-bombs," said Sam.

○          ○

Van had lunch by himself, brooding, his intensity acting as a forcefield that kept his curious classmates at bay. That was good. He didn't want to talk about Andy and the Tunnel Snakes, he didn't want to talk about the nuclear test, and he sure as hell didn't want to talk about the lights in the quarry, an event which—so far at least—seemed to have gone unnoticed by the rest of the town.

Instead, and for reasons he couldn't explain, he had found himself thinking about his dead sister, a nameless baby he had never seen. Perhaps it was the effort of not thinking about the other stuff, perhaps it was the knowledge that he was going to be seeing his mother that evening, but she had just popped into his head. The short version of the story was that his mom had been pregnant when they moved from New Mexico to Nevada but the child hadn't survived. He didn't really know what had happened. He'd been about to have a little sister. And then he wasn't. One day his mom was in hospital and then she was out, and the room they had set aside as a nursery had been stripped and turned into storage. His dad had installed a gun safe in there, and had taken to staring out of the windows, looking for strange cars, and the agents of a conspiracy only he understood.

It had never occurred to Van that the two events were somehow connected, though he knew that they had led to his mom's leaving less than a year later. For eighteen months she had lived alone in a rented apartment close to the insurance agency where she worked as a secretary. And then . . .

He couldn't think about what had followed, though he was going to have to deal with it in person later that day.

"Mr. Lopez?"

Van looked up.

It was Miss Vanleash, the art teacher. He stared for a second, as if she had spoken to him by mistake, then got clumsily to his feet.

"Miss Vanleash," he said, flustered. "You need something?"

"No," she said, calming him with a gesture and a faintly bemused smile. She was in her 40s, solid looking, her hair lank and uncared for in a way that somehow made her more interesting. To Van, at least. Her spinsterhood was a source of much amusement in some quarters, even from those who acknowledged that she cared for her students, and—and this was rare for Trinity High—inspired them to achieve great things. "I heard you were looking for me. Yesterday."

"Oh," said Van, wrong-footed. "I was, kind of."

"Kind of?" she repeated, not unkindly.

"I had wondered about the art club. The after-school thing. I know we're already well into the semester but . . ."

"You'd be welcome any time," she said. "I was disappointed you didn't take the painting and drawing elective this term."

"You were?" he replied, stunned. "Why?"

"I saw your work in the file that came with you when you transferred."

"My work?"

"Paintings and drawings from when you were in middle school. One of your teachers saved them. You didn't know?"

Van shook his head in stunned disbelief.

"They were really quite good," said Miss Vanleash. "You painted a lot of desert landscapes with mountains, nocturnal scenes but with splashes of brilliant color in the sky like stars, planets. I assumed I'd have you in class one day, but here you are, about to graduate."

"Yeah," said Van, not wanting to think about mountains and lights in the sky. "Sorry. I just . . . I guess I didn't have room in my schedule."

"I guess not. It's too bad. I do hate wasted potential. But I am sure you have done well in other subjects and you are welcome to join us after school whenever you can."

"OK," said Van, still a little stunned. "Thank you. I'll seriously think about it."

The teacher considered that, hearing the note of caution, and nodded, smiling a little sadly.

"Just don't feel that you are responsible for everyone and everything except your own wishes," she said. "Time goes by so very fast. Don't waste it. You don't want a life full of regret for chances you didn't take."

She smiled again and walked away. Van watched her go, wondering about the implications of what she had said, and the way she had touched on something that felt so absolutely true and, simultaneously, unfixable. He pondered how much she was aware of his home life, then reminded himself that everyone in Trinity knew everything about everyone, particularly about relative newcomers.

*Strangers*, he thought. *In every sense of the word.*

Suddenly Van felt something close to breathlessness and wondered how something as tiny as whether or not he joined an after school art club could leave him feeling like he was having some kind of existential crisis. It wasn't until later that he realized the only person who might have mentioned him to Miss Vanleash was Stacy. He didn't know how he felt about that either.

# CHAPTER SIX

Van and Andy's mother, Tammy, lived on the south side of town in a housing development not unlike the one under construction out on the corner of Gamebird and Sagebrush where the boys had liberated some of the building supplies. Trinity wasn't big enough to have suburbs, but that was clearly what the planners had gone for: tract housing with little yards, identical floorplans but semi-customized trim packages. The houses were bright and clean and modern: "executive homes," whatever that meant. Van had hated the place on sight. It looked like a doll's house and felt prim, fake, a version of life modeled on TV shows. Against the backdrop of the mountains and desert, he thought the houses looked absurd. And, of course, under the resentment, the hint of envy, what he felt mostly was sad.

There was a powder blue Plymouth parked outside. In spite of his mood, Van couldn't help but be impressed. It was low-slung, long, and sleek, shining with chrome, particularly in the front, where the grill and bumper were set off by double headlights, each with a distinctive eyebrow trim. The taillights were on little jet-pack nacelles, and the rear wheels were half hidden by the paneling, so the whole thing looked like a boat, or a space ship. By comparison, the pickup Van was riding in, the thing he had spent half the morning working on, really did look like a piece of crap.

They had driven over in the pickup with the radio on, and though Andy had rolled his eyes, Van—for once—had not objected to having Stevie Fly on.

"Lights in the sky," Stevie half-crooned. "Right here in Trinity, last night. That's what we'll be talking about tonight, and I got a whole line of callers who want to share the full on freakiness of what they saw . . ."

Before Van could stop him, Danny switched the radio off.

"I'll pick you up at nine," he said.

"You not coming in?" asked Andy. He was still stiff, and his face was a mass of bruises and swelling, but he had insisted on coming along.

"This is about you guys and your mom," said Danny.

He didn't say that she wouldn't want to see him, that it would only make an awkward situation 50 times worse, that it pained him to be around her knowing she wouldn't be coming home, but they knew all that, and the thought of it tore Van's mind from what he was missing on KTNT.

"And keep your cool," Danny added. "No point punishing her."

Van and Andy felt the weight of that, the generosity of it, and how much it cost their father to say it, and they both responded with a murmured "Yes, sir."

As Danny drove off, Andy stood scowling at the Plymouth. "Welcome to 1962," he said sourly. "Gateway to the future."

"Might be better than the past," Van said.

"I wouldn't bet on it." Andy winced and put a hand to his tender jaw.

"You sure you're up for this?"

"Yeah," said Andy with resolve. "But why did she have to marry *him*?"

He gestured vaguely, and his motion took in the car, the house, the street, a whole world of difference from the one they knew.

Van shook his head and shrugged, but said, "Guess we have to put up with it. Come on. It'll only be a couple of hours."

"With them," said Andy bitterly.

"With them," Van concurred. For a moment they both stared at the car which glittered smugly back at them, then they approached the front door.

It opened before they could ring the bell, and there was their mother, looking harried and anxious under the wide, welcoming smile.

"Come in, come in!" she said, then caught herself and became all shocked concern. "Andy! What happened to your face?"

"It's nothing. Came off my bike."

"It looks terrible! Come inside and I'll get you some antiseptic anointment."

"It's fine, mom," said Andy a little stiffer this time.

"It needs dressing."

"Dad already took care of it," said Andy pointedly. "Dad and Van."

He didn't say "my family" but the possibility was in the air, and his mother hesitated, her cheeks pink, and she looked down at her hands, her mouth open. She had put on a little weight since the last time he saw her and wore the kind of weariness that comes from habit.

"He's OK, mom," said Van quietly, but she was already bustling off, urging them to follow her into the dining room.

"Come on through," she said, flustered. "Dinner is almost ready. Maybe Dylan can get you a soda."

And there he was, Dylan Sweet, looking resentful and smug as the Plymouth. Behind him was his father, Hank, tall, square jawed and clean-cut in shirt sleeves with starched collar and cuffs. He looked like the model whose image would appear on a realty listing for the house. Or an ad for the car. It wasn't just his jaw that was square. He smiled and offered a strong hand as Van nodded and said, "Mr. Sweet."

"Welcome," he said by way of introduction.

They had met before, of course, but Hank Sweet always greeted Van like he was a prospective customer or someone he'd just bumped into on the golf course. Van and Andy had even attended their mother's wedding three months earlier, an excruciating affair at which they had kept to themselves and ducked out as early as wouldn't give offense. Since then they had met up twice for burgers and shakes at Monty's, each occasion tense and awkward, the conversation like lead and molasses. But before tonight, they had never visited the Sweets' house.

"You have a lovely home," said Van.

"Not too grand," said Hank airily. "But it suits us. Hi, Andy. That's quite the shiner you got there."

"The other guy's even worse," said Andy. His mother gasped, and there was a momentary hollow in the evening, an uncomfortable space which Andy hastily filled. "Just kidding. Fell off my bike."

"That's good to hear," said Hank. "I mean, not that you got hurt, but that you weren't involved in anything unsavory. You hear awful things these days—right, Tammy?"

"Juvenile delinquents," said their mom.

Van winced at Hank's casual use of her first name, though he didn't know what he had expected him to call her. Mrs. Sweet? That would be dumb. And worse.

"Anyway," Hank concluded. "Glad you're doing better. Have a seat. Dylan, how are those Cokes coming? I put some in the refrigerator an hour ago."

"Hank is very proud of that fridge," Tammy said with a teasing smile.

"It's new!" Hank protested, smiling back at her. "GE Spacemaker fridge-freezer! Pull-out bins, ice trays, pivoting shelves, even a place for eggs!"

"It's very impressive," said Andy, glancing through the state-of-the-art kitchen to the appliance.

"Top of the line," said Hank with a secret smile, like he was confiding a fetish. "I do like new and shiny things."

"Yeah, I got that," said Van, looking directly at his mom. There was another momentary hesitation, a teetering uncertainty as to which way the evening might go. "Everything looks fantastic," he added, steadying the seesaw.

There was music playing on the radio: Connie Francis singing "Stupid Cupid," if Van could believe his ears.

Dylan returned from the kitchen with a pair of Coke bottles held by the necks between his knuckles. He didn't so much offer them as thrust them in the direction of Andy, then Van, his face a mask. The Lopez boys took the sodas but found they were still capped. Dylan waited a second, an insolent smile on his face, enjoying their helplessness, then swept a bottle opener from his back pocket like he was pulling a gun, and handed it to them.

"Sit, sit!" Tammy crooned. "I hope everyone is OK with pork chops. They looked so good at the market that I couldn't resist."

Van had a wild urge to say he'd gone vegetarian, though that would probably get him run out of town.

"Great," said Andy.

"Wanted to give you fellas a treat," said Dylan, cryptically.

"Yeah," said Van, understanding the jibe, "we usually eat grass and stones."

Tammy laughed a little louder than was necessary, and Hank joined in, uncertain exactly what the joke had been. Van and Dylan eyed each other with undisguised hostility. The radio—which Van figured was tuned to WKRT Favorites, moved from "Stupid Cupid" to Guy Mitchell singing "Sippin' Soda."

Van rolled his eyes at Dylan. *You listen to this shit?*

Dylan's jaw tightened, his eyes hard.

"So, who's hungry?" asked Hank, glancing around as if he expected a show of hands.

"You boys get comfortable," said Tammy, "and I'll start serving."

"Sounds good," Hank pronounced. "Only four months to graduation, eh boys? That's got to feel good, right?"

Van barely heard him.

"Van?" said Tammy gently, hovering at the kitchen door.

"What?" said Van, focusing. "Oh yeah. Sure. Real good."

"And what will you do after?" asked Hank.

"Not really sure yet," Van began but Andy cut him off.

"College," he said. "Out in California probably. If his grades hold."

"Really?" said Hank. "Impressive. What do you want to study?"

"I'm not really sure." Van shot Andy a reproachful look. "Figure I'll see what seems interesting. If I go."

"He'll go," said Andy. "First Lopez to go to college. Pretty cool, huh?"

He said it with such wonder, such strange and genuine joy that Van stared at him in amazement. Dylan gave a little snort of derisive laughter.

"First Lopez to be able to read," he muttered.

"What was that?" snapped Van.

Dylan gauged the moment, one eye on his father who had missed the remark, and shook his head. "Just clearing my throat."

"Costs money, college," said Hank sagely. "If you go, you make sure you study something that will earn you a decent wage. They're teaching all kinds of weird stuff these days. Art and social science subjects, though they don't seem very scientific to me. You get yourself a business degree or something. Pre-law, maybe. Stacy Nicholson's going to be a nurse or something, right Dyl?"

"Right," said Dylan.

Van's hackles rose and he shifted in his seat. "I heard she wanted to be a doctor," he said.

"That seems a bit ambitious for a young lady," said Hank, with an indulgent smile. "Not sure many men would find that appealing."

"Maybe that's not why she wants to do it," said Van.

"Now Hank," said Tammy teasingly as she emerged from the kitchen with plates of chops and mash, "women can be all kinds of things today. Dyl, bring those green beans through, will you?"

"I guess I'm just old fashioned," said Hank, smiling and holding up his hands in surrender. "Now Dyl here, he's going to be an accountant, right Dyl?"

"Something like that maybe," said Dylan grudgingly. He had not moved to help with the vegetables.

"What about you, Van?" said Hank. "Fancy giving accountancy a shot? Steady, respectable job, good money."

"I don't think it's my kind of thing, sir."

"Well, you've got to be able to count, so . . .," Dylan quipped. "Instead of drawing pictures in class."

"What's that?" asked Tammy, anxiety flickering across her face. "What does he mean, Van?"

"It was nothing."

"Sure it was," said Dylan, warming to the subject. "We were doing calculus in Fleischman's class but Van was doing *art*. All intense, you know?" he added, laughing out loud. "Scribbling away like he'd forgotten the rest of the world existed. And Fleischman showed it to the whole class."

Van caught his mother's apprehension and forced a smile. "Math's just not my thing."

"*Not your thing*?" said Hank with just enough scorn that, in a flash, Van saw exactly how far the acorn had fallen from the tree. "What does that mean?" he said, in a falsely hearty tone. "It's numbers. You don't have to be *into* them, or whatever you kids say these days. It's work, not a hobby or a vacation. You do it because it's what puts food on the table."

"And buys a house like this," Andy cut in with the kind of enthusiasm that had to be sarcastic, but Hank missed it.

"Exactly," he said. "Life isn't all fun and games. Your generation doesn't seem to get that. When I was your age we were fighting a world war and everyone had to . . ." He caught a look from Tammy and raised his surrender hands again. "But as I said, I'm old fashioned."

"Accountant, huh, *Dyl?*" Andy said with mock approval at Dylan. "That will certainly draw the ladies."

"I've never met a woman who didn't want a man with a stable income," Hank announced. "They don't always know it right away, but they always come round. It's the natural order of things."

Dylan was glaring at Andy. "Beats being a ranch hand."

Andy's good humor vanished. He glared at Dylan who, pleased to see his point had stuck home, smirked.

Van got up. "I'll help Mom with the beans," he said.

Dylan bristled at "Mom" but said nothing and remained sitting.

In the kitchen, Tammy was standing still, her head hung, her face drawn with tension and worry. She brightened deliberately when she saw Van, framing a smile that didn't quite reach her eyes.

"You've come to help?" she said. "Isn't that kind of you."

Van just nodded and reached for the serving dish of beans. There was an old photograph on the wall by the stove: Dylan when he was maybe 12, a laughing Hank, and a woman Van assumed was Dylan's mother. He wondered vaguely when she had left and why.

Tammy watched him for a second, biting her lip then said, "Don't mind Hank. He's a good man and he's really making an effort. It's not easy for him to have you guys around. I think if he had the choice he'd want us to move away, start over . . ."

Van couldn't think of anything to say, so he just stood there, cradling the beans like a servant in the background of some old painting, waiting for instructions.

"You OK, Mom?" he said finally. "You seem . . ."

Sad? No, it was more than that. He remembered her as sprightly, nimble even. Now she seemed sluggish, every movement at three-quarter speed. There was a puffiness to her face and neck he had not noticed till now.

"I'm fine," she said breezily.

"Yeah?" said Van.

Her forced brightness flickered a little and she smiled wanly. "Just don't seem to have much energy these days. Finding it hard to concentrate at work. Stress, I guess."

"You should see a doctor."

"It's nothing." She put her hand to her throat as if feeling for tender spots on either side. "Age, probably," she added with a self-deprecating smile.

"You're only 40!"

"It's amazing what time can do to you."

"Still, you should get checked out."

"Hank has already insisted," she replied. Van said nothing to that, and she went back into her entertaining-housewife mode. "Let me put some butter on those before you take them through," she said, opening the famous fridge. It was indeed impressive, Van thought, to his dismay: sleek and modern like everything else in the house. Compared to theirs, at least. "How's your father?"

She had waited to say the words till she had her back to him, as if that would make it sound more casual, or so she wouldn't have to meet his eyes.

"Not good, mom," said Van. "Worse."

She paused for a moment before turning to face him, her eyes full of a pleading desire for him to understand, to forgive. "I stayed as long as I could," she said.

Van nodded, mute.

"I just couldn't—"

"I know, mom," he said. There was another loaded silence, and then a question tumbled out of Van's mouth before he had even decided to say it. "Was it about the baby?"

He hadn't intended to raise the matter, but it had been weighing on his mind all day, or rather it had wormed its way into his brain like a parasite, and now lay pulsing faintly in his head, ever present and swelling.

Tammy stared at him, her eyes wide with surprise. She blinked and wiped them with unsteady fingers. "What made you . . . ?" She stopped and considered before she spoke again. "It was part of it," she admitted. "Maybe it was the thing that forced the issue. But it had been building for years. You know that. You know how your father can be. He wasn't always like that, you know? The paranoia, the obsession. He had none of that when we first met."

"When did it start?"

"A year or so after you were born." Her voice was distant, as if she was recalling things she hadn't considered in a long time. "Not that it was anything to do with you," she added hastily. "One day it just started, got worse over time.

Then the ranch in New Mexico closed and we had to come here. I thought a new baby might help but . . ."

She gave an oversized, helpless shrug and her eyes finally brimmed over. Van wanted to hug her, but he was still holding the dish of beans in both hands, and before he could set it down, the moment had passed.

"You doing all right?" called Hank from the living room jovially. "We're starving out here!"

Tammy blinked again and wiped her face. "Go on through," she said to Van. "I'll be right there."

Van did as he was told, setting the beans in the middle of the table.

"Got a serving spoon?" asked Dylan. "Or did you expect us to eat them with our hands?"

"I have a spoon," said Tammy as she came in.

"You folks eat a lot of beans, right?" Hank asked.

"Different kind of beans, dear," Tammy inserted quickly.

"What folks?" asked Andy warningly.

"With a name like Lopez, I just figured . . ." Hank said innocently. "What?" he said off Tammy's look. "Just asking a question. It's good to be curious about other peoples, right?"

"We were born here," said Andy.

"Well," said Dylan. "Not here. New *Mexico*."

"Still the U.S.," said Andy, his face rigid. "We're Americans."

Hank did an odd tilt of his head and made a questioning face followed by shrug and a smile as if the point was debatable but he was prepared to let it go.

"These chops are cooked to perfection, dear," he said.

"I'm glad you are enjoying them," said Tammy.

Andy bit into one then raised a hand to his bruised jaw, wincing.

"You OK, hon?" said Tammy. "That looks very painful. You did that falling off your bike?"

"It's fine, Mom. Guess I was going a bit fast."

"Yeah, right," muttered Dylan.

"What's that?" said Andy.

"Oh, come on," said Dylan. "You got beat up! It's obvious. Probably by your dad."

"What did you just say?" said Van.

"Now boys," Tammy cut in, but Dylan had had enough of playing nice.

"We're just gonna sit around and pretend we don't know their dad's a wacko?" he said, leaning back and making the pronouncement like it was something they were all thinking. "Every single person in this town knows Danny Lopez is a freak and a drunk and a dangerous loon—"

Andy launched himself across the table like a grizzly. The sheer suddenness of the attack rocked Dylan back, and though Andy landed only one punch, he fell out of his chair and sprawled heavily on Hank's immaculate carpet. Andy, as if struck with doubt, even horror at what he had just done, hesitated, even looked as if he might climb down and apologize, but in the stunned silence, Dylan was up and raging.

He rounded the table and clocked Andy who was just standing there looking shame-faced at Tammy, catching him squarely on his already battered jaw. Andy, who made no attempt to block the punch, staggered backwards, banged his head against the wall, and slumped down, but Dylan was still coming, spewing outraged obscenities and a vague stream of racist insults.

Van leapt for him, grabbing his arm as he was about to bring his fist crashing down on Andy's dazed and bloody face, and in the melee which followed, the table cloth snagged and dishes of food crashed to the floor.

"Stop that right this moment!" bellowed Hank.

"Boys, no!" Tammy shouted, hands to her anguished face.

But Van and Dylan were locked together, wrestling, kneeing, and then they went down hard, rolling on the floor as they fought to get free enough to punch. Van was blind with fury, all the frustrations of his life coming screaming out in a rush of blood. His mind went blank, and all he could feel was rage and hatred, so that he was barely a person anymore. Dylan got a hand free and thrust his fist into Van's belly, once, twice, three times as Van doubled up, the air driven from his lungs. He rolled to get clear, gasping, trying to suck the oxygen in, his eyes wide with panic, but Dylan threw himself on him again and went for his face.

Van felt a smashing blow to his right cheek which bounced his head off the floor, but in the same instance his breath came back, and he fought back like a demon, throwing his elbows, knees, fists, anything. It was an ungainly maelstrom of fury and bitterness, but suddenly he had

Dylan on the ground, his right wrist seized and wrenched halfway up his back till the boy shouted out in pain.

"Get off him!" roared Hank, all trace of the genial host gone. "You'll break his damn arm."

He grabbed Van from behind and hauled him off. Free and furious, Dylan turned and threw one more punch which Van, held firmly in place, couldn't block or dodge. It caught him in the teeth and for a moment the room spun.

"That's it," said Hank with a chilly calm as he twisted around to point Van at the door and thrust him out toward the hall. "Get out. Both of you."

Van stumbled and turned. Dylan looked ready to come at him again, but Hank had grown glacially hard, as if only restraining himself from joining the fight with the greatest degree of self-control. Andy was on his feet again, but he looked dazed and his nose was bleeding. Van's eyes went to his mother. He gave her a long, appealing look, but she was standing beside Hank and her face was oddly blank.

"You'd better go," she said.

"Mom," said Van. "You can't stay here with them. Come with us."

Tammy looked back at him as if she was carved in marble. The blood still sang in Van's ears, but the sudden silence after the chaos of the fight was strange and unearthly.

"Mom" he said, beseechingly this time. "Please."

There was a long, still moment in which any number of things might have happened, and then she shook her head. Her mouth had grown thin, as if she had locked down all her feelings and did not trust herself to open her mouth. At last she said simply, "I live here now."

Van stared, aghast, speechless, and then Andy was tugging at his shirt.

"Come on," he said. "Let's go home."

Van continued to gaze desperately at his mother as if there was no one else in the room, in the world, and then he nodded and backed out.

# CHAPTER SEVEN

In the week leading up to the atomic test, Trinity swelled with both visitors and anticipation. Some of the former were what Monty at the diner referred to as "nuclear tourists." He was happy to take their money and smile, regaling them with stories of past detonations, how far away they could be seen, how the shock waves shook the windows, and any number of other strange phenomena, some of them fairly truthful, others he just plain made up. The tourists couldn't get enough, and soon the local paper ran a story on Monty, proclaiming him a "character" and his diner the "perfect place for a bite while soaking in some local color." Sam Jenkins, Van's army-bound buddy, had it on good authority that Monty had paid for the privilege, but his source was "a friend of a friend," so no one took it too seriously even if, as Red Hauser observed, it was exactly the kind of thing Monty would do.

Rumors of an expanded military presence at the base also floated around Trinity, but this was taken to be normal and not much worth discussing. The town was just homespun enough to still assume that the government and the military acted in their best interests. Subsequent events, particularly the escalating war in Vietnam, would change that, for some at least, but for now the default position in Trinity's mostly white populace was that whatever happened at the base was being done to protect them and their way of life. There was a generational gap, of course, one that would widen significantly over the next decade, but much of what young people did, and who they aspired to be, still looked like a version of what their parents did and aspired to, and the only people outside the bubble were criminals like the Tunnel Snakes and folks who—by reason of race, ethnicity, and other things that kept them out of the mainstream—were simply not on Trinity's radar.

So the steady influx of military vehicles and personnel into the base drew little comment and the attitude to the upcoming test mingled excitement at the sheer spectacle of the thing, and pride at what it represented to them as Americans. Outliers like Danny Lopez were baffling, crazy, and probably dangerous. Van feared his father was all these things, and, for as long as he could remember, he had dismissed Danny's anti-government leanings as mere paranoia. But something had been nagging at him since his experience in the quarry, and however much he tried to bury it deep in the recesses of his mind, it kept resurfacing, bright and hard.

Over dinner on the Thursday night before the test he casually asked his father about New Mexico and why they had moved.

"You were there," his father said, frowning. "The ranch wasn't workable. The cattle died or had to be put down. Government bought the land from old man Fenning. We couldn't live on the site anymore. There was no other work in the area, so we came here."

He said it with a shrug, a story he thought common knowledge, but it had the inflection of a question. He gave Van a wary, searching look.

"What killed the cattle?" asked Van.

"Water and feed went bad," said Danny. "The whole valley. Why are you asking this?"

Andy—now much recovered from his beating—gave Van a warning look. They knew that tone in their father's voice. It was like seeing storm clouds rolling in from the mountains, loaded with rain and lightning.

"When did it start?" asked Van.

Danny was getting edgy, shifting in his seat and rubbing his hands together like he was washing them.

"Late '40s," he said. "Fenning toughed it out for six or seven years, thinking things would recover, but they never did. Why are you asking this?"

"No reason," Van lied. "Where are you gonna watch the test from?"

"I ain't watching that," said Danny. "Staying home. You should too."

"No way!" said Andy. "I wanna see it."

"You've seen them before," said Danny.

"A few. Not many. And people say this is gonna be a big one."

"Yeah," said Van carefully. "It's not like we got to see them growing up."

He watched his father. Danny's eyes had gotten a furtive, hunted look. They flashed around the room as if unable to focus on anything, and his fidgeting hands couldn't keep still. "You did, though. Right, Pops?" Van asked.

His father said nothing, but got up abruptly and went to the fridge. He pulled out a can of Coors, opened it and downed half of it in a series of long swallows. Andy's look to Van this time was inquiring.

*What the hell are you doing?*

"The first nuclear tests were out there in '45—right, Pops?" Van continued. "Right over Fennings's ranch. I would have been a year old, right?"

His father hurled the beer can away and glared at them. He looked both distraught and furious. Andy blanched and got quickly to his feet in case they had to make a run for it.

"Why are you talking about this?" Danny demanded. "I told you not to. *They* might be listening. They have eyes and ears everywhere!"

Knowing he had gone too far, Van spread his hands and made a calming gesture. "You're right," he said soothingly. "I'm sorry, Pops. Forget I mentioned it."

In the silence the beer can rolled across the floor, trailing thin, yellowish fluid. Van took a step toward his father, who stiffened, on his guard, but Van made the gesture again, then approached more slowly and put his arms around his father's shoulders, drawing him into an unequal embrace. He was alarmed to feel his father's body shuddering with emotion.

"I'm sorry, Pops," he whispered. "It's OK. It's OK."

It took 10 minutes for his father to fully stabilize, and he insisted that they lock themselves in the basement with their weapons until the van parked across the street left, just in case. Van avoided Andy's what-the-fuck? stare, and silently thanked God that he hadn't said anything about the lights over the quarry.

After school the next day, Van went to the art club, mostly so he wouldn't have to go home. He sat next to Stacy Nicholson and painted in quick, confident, sweeping strokes, roughing in figures in strong reds and blacks, moving swiftly, from one painting to the next. He did five or six in under an hour, impressionistic visions of a man on a horse in the desert, soldiers with rifles, a screaming, desolate child, and what looked like a great exploding planet with four stars perfectly aligned in the sky above. He worked in silent intensity, unaware of Stacy, the other students, or even the teacher as they all watched him from the corners of their eyes, impressed but cautious, maybe even a little scared by his intensity.

*We shouldn't be here*, he thought vaguely, though as soon as he thought it the phrase became inexplicable to him.

"You wanna go get a soda or something at Monty's on the way home," Stacy asked when the club ended.

"Can't," said Van. "Something I need to do." She looked a little affronted and he shook his head, trying to shake off his mood. "I'm sorry. Sort of . . . out of it today."

"Yeah, I saw. Everything OK at home?"

"Yes," Van snapped. "Everything is fine at home. Why does everyone keep asking me that? Why do people look at me like I'm about to explode or get beaten to death by my crazy father and my hellion brother?"

Stacy looked offended but quickly hardened. "That's not what I meant," she said, "but if you're going to be like that, fine. Whatever. Do what you like."

Van caught himself. "I'm sorry," he said, reaching out and taking her by the hand before she could stalk away. "I didn't mean you. I'm just . . . I don't know. There's been a lot going on."

Stacy considered this, then nodded. "OK," she said. "Just remember that not everyone in Trinity is the same."

"Not the same as me. That's for damn sure."

"Or me," she said pointedly. "And you can let go of my hand now."

Van looked down and blushed. "Right. Yes. Sorry."

Stacy smiled. "Just teasing."

Van blew out a long breath and shook his head at his own behavior. "Well, at least I can say I held the hand of Trinity's first female doctor."

Stacy beamed with pleasure and surprise. "Who said that?"

"It's in the air."

"As a joke, I'll bet, for most people."

"Not for me," said Van. It came out more earnestly than he had meant it, and he glanced down embarrassed.

"I'll take that as a compliment," Stacy replied. "And if Trinity doesn't like the idea of female doctors, they can bite me."

Van looked up and nodded, his eyes distant. "Oh brave new world that hath such creatures in it."

Stacy tilted her head on one side, her eyes narrowed. "Is that Shakespeare?"

"*The Tempest*," said Van.

"Which class did you read that in?"

Van looked away, abashed. "Just found it in the library."

"You are an unusual person, Van Lopez," she said.

"For Trinity," he said.

"For anywhere."

"Well, it takes one to know one, Stacy Nicholson," he said.

She beamed again. "Say." The words tumbled out of her mouth before she could stop them. "You gonna watch the test?"

"Seems like I don't really have a choice," he said. "Why?"

"A few of us are heading up to Baldy Lookout. You should come."

Van hesitated, then nodded. "OK, yeah. I'd like that."

"Maybe grab that soda beforehand?"

"I'd like that, too," he said.

"Then it's a —" She caught herself, but gave him a considering look and finished the statement. "A date," she concluded.

"Sounds good," he said. "And here was me not having anything to look forward to."

"Come pick me up?"

"Sure. Great."

She returned his bashful look and was about to leave when he said, "Listen, can I ask you something? It's a bit out of left field, but I can't think of anyone else who might be able to help."

She gave him a slightly coy smile, as if this was more flirtation. "What do you want to know, Van Lopez?"

"How would I get access to a death certificate?"

It was as if someone had dropped a bell in a church. She stared, her demeanor changing completely. "What?" she asked. "Why?"

"I want to see if there was a cause of death recorded for ... someone. Like, if there was an autopsy or something."

Her brow furrowed. "And you are asking me because ... ?"

"You're going to be Trinity's first female doctor," said Van sheepishly. He knew it sounded like a line, but it was also true.

"The dead person," she replied, her voice low. "You suspect some kind of foul play?"

He almost grinned at that. It sounded like something off the TV. "No," he said. "Nothing like that. I just want to know."

"Where did they die?"

"Here. Trinity Hospital."

She went thoughtful then, weighing something privately.

"What?" Van asked.

"I volunteer there," she said. "Wanted to build my résumé and get some real experience before I start my pre-med college work. "

She said it carefully, laying the words out as if testing him, gauging his response. For a moment he stood there, waiting for more, then realized what she was asking.

"I had no idea," he said. "I wasn't, you know, trying to get anything out of you."

She laughed suddenly; a musical peal that took years off her age. "This has to be the first time a boy has tried to get something out of a Trinity girl and it was access to an autopsy report." She got thoughtful again and then shook her head. "I don't know, Van. I don't want to do anything that could jeopardize my college application. I have a good thing at the hospital and they've already said I can do some kind of orderly work or internship there after my first year."

Van nodded hurriedly.

"Absolutely," he said. "I wouldn't want you to. Honestly, I didn't know. I was just asking for your advice, not your help."

She considered that. "Who is the dead person?" she asked.

He looked away as if he didn't want to say, but then turned back and looked her full in the face. "My baby sister."

There was a long silence between them. It stood like summer heat in the desert, a physical thing.

Stacy looked at her watch. "The hospital records office will still be open," she said. "We can go there now."

○        ○

Stacy stared at the forms in the manila folder, unsure what to say. It had begun as a lark, a flirtation, and a curiosity, but as soon as Van had said who the deceased was, it had grown heavy with significance, settling in the pit of her stomach like a stone.

Getting access hadn't been hard. The staff at the hospital knew and liked her. Van was a blood relative of the deceased. The findings were a matter of public record. Still, it felt like they were looking into something which was best kept dark, as if they were casually flipping stones in the desert, knowing full well that they would eventually reveal a scorpion or a rattlesnake.

"Take your time," said nurse Harvey. "If you have questions, let me know. If I can't answer you, I'll find a doctor."

She left them in the examination room with the folder, like they were opening a safety deposit box on one of the TV cop shows. When the door closed they both stood, looking at the folder, saying nothing. Finally, Van reached for the file, opened it, and read in silence. Eventually he shook his head, baffled and disappointed. He shoved it across to Stacy with a shrug that said he hadn't learned anything.

"Thyroid hormone deficiency," he said. "Whatever that means."

Stacy scanned the chart. "The thyroid gland was damaged," she said quietly. "It affects the baby's development."

Van nodded a little too emphatically, and his eyes were glassy. "So . . . natural causes?" he said.

Stacy frowned. "Well, hypothyroidism is associated with Hashimoto's disease," she said, glad of being able to use some of what she had been reading about. "There was a piece recently in *The Lancet* about it. It's an autoimmune disease but . . ." She hesitated, flipping the chart. "The patient's mother . . ." She caught herself and blushed. "Your mother," she corrected, "would probably have shown symptoms."

"Then where did it come from?"

"I don't know. There was no real autopsy. They aren't common for miscarriages unless there was reason to look for something in particular, and with your mom being on the older side for child bearing . . ."

Her voice dried up. Van looked blank, vacant as an empty lot, lost. She wanted to reach out to him, but didn't know how. Even a touch would feel presumptuous. "Thyroid," she said musingly. "It can be tied to other issues."

"Like what?"

"Well, it's probably not related but we've had a few cases of thyroid cancer lately," she said.

"Cancer?" said Van, shocked.

"It wouldn't affect the baby like this," said Stacy quickly. "I just seem to have come across a lot of references to it lately."

"In books?"

"No, I mean here in town. Dylan Sweet's mom died of it."

Van looked up suddenly as if she had slapped him.

"Dylan's mom?" he said.

"Yeah. Three years ago. What?" she said, reading his face.

"I thought she just left," he said. "I thought . . ."

"No, she died. Why?"

For a moment Van just stared, then shook his head. "Nothing," he answered. "Can I tell you something, even if it sounds crazy?"

"Of course," she said, cautious, but meaning it. "About your mom? Your sister?"

"No," said Van, shaking his head. "Nothing connected to that. It's about something that happened here the night you brought my brother home, something I saw at the old marble quarry."

O      O

That night, in the mountains overlooking the base, a whip-poorwill called, low and plaintive, and a cloud scudded slowly across the face of the moon. In the carefully chosen shadows of a ravine, the agent known as Skylark, still in a quilted trench coat, moved quietly up the ridge. It skulked to a stand of scrubby mesquite trees, settled, and drew out a pair of high-powered binoculars and a camera with a long lens. Below was a grid of lights: buildings, parking and loading lots, runways, and the headlamps of vehicles crossing the barren emptiness of the compound. It was like watching an ant farm or a beehive, in which each creature has a role, a purpose, organized and specific but operating according to an internal logic impossible to read from the outside. Among them were Emil Washington and Mike—Sourface—Sourstein, a couple of soldiers following orders, as unaware of being watched as they were unaware of the larger machine in which they were the smallest of gears. To a casual observer, the activity, like that of ants and bees, meant nothing, but just as the trained entomologist could discern patterns from long, meticulous study, turning them eventually into meaning, so could the movements of the base be at least partially decoded by someone with the necessary focus, experience, and dedication. For the next two hours, Skylark stayed still and silent, shifting only to make notes in a pad, writing not words but a complex pattern of shapes and symbols, closer to hieroglyphics than English. Mostly the binoculars were trained on the base itself, but from time to time they would sweep the skies above, hunting.

The Berlin wall had been up only for a year, a structure designed to stop the flow of data from east to west. The year before that, the United States, after failing to bluff the world with tales of meteorological research equipment, had been forced to publicly acknowledge its surveillance of the Soviet Union when its U2 spy plane had been shot down over Sverdlovsk. Only a few weeks ago that aircraft's pilot, Francis Gary Powers, had made the long, tense walk across the Glienicke Bridge—the so-called Bridge of Spies connecting West Berlin with Potsdam—in exchange for a KGB colonel named Rudolf Abel. Information was currency, and covert operations were quickly becoming the hottest part of the cold war.

Atomic spies had been embedded in the United States since the '40s, some of them actively engaged in the Manhattan Project—Klaus Fuchs, Theodore Hall, Morris Cohen, David Greenglass, Saville Sax, and others. They had funneled stolen plans and other data to the Soviets across the Iron Curtain from the earliest days of nuclear testing when the atomic detonations had taken place not here in Nevada but several hundred miles east, in the deserts of New Mexico, directly adjacent to the ranch land where a young Danny Lopez had just started his family.

That had been the beginning.

Now the figure on the ridge stowed the binoculars, pocketed the code book, and moved silently down the rocky slope. Skylark had things to report, and time was short.

# CHAPTER EIGHT

**V**an spent another morning under the hood of the F100, thinking of Stacy, the way she had listened thoughtfully to his tale of lights in the quarry. She had been quiet, wary, but when he finished, she had nodded soberly as if it all made sense.

"You thought it—or something in it—was looking at you?" she clarified when he finished.

He nodded, glad that she had picked up on what he thought was the most remarkable part of the story. If he'd told Sam, they'd be talking about the lights: how fast they had moved, how high they were. If he'd told Andy he'd be explaining that no, he hadn't been drinking. Both Andy and Sam would have made a lot of noise. Stacy had gone quiet, not—he felt sure—because she thought him crazy and didn't know what to say, but because her sense of the world had shifted a little on its axis.

As he replayed it all in his head, Van beat out a dent in the passenger side fender with a ball-peen hammer, then brushed out the interior, washed and buffed up the bodywork.

"Check you out," said Andy. "I guess the rumors are true."

"Just want it to look nice, is all," said Van, focusing on the broad, circular sweep of his cloth.

"For your date."

Van was about to say it wasn't really a date, but he remembered the way Stacy had called it exactly that, and he shrugged.

"What are you going to wear?" asked Andy.

"Wear?" Van answered. "Hadn't thought about it. Does it matter?"

Andy gave another extravagant eye roll. "You are supposed to be the wiser elder brother. How are you so clueless about this stuff? I've had three girlfriends in the last year! That beats your lifetime achievement by—hmmm, let me see—three!"

"I'm not good at that stuff," Van muttered.

"It's not even that girls don't like you, which is weird. They do! But you're always up to your elbows in grease, or have your head buried in a book, or are drawing. Sorry, *sketching!* Sometimes I think you were born in the wrong place. Or the wrong century. Maybe you should be some brooding French painter in a wig or one those English Romantic poets writing about flowers and shit."

"Whatever," said Van, brushing the remark away.

"C'mon," said Andy. "You need to plan this properly. Clothes, music, flowers, topics of conversation, things that make you look cool, stuff you know she's into. We need to do some prep."

Van smiled and shook his head. "I'll be fine."

"Have you done the prep?" asked Andy pointedly.

"Gonna wing it. Be myself."

"Oh, this is bad," said Andy. "Don't be yourself. Be someone interesting and cool."

Van sat on the pickup's running board. I'm good."

"You are not good. You are terrible. The worst. You need to study this stuff."

"Which you have been doing," said Van, amused, watching the way the sun sparkled on the truck's chrome.

"Every day, man," said Andy. "While you have your head in the truck or are out sketching, I'm studying the ways of the fairer sex. Sketching, for God's sake! Empires can crumble while you're sketching. The house could collapse around you and you wouldn't notice. Naked women could dance in front of you and you'd be scribbling away on your pad, drawing fucking trees. And now you're going to *wing it* and *be yourself*..."

"I'll be fine," said Van.

"Don't say I didn't try to help," Andy replied, palms raised.

"Duly noted. Now beat it."

Andy backed off, hands still up. "See you at Monty's before the show?" he asked. "I'm gonna get together with Sam. Hang with Red."

"Sure," said Van. "But don't give us a hard time, OK?"

Andy grinned wickedly. "Would I do that?"

After Andy left, Van wondered why he hadn't told him about the lights in the quarry, then wondered why he had told Stacy.

*Winging it*, he thought. *Being myself.*

It was amazing she hadn't run for the hills.

o          o

In the parking lot outside Si's Pawn Shop on Haybrook Lane, four motorcycles sat cooling like horses at a trough by the saloon in some movie Western. Inside, their owners haggled, Vince holding back while Moe wheeled and dealed, instinctively knowing that the longer and quieter he sat, the more bargaining power he had. Si wasn't easy to intimidate. He was a big, barrel-chested man with an unfashionable handlebar mustache and a mane of wild, iron-gray hair. He had been around the block a few times before setting up his hock shop, much of it on bikes like the Harleys the Tunnel Snakes had ridden in on, and he wasn't impressed by all their *Rebel Without a Cause* bullshit.

"Twenty," he said. "Take it or leave it. And since it's obviously hot, I'd say take it 'cause you won't get a better deal anywhere in the county."

The items in question were construction tools newly liberated and currently sitting in a pair of duffels on the counter.

"No way!" Billy chimed in. "That stuff's worth way more than that! The drills alone would fetch . . ."

"Where?" Si demanded.

"What?" Billy replied, annoyed and confused. "Here! These right here."

"No," said Si with exaggerated patience. "You're saying what the drills would fetch, and I'm asking where they would fetch that, 'cause if you can tell me, then maybe you have a point. But so far as I can see, they won't fetch any more than I'm saying, because they are, as I said, hot. Stolen."

"You can't prove that," said Moe.

"I don't need to," said Si. "But can you prove that you bought them legally? You have receipts? These are practically brand new tools. Look at that." he said, picking up a set of socket wrenches. "No rust, no scratches or dings. Barely used. You show me how they came to be in your possession in ways that won't bring the fuzz down on me and we can talk, but if I have to stick 'em under the counter every time Watts walks in, that's . . . inconvenient. Inconvenient gets you 20. Not a dime more."

"This is bullshit," sputtered Moe.

"You are free to go any time," said Si serenely. He was sitting with his back against the wall, hands by his side, an attitude of complete composure.

"Maybe we should use some other methods of persuasion," said Moe in what he thought was a suggestively menacing tone. He flashed a grin at Vince who didn't respond.

Si blew out a long, slow breath and got slowly to his feet. His expression was all bored exasperation, but he had picked up a two-foot wrecking bar with a cruel hook at one end and a chisel point on the other. He didn't look at it.

He didn't have to. It pulled the Tunnel Snakes' gaze like a magnetic field.

"Time for you boys to make tracks," he said pleasantly.

"Twenty," said Vince, knowing when to cut his losses. "Deal."

Billy gave him an open-mouthed look, and Moe exclaimed "Vince!" but Vince ignored them, holding Si's eyes with his.

Outside a truck rumbled past and the windows rattled, then Si nodded, reached into the register and pulled out a pair of rumpled bills.

"And everyone is happy," he said. "But for future reference, tools are too easily recognized. I'd recommend you go back to girders. Those I can move a whole lot easier."

Vince's eyes narrowed. "Like the ones Andy Lopez sold you?"

"That's right," said Si. "But he closed out his account."

"Loser," said Len, speaking for the first time. "No-good, lying, yellow . . ."

"What did you pay him?" asked Vince.

"Twenty," said Si. "Same as you. Why?"

"Twenty?" exclaimed Moe.

Si shrugged. "Fair price for what he was bringing. Too bad he quit. I could have used some more."

"For the stuff from last week? He said he sold you one girder," said Len.

"Sold me four," said Si. "The full-sized ones, too."

"That little shit!" snapped Moe. "He gave us two lousy bucks!"

Vince shot him a look and Moe went quiet, but Si couldn't help grinning.

"The kid got you," he remarked.

"Yeah, well we ain't done with him," said Vince.

And though Si was as unflappable and used to trouble as any man in Trinity, looking into Vince's eyes it was clear that he felt a stab of pity for the Lopez boy. Vince just smiled.

O     O

Monty's diner was positively hopping. Most of the tables were already full, many with out-of-towners here for the atomic spectacle. Even the counter, which old George Singer usually had to himself, was packed. Andy ordered a cheeseburger with fries and told Red to be quick about it "my good fellow" in what he thought was a haughty British accent but sounded more like a deranged Australian with a speech impediment. Red grinned and rolled his eyes, using the cloth he had wiped the table with to give him a quick snap to the back of Andy's head while Monty wasn't looking.

"See, there's that temper of yours again," said Andy. "Gonna get you in trouble one of these days."

"Hilarious," said Red. There weren't many people in town who could joke with him about his infamous flare-up on the football field, but the Lopez boys were in that exclusive club. They teased him about it constantly, partly because he flatly refused to explain his actions. Though he had acquired the hothead reputation and the nickname—"Red," because that was what he saw—he was actually a placid, easy-going kid. As part of the only Black family for miles in a state that *Ebony* magazine had called the Mississippi of the West, he had to be.

Red's great grandparents had settled in Trinity after moving from Georgia during what they called the Great Migration, when Black folks fled the Jim Crow south. Family lore said they had been heading for California but decided that their money would go further in Nevada and, instead of merely passing through, had stayed, helping to found a small Black community—mostly made up of laborers, construction workers and their families—on the southern edge of Trinity. Some had worked the railroad that ran through Vegas, others helped build the Hoover dam. Decades later, with Nevada comfortable in its own version of Jim Crow and half the stores, hotels, and restaurants of Trinity quick to let him know that he wasn't welcome on their side of town, Red had good reason to wish they'd kept going west. But he kept his head down as his daddy had taught him, and though he dreamt of shaking the little town's dust from his feet, he hadn't figured out a practical way to make that happen.

Yet.

"How about a change from the burger?" he said.

"I always have a burger," said Andy.

"Exactly."

"They're good here," said Andy. Sitting opposite him, Sam Jenkins, who looked like he could probably eat about six a day for a month and still be underweight, nodded fervently.

"Best burgers in the county," he said.

"Burgers are easy," said Red. "Basic. So long as the meat is decent and you don't cook 'em too long, it's all about the trimmings. Where's the challenge in that?"

"OK," said Andy cautiously. "What are you proposing?"

"Wait and see," said Red, flashing him a smile and heading off to the kitchen.

"Not sure I like the sound of that," said Andy to Sam.

"I'd be concerned," Sam agreed. "Who knows what he has back there. Snails, maybe."

"Snails?" Andy exclaimed, more bemused than revolted.

"They eat snails in France," said Sam wisely.

Andy made a show of looking around the diner. "You noticed we ain't in France, right? If we'd gone to Paris, instead of, you know, Monty's in shit-hole Nevada, I'd have noticed."

"Just sayin'" said Sam, unflustered. "You don't know what he might be cooking up back there."

"Why do you always look for the most sinister explanation for everything?" Andy demanded, only half joking. "Why is everything a conspiracy with you? Why can't things just be what they look like?"

"Nothing," said Sam gravely, "is as it seems."

"You're watching too much goddamn *Twilight Zone*," said Andy, shaking his head. "Right now, our pal Red is back there making me something kind of like a burger but a little bit different. Maybe it's got some nice onions grilled in there with the beef, or maybe it's a sandwich with melted cheese or something, but you know what it won't be?"

"What?"

"It won't be fucking snails."

Sam raised his hands and made an *I'm just sayin'* face. "The world is far stranger than you think."

"Oh my God. Now you sound like Stevie Fly."

"Stevie Fly gets it, man."

"Come on," Andy said dismissively.

Sam leaned forward across the table. "Last night this one woman called in. Eunice, her name was. Said she's seen those lights over the quarry that everyone was talking about. Anyway, she said that later that night she woke up and her room was full of this weird glow, and there was like a *presence* in the room . . ."

"Probably one of the Tunnel Snakes," scoffed Andy. "Len, I'd bet. That guy needs to get locked up."

"Not a *person* kind of presence," Sam cut in. "An *otherworldly* presence. Something from beyond the stars . . ."

"Some jack weed trying to catch her in the buff, more like," said Andy, unimpressed.

Sam shook his head with renewed vigor. "No, man. She said she's had these dreams before, but they feel real, and she thinks she's kind of remembering something that happened a long time ago . . ."

"You gotta shut that stuff off, Sam. You're sleep deprived."

"But other people have been saying the same thing," Sam pressed on. "Just this week, there've been like five people reporting the same dreams, the same sense of, like, repressed memories, and Stevie says—"

"Oh, *Stevie* says!"

"Stevie says it feels like something is coming, like there's a building intensity, like when you can feel the air change before a storm, and all the cows go under the trees, and the dogs stop barking and—"

"Except those are real things, not made-up shit."

"It's not made up!" said Sam, a little louder this time, and just sharp enough that Andy sat back startled.

"Whoa, there. Take it easy!"

"You guys don't take me seriously. And you should, because this stuff is real and it's serious and it affects you more than anybody."

"What does *that* mean?"

"Because you were there at the start," said Sam under his breath.

"At the start of what?"

"The tests, man! The nukes. Stevie says that's where all this weird stuff began."

"Weird stuff?"

"Lights in the sky! Abductions! Fucking aliens, man!"

"I thought you were talking about the A-bomb tests?" said Andy.

"Same thing!" said Sam. "The tests started back in the forties, not here but out in New Mexico, when you were kids. Before you moved here. You were there! The first A-bomb went off right by the ranch where you lived, and it was way bigger than they intended it to be, and . . ." Here he leaned all the way across the table and spoke so softly that Andy barely heard the words. "And Stevie says some-one—or some*thing*—noticed."

In spite of himself, Andy found Sam's earnestness a little spooky. The back of his neck tingled where the hairs stood on end.

"What do you mean *something*?"

"The A-bomb was a giant technological leap forward, right?" said Sam. "And it got someone's attention. And maybe that someone wasn't from this world."

Andy thought for a moment, then shook his head.

"Nope," he said with the kind of finality Sam couldn't ignore. "That's all Buck Rogers/Flash Gordon horse shit. Where's my damn burger?"

He looked around, and at that moment the diner door opened and a group of boys came in, all wearing preppy sweaters and pale slacks: the jock crew. Dylan Sweet with his brain-dead lackey, "Tank" Matthews, and their underlings, Johnny Simmons and Chuck Carter. Andy grew quiet, watching them as they walked by, and Dylan gave him a long baleful stare. Andy was pleased to see you could still see a little color to his cheek when Van had thwacked him, though the cuts had healed cleanly.

Dylan made a show of sniffing the air and making a sour face. "What's that, beans?" he said, shaking his head. "Better sit over by the far wall."

"Don't put any of your shitty music on the juke box," Andy snapped after them.

Tank glared at him and reached into his pocket for a coin. He slotted it into the juke box and moments later the diner was awash in the faintly Germanic strains of Lawrence Welk's instrumental polka, "Calcutta."

"Oh, man," Andy groaned. "You have got to be fucking kidding."

"That's on you," said Sam, miserably.

They listened aghast as the plinky band and the wordless la-la-ing of the jaunty choir gave way to the accordion solo.

"I can't take much more of this," said Sam. "If we don't get some Chubby Checker or Little Eva on there fast I'm gonna turn into my mother. Frankly, I'd rather turn into my grandmother. At least she's dead and wouldn't have to listen to this shit."

Some girls came in, Candy Green and a couple of other cheerleader types Andy didn't know. They made a beeline for the jocks as Monty came out from the back to welcome them.

"Don't you ladies look delightful!" he enthused. "All ready for the big event, huh? What can I get you? Burgers, hotdogs, ice cream floats? We're all stocked up."

The diner door opened again and Van and Stacy came in, self-conscious but happy. They had both dressed up for the occasion—starched shirt and new jeans for Van, frilly blouse and poodle skirt for Stacy—but the unusual formality, and the way they carried it, somehow made them look younger than they were.

"Ding!" said Andy, "Table for Cupid!"

"Cut it out," Van muttered. "Hey guys. Can we join?"

"You gonna need a candle?" asked Sam.

"I said cut it out," said Van.

"Stace!" called Candace from the back of the room by the juke box. "There's room over here."

"Yeah, Nicholson," said Dylan. "Still time to save your social life."

"I'm good here, thanks," Stacy reposted stiffly. She made a show of sitting with her back to the jocks, who let out an "Oooh" of mock fear before erupting into laughter.

Red appeared at the table. "OK," he said, producing a plate like he was unveiling a new car. "Try this."

It was a sandwich of sorts, but the filling looked like some kind of stew. Andy regarded it skeptically, then took a bite. He paused in thought, then his face lit up and he began to chew with relish.

"Holy shit!" he said as soon as he had swallowed enough to speak. "What is this?"

"Kind of a family recipe," said Red. "Smoked pork barbecue simmered like a pot roast."

"It's fantastic!" said Andy. "Man, I may never eat another burger."

"Where is it?" asked Stacy, scanning the menu.

"It ain't on there," said Red. "It's new. For here at least."

"Let me try a bite," said Sam, taking it before Andy could object. He bit a corner off and made stunned, enthusiastic noises.

"You made that?" Andy asked.

"Course I made it," said Red.

"You, my friend, have a talent for more than catching footballs and decking refs. My compliments to the chef," Andy intoned, reverting to his terrible British accent.

"Can we get some service over here?" called Tank from the table by the juke box. He was looking pointedly at Red.

"I thought Monty took your orders," said Red with just a hint of defiance.

"Yeah," said Dylan. "Well, now we want to make some more orders and he isn't here, so why don't you quit flirting with your girl friends and do your job?"

Van stirred in his seat but Red stilled him with a look.

"It's fine," he said under his breath. He walked over to where the jocks and their girls sat waiting impatiently. "What d'ya need?"

"*So* polite," said one of the girls, a blond sporting a beehive do.

"Ain't the Ritz," said Red, his patience starting to fray.

"Clearly," said the girl, who Red thought was called Linda, with a smile suggesting she had just won some lengthy intellectual debate.

"You want to order or are we just gonna banter?" said Red.

"Maybe I should speak to your manager," said Linda.

Red snapped his note pad shut.

"Knock yourselves out," he said. "Monty!"

"Just get us some chocolate milks," snapped Dylan.

Red met his eyes, his gaze lingering just long enough to take in the bruising around his eye, nodded once and left.

"What was that about?" asked Monty as Red entered the kitchen.

"Nothing," said Red. "They want chocolate milks."

"You aggravating my customers?"

"Try that the other way around," said Red.

Monty frowned and Red sensed a scolding coming, yet another reminder of why he wasn't really up to the job and should be grateful that Monty didn't fire his ass months ago, but at the last second the proprietor seemed to relent.

"Yeah," he said. "They do that. Especially that crowd. Think they're too good for the place."

Red blinked, so unaccustomed to this moment of solidarity from his boss that he didn't know what to say. Eventually he just grinned, a rare flash of genuine gratitude. Monty touched his arm.

"You take care of the Lopez crew," he said, "and the out-of-towners at table five. I'll handle Sweet Dylan and his buds."

Red raised his eyebrows at the ironic pun, but the big man raised a finger to his lips and winked.

Sam Jenkins stuck his head around the door. "Hey, Red, can you do another three of those whatever-you-call-'em sandwiches?"

"Sure," said Red.

Monty gave him a quizzical look.

"Trying out a new menu item," said Red, not sure how his boss would react. Monty had served practically the same range of dishes for at least 10 years.

"What is it?" he asked.

"Twice-cooked barbecue pork," Red answered.

Monty considered this and nodded. "Sounds good."

"It's great!" said Sam.

"Well, all right," said Monty, fishing the chocolate milk from the fridge.

As Red worked on the sandwiches Sam took the good news back to the group. "More sandwiches on the way!" he announced, like a prospector who had struck gold.

"Man," said Andy, "these really are good. We should commemorate the moment when Red brings them out." He fumbled in a bag under the table and brought out a steel and black Kodak Pony: the Lopez family camera. "Was gonna try to get a shot of the blast," he explained.

"Where did you get that piece of junk?" sneered Dylan who was on his way to the rest room. "The Truman administration?"

Andy considered that and shrugged, unabashed. "Probably. Still works."

"Mostly," said Van.

"Like I said," Dylan went on. "Junk, like your truck."

"I'd put that truck up against your Daddy's Plymouth any day of the week," said Van.

"You're crazy," sneered Dylan. "Another family trait."

Van almost stood up, ready to go as he had been at Dylan's house, but instead he smiled.

"Yeah?" he said. "Prove it."

"You mean, you wanna *race?*" said Dylan in delighted disbelief.

"Sure, why not?" said Van. "My piece of junk against your Space Age rocket ship. What do you have to lose?"

"Oh yeah," said Tank, joining them and looming over the table, rubbing his hands together in showy anticipation. "You're gonna get creamed, Lopez."

"We'll see," said Van.

"Yeah, we will," said Dylan, warming to the idea. "Dead Man's Wash, tonight before the bomb goes off."

"Forget the Wash," said Van. "You want a real place for a real race, there's only one place to go."

"Wait," said Andy, his eyes wide "You mean—?"

"Old Eastman Runway," said Van.

Someone whistled. It was like one of those movies when the guy playing poker goes all in, shoving his stack of chips into the middle of the table, and you know he's either gonna go home very rich or very, very poor.

"You'll never get near the runway," said Tank. "Tonight of all nights."

"Actually," said Sam, their resident military expert, "tonight is the perfect night. They'll be mostly guarding down at Yucca Flats. The test will be at Area Four or Seven, maybe Two or even Nine, but nowhere near Five."

"You speak English?" said Tank, flicking Sam's earlobe so he winced and uttered an "Ow!" of protest.

"The old runway is in Frenchman Flats," Sam said. "Area Five, dumbass. They won't be watching there. And I know where we can get in."

"We'll get a hell of a view of the blast, too," said Andy. He eyed his camera thoughtfully.

"I wouldn't bother," said Sam. "At that range your film will be contaminated by whatever comes out of the bomb. Stevie Fly says . . ."

"Yeah, I heard," said Van, waving the remark away.

Stacy frowned, but when she opened her mouth to speak, Sam continued quickly. "I can show you where to go and how to get past the patrols. No problem. You in or not?"

"Hell, yes," said Dylan, giving Van a baleful stare. "Time we settled this."

"Fine by me," said Van.

"The film gets contaminated?" said Stacy absently.

Sam gave her a quick look.

"The conversation has moved on," he said. "So, what do you say? Seven o'clock. Quick race, then we all get a front row seat for the fireworks."

"Seven," said Van. "Deal."

"Seven," said Dylan.

"All right!" crowed Tank. "This is gonna be wicked!"

Monty set down a tray of chocolate milks and then walked away, hands held up to the sides of his face like the blinders on a horse.

"I didn't hear any of this," he said.

"So," said Andy, checking his watch and looking around. "We finish up here and go?"

"Cool," said Sam. "Let's do it."

# CHAPTER NINE

Trinity, usually a sleepy desert backwater, transformed as the test loomed; it felt like the town's population had doubled within the last 12 hours. The scrubby little park off Main Street was filled with picnic tables and benches, all hung with patriotic ribbons and balloons. The grass had been mowed, the trash collected, and the gum pressure-washed off the sidewalks, as if they were expecting some dignitary—a senator stumping for the presidency or a celebrity astronaut on some educational tour. Barbecue grills had been set up, and the air hung with the aromas of lighter fluid and roasting meat. There was a popcorn stand and a cotton candy machine. Jim Flinders from the hardware store had set up an industrial-scale hotdog grill, his wife providing the bun-splitting and ketchup application, while his just 21-year-old daughter Justine sold cans of Old Milwaukee from a cooler. Across the way, one of Monty's rivals had gotten permission to set up a soda fountain and funnel cake stall from which a cloud of delicious, sweet-smelling smoke blossomed. It was Coney Island without the rides, and it buzzed with activity and expectation.

Down at Trinity High, one end of the football field bleachers had been opened to the public ("Donations Welcome!"), and over the entrance some enterprising soul had hung a hand-painted banner promising "The Best A-BOMB view in Town!"

There were folks who found all the celebration a bit crass. There were others who objected to the test itself, bristling at the expense and the way it seemed to stoke the fires of the Cold War with its effusive and uncritical nationalism, and who worried about what a war with such weapons might look like and what—if anything—it would leave behind. There were some who were beginning to ask questions about the safety of the tests themselves. But those people were invisible this evening. Some of them had taken the opportunity to leave town for a day or two, but most were at home, their doors and windows closed against the invisible dangers of fallout. A few, like Danny Lopez, were huddled in their basements, sealed up as best they could, anxiously waiting for it all to be over.

But for the most part, Trinity partied, urged on by Stevie Fly, broadcasting live from KTNT.

"Hello out there, all you groovy cats and kittens, hope you've found yourself a primo location because we're closing in on zero hour," he cooed into the mic. "And your pal

Stevie Fly is the guy to get you there and back again. But we've got a whole 55 minutes to go till the world's biggest firework lights up the Nevada sky, and according to Miss Dee Dee Sharp that makes it . . . 'Mashed Potato Time'!"

The music came oozing out of transistor radios all over the park and echoing from bullhorn speakers down at the football field, tinny and thin, but loud and recognizable enough to set off a sprinkling of dancing all over town, some little more than a shifting of weight from foot to foot, others executing a demure form of mini-twist, some really letting loose with flamboyant whole-body gyrations, which—even with the sky poised to explode—drew disapproving looks from watchful elders. It was a Trinity moment, one in which past and present felt balanced on the edge of a knife, as if the turning of the world had paused for the mere fraction of a second before spinning into a wild and unknowable future from which yesterday was separated by centuries.

After Dee Dee Sharp came Little Eva's "Locomotion" and the Isley Brothers' "Twist and Shout," the thrilling, upbeat sounds of a present barely imaginable a few years earlier. Stevie Fly fed the town with music like he was stoking the boiler of some great steam locomotive, an engine that shifted and evolved even as it sped forward, till it became something like a rocket ship lancing right at the moon. And with each new song the town got a little more hysterical, a little more rapturous, and the minute hand inched a little further around the dial—faster and faster, it seemed—toward the main event.

As Stevie fired up the Trinity crowd, Van, Dylan and their respective supporters sped out of town, headed northeast into the gathering dusk. Van sat with Stacy beside him on the F100's bench seat, while Andy, Red, and Sam hung on to the sides in the back, hooting and whistling at the powder blue Plymouth, which coasted easily in their wake. Dylan, Chuck and—in the back seat—Candy and Johnny responded in kind, their various real animosities briefly turned into something lighter and more playful. Tank had brought his own car—a pastel green Oldsmobile 98—and was bringing up the rear. The sense of sport, of a game they were confident of winning, gave the rivalry a gloss as bright as the Plymouth's tail fins.

That mood survived the sudden appearance of the "Access Restricted" signs that appeared by the highway as they approached the abandoned southeast side of the base, the ramping excitement now interlaced with a hot red line of the forbidden that made Candy giggle and sprawl on the cream-colored upholstery. They slowed before a dusty gate marked "Authorized Personnel Only," but the rusty chain looped over the barriers wasn't even padlocked and offered no real resistance to Sam when he hopped out of the pickup and raised them.

He waved everyone through, past an ancient and dilapidated guard house with a sentry box and a two-story tower, all clearly abandoned. Once they were all in, he closed the gates behind them and jogged back to where the vehicles were idling in the amber glow of the sunset.

"The military still owns this part," said Sam, in case anyone was feeling anxious, "but they haven't used it for years, and there's a whole 'nother inner fence a couple of miles yonder that's the real perimeter." He waved vaguely toward the ridge. "They used to patrol out here sometimes, but I haven't seen them do that for months, and tonight they definitely have bigger fish to fry. Our destination, ladies and gentlemen," he concluded with a showman's swagger, "is right there."

He pointed, precisely this time, at a long, straight belt of concrete, 10,000 feet of tarmac as wide as a four-lane highway. It was flanked by the hulking remains of gas tanks and hangars, and, with the military's attention squarely focused elsewhere, it was eerily silent. The spirit of wild rivalry in the group stalled for a moment as they took in the stillness.

"That," said Sam, gazing along the runway and speaking to the universe in general, "is what I'm talking about."

There was a watchful moment, then Andy checked his watch. It had taken them longer to get there than they had anticipated, and the test was about to start.

"We need to get moving," he said, "Or we'll miss the main event."

"We taking passengers?" Van asked.

"Hell no," sneered Dylan, as if the possibility was some kind of dodge. "This is between you and me."

He nodded at Chuck and the others to get out, and they did so without complaint. Candy and Johnny had developed a palpable intimacy on the way over and probably wouldn't be sticking around to watch anyway.

Van shrugged, nodding at Stacy who slid out and dropped to the dusty ground.

"Fine by me," she said, though he thought she looked less excited than she was anxious. The thought pleased him somehow and he gave her an encouraging smile.

"Gonna take him to school," he said.

She frowned in puzzlement. "I don't care if you win," she clarified. "Just don't get yourself killed."

"Oh," he said, the good feelings from a moment before shifting and complicating before becoming simply good again.

"Think you're hot shit, huh, Lopez?" said Chuck. "You ain't. Your truck, on the other hand: that looks pretty shit."

Dylan smirked at him.

"We'll see," said Van, buoyed by the look on Stacy's face.

"Come on!" said Andy again, tapping his watch.

"Start and finish right here," said Sam, striding onto the concrete as he plucked a red bandana from his back pocket. He whipped it through the air like a flag, and Van saw it again, that flash of the showman, as if he was the ringmaster of a circus. "There's a turn-around at the end of the runway," Sam continued. "Pull your vehicles up beside me, and we'll get this party started. Keep it clean, boys, and we'll see you back here just as soon as you can make it. Don't make us wait and don't get arrested. Ready to burn some rubber?"

Again there was that magical sense of expectation, an air of ritual, aided by the setting sun, as if these kids in their cars were the priests of some ancient cult about to engage in a ceremony that would bring life to their village.

Dylan had already rolled the Plymouth past to Sam's right, and was now pushing the accelerator, making the engine snarl. Van pulled forward on Sam's left and gave the F100 a little gas. It growled, a lower, throatier roar than seemed possible from the old pickup, and for the briefest of moments Van thought he saw doubt flash through Dylan's customarily smug face.

"I did a little work on it," he said.

Dylan opened his mouth to say something, but by then Sam had raised his bandana.

"Ready?" he roared. "Set!"

And he brought the makeshift red flag whipping down.

Both vehicles leapt forward. A shout went up from the onlookers, and the moment of magic buckled, turning into something simpler. They broke apart to get a better look, waving away the exhaust smoke and screaming till their throats ached.

The Plymouth responded quickest, shooting out like the rocket ship its taillights suggested. The pale blue nose inched ahead of the battered Ford, and Dylan shot Van a sideways glance. Within 50 yards of the start, the Plymouth was pulling away, its engine singing.

Van shifted gears, urging the pickup on, feeling for the V8's sweet spot as the Plymouth slid ahead. He looked sideways and saw more of the car's long chromed fender, then its rear wheel arches, and finally the fins of its tail. He gripped the steering wheel and floored the accelerator. The truck shook under the strain, bellowing like an enraged bison, and then—without warning—it seemed to settle into a groove, and he could feel that the Plymouth wasn't pulling away anymore. For a hundred yards or so the two vehicles moved as one, their positions in relation to each other frozen as if they were bolted together, but then, very slowly, the pickup began to close the gap.

Outside, the darkening concrete and steel remnants of the base flashed past, but all Van's attention was on Dylan's Plymouth.

Dylan's *daddy's* Plymouth. Dylan's daddy who now lived with Van's mother in a nice house with its George Jetson fridge and its magazine living room.

Van pushed his foot to the floor as far as it would go, eyes on the runway now as if refusing to look at the car beside him. This was about him and his truck. Dylan, and the Plymouth, were irrelevant.

And then all of a sudden they weren't. The Plymouth swerved hard to the left, veering into Van's path. He pulled the pickup wide, but the move cost him, and it skidded as he fought to keep it on the concrete. He'd lost several hard-won yards, but even as he swore out loud he felt a new clarity in his head. Dylan knew he couldn't hold him off without pulling that kind of shit, and that meant Van could beat him.

Van peered ahead. In front of him, and coming up fast was the concrete barrier that marked the turn around. The runway became a wide open pan that swept off to the right, looped around a corner where a huge hangar stood, open at both ends, before rejoining the runway and leading back to where they had started. He feathered the steering wheel, easing the truck to the right and tucking in right behind the Plymouth. He eased off the throttle and let the Ford cruise in its wake like a long-distance runner, waiting for his moment. He saw Dylan check his mirrors and felt his uncertainty.

Van smiled grimly. The barrier was hurtling toward them. Any moment now Dylan would have to brake, but he would feel Van sitting on his bumper and didn't want Daddy's precious chrome getting dented. Even as he thought it, he felt the Plymouth slow a fraction. Van matched the deceleration, opening up the gap between them by a few feet. The Plymouth slowed a little more, and this time its heading changed a few degrees as the car started to bank gradually into a long turn around the hangar. Van pulled the steering wheel hard, veering to the right of the Plymouth, and gunning the engine.

The truck surged forward and, with a shriek of its tires, cut a line inside the Plymouth's. It was a dangerous thing to do at this speed, but Van knew the truck like he knew his own muscles and bones. There was a moment of near weightlessness as the pickup rocked onto its left-hand wheels, but he held it steady and came out of the turn ahead, the old Ford settling back into its flat-out burn. He risked a glance back and saw Dylan roaring his fury, but then they were around the turn and there was something on the runway ahead. Something large.

It was an abandoned fuel truck, long and solid. Though it was big enough to block the turn, it had been screened by the hangar.

Teeth clenched and knuckles white, Van swerved around it, knowing that his only route now was through the hangar itself. The doors were wide open, but the roof cut the light in half, and for a second Van was blind, the truck hurtling through God knew what, aimed at the opening at the far end. In the sudden confines of the building he heard the deafening screech of Dylan's wheels skidding behind him, and knew that he had made the turn successfully. He leaned forward, hoping against hope that there was nothing between him and the exit . . .

There wasn't. The F100 flew through the warehouse-like structure and burst out into the light at the other end.

But that was no ordinary light. As the pickup sped out onto the runway, the Plymouth hot on its heels, the sky went white. Van winced, closing his eyes and throwing his hands in front of his face, the truck hurtling across the strip as he fought blindly to bring it to a controlled stop. A moment later the sound of the blast hit him, like a cannon going off in his head. He cried out but couldn't hear himself. He had no idea where Dylan was. Had no clear sense of where any of the others were or even where he was. The truck was probably still moving but he couldn't feel it. His senses had been overridden, and he was somehow awake but unconscious at the same time. The world had vanished in the terrible power of the nuclear detonation, and for a moment he thought he had driven into the heart of the bomb where he would be vaporized, his very atoms stripped apart and consumed.

After the light came the cloud. The immense, towering mushroom of destruction which, though miles away, seemed to be on top of them. Van dragged himself out of the now motionless truck, which sat canted unevenly on the edge of the runway, shrinking away from the sheer scale of the cloud, as if it was the face of God himself—or his demonic adversary. The air itself was colored impossibly. Some 30 yards back, Dylan had managed to park the Plymouth, and now stumbled toward him, his eyes wide in awestruck horror. Together, their mutual hatred forgotten in the shadow of the monstrous thing that towered above them, they crouched in the shade of the pickup, their silent faces lit by the unnatural fire above. Their hair streaked out and their very skin rippled as the shock wave sent the truck creaking and rocking, and there was nothing else in the universe but them and the infernal power blossoming in the Nevada sky.

And then.

And then . . .

And then, when they had seen enough and were ready to turn away . . .

Only then,

came something else.

# CHAPTER TEN

"**O**h, man, that was a big one!" Stevie Fly crooned into his microphone, a glass of Wild Turkey forgotten in his right hand. He gazed upwards through the studio window and for a second all his studied cool and lazy charm dried up in the face of the sheer immensity of the blast. The mushroom cloud reared up overhead and opened, beautiful and terrible so that for a moment all Stevie could do was stare. Outside, Trinity shielded its eyes, chugged their beers and toasted good-old American know-how, though some of that was shot through with a daunted unease as surprising as the explosion itself. At his makeshift hotdog stand Jim Flinders hung a little more tightly to his wife than she had known him do for many a long year, and if anyone looked closely at him they might have seen him wipe away a tear he couldn't explain.

No one did. They were all looking up, or looking in. It was funny, the way something so immense could make you think about yourself. Then the blast of wind came, shattering windows and sending garbage cans rolling down the alleyways. Trees bent, some to breaking point, and dogs that had been strangely silent suddenly howled.

And then it was over and with the return of stillness to the desert night came something like relief. More beers were drunk, and even the daunted and fearful recovered their swaggering confidence, as if cheering a long touch-down pass that had snatched victory from crushing defeat. Briefly they had been mere specks floating in a vast and frightening universe. Now they were Americans again.

"A little early for the Fourth of July," said Stevie Fly, recovering his languid swagger, "but absolutely worth the price of admission. That, cats and kittens, is one almighty firework. And while the skies boil for our entertainment, we are 'Having A Party'!"

With that, he cued up the Sam Cooke song and toasted the mesmerizing mushroom cloud with his whiskey glass. He raised it to his lips, but before he could take his first sip he saw something high in the evening sky, a bright point of light well outside the infernal cloud, a point that seemed to brighten even as he watched.

*Like it's getting bigger*, he thought, then hastily corrected himself. "Like something's *falling*," he said aloud. "Like something's coming down."

All over Trinity the cheering and toasting stalled. Conversation sputtered to a halt. Everyone was looking up again, but now their eyes were narrowed with confusion and doubt.

Was this supposed to be happening? Was it some off-shoot of the explosive material? Whatever it was, it looked dangerous, which was saying something, given what they had all just witnessed.

Heads tilted sideways slightly. Mouths opened. A hundred exclamations of wonder and curiosity began, half muttered, then interrupted by a collective intake of breath. The point of light flared and separated into two, their paths diverging, but both still headed down.

At his window, Stevie Fly made some hasty estimations and decided that one of the lights, the one that now seemed larger than the other, was heading for the mountains just north of town. It was hard to judge the distance but yes, that's what he thought. The other executed a strange spiral arc and then plummeted toward what, if he had to guess, was rather closer.

"That's gonna hit the base," he mused, all trace of the hipster cat gone from his voice.

O    O

Van Lopez and Dylan Sweet stared upwards, coming to the same conclusion. One of the lights had become a fireball, swelling as it crashed earthwards, like a guided missile. Coming right at them.

"Go!" roared Van, throwing himself back into the pickup and gunning the engine. It sputtered for an agonizing second or two, then caught. He had it in gear and moving before Dylan had reached the Plymouth.

Overhead the fireball seemed to fragment, filling the sky like a dozen falling stars. The air roared with the sound of their descent and Van felt the hairs on the back of his neck stand on end. He spun the steering wheel to aim the truck down the runway, then slammed the accelerator hard. The engine bellowed its protest, yanking the pickup forward like an unruly horse. Van rocked in his seat, then leaned forward to look up. As he did so there was a brilliant flash and, after a hair's breadth delay, a crash like a mortar shell exploding mere yards behind him. Chunks of concrete flew in all directions. Grit and debris peppered the bed of the truck and with a snap, a long crack flicked across the cab's rear window. Van ducked instinctively in his seat, then hunkered down and urged the pickup forward.

*Got to get out of here.*

As he did so he saw Dylan's Plymouth surging forward alongside him. For a mad moment it was as if they had resumed the race, but then there was another fiery flash as another fragment of whatever had been up there hurtled into the desert off to their right. It raised a cloud of dust, which glowed improbably with the light of strange fires, and Van remembered that phrase from his dream.

*Got to get out of here.*

The two vehicles hurtled back to where their friends had been watching, though the way the evening had started now felt a world away.

There was another incoming rush of burning air, and the road in front of Van exploded. A yellow light filled his vision, so bright it was almost white, then vanished, plunging him utterly into darkness. In the same instant he felt the front wheels of the truck drop into a crater so deep the pickup tipped forward, its tail end momentarily airborne. The impact rocked him forward hard. He hit his forehead on the windshield, and felt the thump of the steering wheel like an anvil on his chest. For a moment he had no idea where he was, he may have even blacked out, but the truck labored up the other side of the crater and rolled on.

Van blinked and held his face, forcing himself to stay awake, to focus, and that was when he realized that the Plymouth was no longer coasting beside him. He looked wildly around but couldn't make out anything in the leaping firelight and deep evening shadow. Reluctantly, he hit the brakes. The truck stuttered to a ragged halt, and he shouldered the door open, leaning out and looking back.

The Plymouth was maybe 50 yards behind. One side and most of the rear, fins and all, had been torn completely off, and the car was trailing a long plume of flame as it tumbled and then came to rest on its roof and slid, slowing, along the runway.

All around, wreckage fell from the sky, some of it burning, though Van couldn't tell which parts were from the Plymouth and which were from whatever had caused the crash in the first place. Not that it mattered. The shattered car was burning and Dylan was trapped inside.

O          O

At the end of the runway, at what had been—only minutes before—the starting line of the race, the remaining teens stared in mute horror as the sky came thundering down. Tank, Candy, and Johnny had already gone, taking Tank's car and heading back toward town as soon as they realized the test had begun. Red, Stacy, Sam, Andy, and Chuck had all stayed. They had hunkered down behind a vast cylindrical fuel tank to watch the A-bomb go off, but now had spilled out onto the runway, faces turned up, as the evening sky filled with unnatural stars, all falling.

Stacy's gaze fastened on a particularly bright shard which turned end over end as it streamed right at them. "Run!" she shouted.

And they did, scattering for distance and cover. The blazing fragments pelted the ground, pocking the concrete and kicking up clouds of dust and shards of debris as they ran. A larger piece slammed into the fuel tank, punching a ragged hole through the steel. A plume of burning gas stabbed briefly upwards from the ruptured metal, then the whole tank blew apart in a brilliant orange flash. The running teens ducked instinctively, then redoubled their speed. Red and Sam veered left into the cover of a hangar, even as they could see its thin roof punched with flaming holes by the falling debris. Stacy, Andy and Chuck went right toward a cinder block office, but before they reached it something inside caught and blew. There was a momentary silence as the light burst from the door and windows, and then the sound of the blast hit them and they shrank away, hiding their eyes and running wild and sightless.

Then Andy stopped. "Where's Van?" he shouted, gazing back through the horrorscape of fires and explosions. Chuck ran right by him, but Stacy came to a stuttering halt, her eyes wide with fear and concern. She gazed at Andy, who stood rooted to the spot, screaming back down the runway.

"Van!"

o          o

Van stared at the burning Plymouth. Then he was out of the truck and running.

The inverted car came to rest, and as the drag on the fire stopped, the flames seemed to spread, engulfing the entire rear half of the car and reaching forward. By the time Van got there, the driver's side was already ablaze and the air was rank with the scent of spilled gasoline and acrid smoke. He shielded his face from the heat with one hand, ducked around the chrome grill with its Space Age headlights, and tore the passenger side door open. Inside the air was thick and rank with the stench of burning plastic and rubber. The door frame was hot to the touch.

Van leaned in. There was too much smoke inside to see properly, so he closed his eyes, blind fingers searching till they found Dylan's slumped body. He grabbed him by the shoulder and started to pull. The other boy didn't respond.

*Dead or unconscious?*

Van kept pulling anyway, reaching in with both arms now, face mashed up against the door frame, even though it was roasting hot. He strained, leaning back and dragging with the muscles of his lower back and legs, until finally Dylan was sliding out.

*Dead weight*, Van thought with a stab of horror, but he kept pulling till he had the body out on the concrete.

"Come on," he muttered. "Come on."

Dylan was on his back. His face was sooty and blood streaked, his eyes closed.

"Come on, you smug prick," Van muttered. "Breathe."

And Dylan did. He gasped, sucking the awful air into his lungs, then rolled, coughing spasmodically, retching and spitting to get the filth out of his airways.

"We gotta go," said Van, hiding his relief.

"Wait . . ." Dylan managed to say, and Van realized that some of the hesitation in the other boy's face was doubt. In spite of all his fear and pain, Dylan didn't trust him.

But Van was already dragging him to his feet. Trust, if it came at all, would come later. He got him as close to upright as he could, then threw one arm around his shoulders and forced him toward the F100, all his attention fastened on the truck, willing it not to go the same way as the Plymouth. It seemed a long way off, and Van's strength was failing. Around them, debris was still falling like grenades. The runway was lit with a shifting and uncanny light, as if from flares or lightning.

The Ford was in rough shape, pocked as it was with little impacts, but it was still in one piece. With a last surge of effort, Van reached the truck and managed to labor around to the passenger side.

"In," he wheezed. "You gotta climb. I can't lift you anymore."

As if to make the point, there was another explosion over on the edge of the runway, and in the resultant flash Van felt the sting of concrete fragments on the side of his face. He winced, shrinking away, feeling the wetness run where the skin was broken. He manhandled the door open and felt Dylan stiffen as fear gave him back some of his strength.

It took only seconds but felt like an eternity to get the closest thing Van had to an enemy into the truck, and then they were driving, weaving around the worst of the craters as the night continued to burn around them. Van felt Dylan staring at him. Some of that was because he was slumped sideways on the bench seat and had barely moved since they started driving, but there was something in his eyes, a fixed puzzlement that smacked of alarm.

"What?" Van snapped, in no mood to be questioned about his motives.

Dylan shook his head fractionally, and when he spoke it was like the words came unbidden from somewhere deep inside him. They dragged bafflement and horror like the tail of a comet.

"What happened?" he said. "I don't get it." He shook his head and some of the woolliness in his mind seemed to dislodge, revealing something closer to panic. His voice went up an octave and the flesh around his eyes tightened as if fighting back tears, "What's going on?"

But Van was suddenly miles away. He was on a horse in the desert, peering around the body of someone much bigger but whose presence was somehow reassuring.

*What he had drawn in math class, minus the Mayan temple . . .*

Just the horse beneath him, warm and smelling musky, its flank smooth to the touch unless you ran your palm against the grain of its sleek coat, when the bristles would prick and catch like spines. They were paused on a ridge gazing at the sky where something impossible had been, something that had come down plowing a rough, blackened trough in the desert and was now burning.

*We shouldn't be here . . .*

Van blinked, feeling, despite the fires around him, oddly, unnervingly cold. The old dream felt more than familiar. It felt real. It felt . . .

*Like memory.*

He reached for it . . .

"Drive," muttered Dylan. "What are you waiting for? Go!"

Van realized that in his reverie he had let the truck coast almost to a halt. He sat up, eyes wide with alarm at his own stupidity, and gunned the engine. The truck leapt forward but moments later Van brought it to a skidding stop. Two figures had blundered out of the smoke and into their headlights.

It was Sam and Red. They looked shell-shocked, their hands held vainly over their dust-streaked faces, their eyes wide.

"Where are the others?" roared Van. "Stacy and my brother?"

"Chuck?" added Dylan vaguely. "Where's Chuck?"

"Tank drove back to town with Candy and Johnny before the explosion," said Sam. He pointed to the right. "Chuck and the others took off that way."

Van bit his lip. "Get in," he shouted. "Fast!"

He had the truck in motion before they had completely scrambled over the tail gate, the more athletic Red hauling Sam in after him.

They drove, faster than Van had ever driven his life. They drove as if the devil himself was after them.

O     O

Stacy, Andy, and Chuck ran. They were near the end of the runway now, and Stacy could see a canted concrete wall set up as some kind of blast shield for ground crew during take off. She was so focused on it that she didn't see Chuck, half-blinded by smoke and panic, put his foot in a crater and turn his ankle. He collapsed with a shout of pain, and came up gingerly. Andy slowed to give him an arm to lean on, and in those few seconds of delay the events of the evening turned. Only when she heard the sirens did Stacy—already in the cover of the blast shield—spin around to face them, realizing in the same instant that the flicker of red light on the concrete was too regular to be firelight.

A pair of military fire trucks with a couple of jeeps and something boxy that might have been an armored car was streaming in from the entrance, headlights blazing. The convoy pulled up and soldiers spilled out shouting orders. Andy and Chuck had nowhere to go, and raised their hands, even as the fiery debris continued to rain down around them. Stacy shrank back out of sight.

"Don't move!" shouted a young officer, but he wasn't talking to her.

Stacy was used to seeing soldiers around town, but never one in a uniform like this. It looked like a single-piece jumpsuit with a hood and a face mask. His voice had come through some kind of speaker and it sounded flat, tinny. Tubes ran to a cannister on his back. One of his men held a device that was clicking rapidly.

*A Geiger counter?*

Something like that, she thought. In his gloved hands he held a squat-looking pistol, but the men on either side of him had much more serious looking firepower: semiautomatic rifles with short barrels. The face masks made them alarmingly anonymous, like automata, but almost as scary was their body language. They looked uncertain, jumpy.

Chuck looked wildly around.

"I said don't move!" shouted the electronic voice of the officer.

"We're gonna die out here, man!" Chuck wailed.

"Stay where you are!" said the officer flatly.

Another hunk of whatever was falling from the sky slammed into the ground only yards from where Chuck and Andy stood and both boys flinched.

"Fuck this," said Chuck, and started to run.

"No!" shouted Andy.

Involuntarily Stacy started to move toward them but it was too late.

She counted three shots, three rapid pops, small and anticlimactic compared to everything else that was going on. For a second she thought they had been warning shots, but then she saw the look of surprise on Chuck's face, the way it froze as he crumpled and fell face forward. She knew beyond a shadow of a doubt that he was dead before he hit the concrete.

Andy yelled and made the smallest of movements as if ready to run to the corpse or at the men who shot him, but he managed to contain himself. Stacy slammed her hands over her mouth and pulled back into the shadows, her eyes brimming. Her muted scream came out as a terrible gasping sigh, but no one heard her. The soldiers were too rattled. The officer turned on the men beside him and sputtered furiously, "Hold your fire!"

There was a terrible silence, and then the soldier who had fired started babbling defensive explanations before the officer bellowed at him to shut the fuck up and hand his weapon over to one of his colleagues. This was not how things were supposed to go. For a split second, as the officer checked the body and tried to decide what to do next, Stacy almost felt sorry for him, but she was too angry, too distraught. How could the evening have gone so terribly wrong?

"Get him in the truck," said the officer to two of his men, nodding at where Chuck lay, his blood darkening the concrete. As they moved to pick him up he turned to Andy. "Where are the others?" he demanded.

Even at this distance, even with the chaos of the night and the shadow of death cast over them, Stacy saw the moment of calculation in Andy's face before he replied.

"Dead," he said. "Or trapped over there. The hangar." He nodded toward a blazing ruin off to the west. "They went in for shelter but it collapsed. If they didn't die right away, they did by now. Only the two of us got out."

The officer hesitated.

"Take him into custody," he ordered.

Two men rushed toward him, seemingly glad of something they knew how to do, one covering him from the front with his weapon while the other went behind him, tugged his arms behind his back and cuffed him. Risking only the smallest fraction of her face around the corner of the blast shield, Stacy watched as Andy was led roughly toward a covered truck and bundled in. Just before he vanished inside she thought he threw a glance her way. His face was tight, stricken, as if all his will was concentrated in keeping it together. Then she heard the officer speaking into a radio.

"There's just one survivor," he said. "We have him. But it's a hell of a mess out here and we have some . . . collateral damage." There was a pause. "Yes, sir. Setting perimeter around Bravo site then proceeding to Alpha site."

Stacy could watch no more. She knew that as they locked down the area she could risk being trapped inside. She wanted to grieve, to bellow her rage at the lunacy and injustice she had seen, she wanted to bleed tears for the boy who had died and the others whose fate was unknown to her, but she knew that would not help. She had to go. She had to stay alive, if only to tell others what she had seen.

○　　○

In Trinity, at the lonely phone booth on the corner of High Bluff and Main, the figure in the quilted trench coat recited the code words and waited, scouring the empty streets.

"Foxtail. Monsoon. Pebble. Desk."

There was a now familiar series of clicks and a voice at the other end said, "Skylark."

"Control," said the agent.

The conversation switched into Russian as the figure reported what had been seen and heard so far. There was a lengthy pause before the distant voice spoke again, confirming the enormity of what had been said.

"Please repeat," said Control.

"Debris fell after the detonation," said Skylark. "Material is present and in play. Repeat, material is present and in play."

Another breath-held pause before Control's words came over the line.

"Understood, Skylark. Your diligence honors the party and its people. Locate the material and collect it. At all costs. Confirm please."

The agent known as Skylark swallowed then nodded.

"Confirmed, Control. At all costs. Understood."

# CHAPTER ELEVEN

**V**an drove grimly along the desert road, putting as much distance between them and the base as possible, but his mind was in turmoil, a mixture of baffled and partial memory from long ago and the dread and strangeness of the immediate present turning over and over in his mind. What had come down in pieces was, he felt sure, the same thing he had seen over the quarry. But he was now convinced that that encounter had not been his first. He wondered about his father. He had grown so used to Danny's paranoid and antisocial behavior that he had hardly ever bothered to ask where it came from. Suddenly that question pressed in on him like the darkness of the desert all around.

The F100's headlights picked up little more than the road a few yards ahead, but they were moving flat out, so he had to brake hard when he saw the pale figure stumbling blindly along the road ahead. It turned and stared at them, and Van realized it was Stacy, her face filthy and tear-streaked. She hesitated, seemingly caught between the impulse to flag them down and another impulse to run from them, a moment that dragged well beyond the truck rolling to a halt and Van leaping out.

He caught her in his arms without thinking and asked if she was hurt.

She shook her head no, but couldn't meet his eyes.

"They shot him," she said. "Killed him right in front of me," she said.

Van stared.

"Andy?" he gasped. "They killed . . . ?"

She shook her head fiercely.

"Chuck," she said. "They told him to keep still and when he didn't they . . ."

Her tears began again and Van hugged her to his chest, caught between the impulse to comfort her and to demand more information about his brother. As if sensing it she pulled back.

"They took Andy," she said. "The military."

"Was he—?"

"He was fine," she said. "But they arrested him. Put him in a truck. I ran. I'm sorry. I didn't know what to do. I should have . . ."

"You did the right thing," said Van. "We'll get him out. Somehow."

"But Chuck?" said Dylan, as if still getting his head around it. "You sure?"

Stacy closed her eyes for a moment, then looked him full in the face and nodded.

"I'm sorry," she said.

"What do we do?" said Sam.

"Get into town," said Red. "There's a phone at Monty's."

"Who do we call?" asked Van. It sounded like such a stupid question but he meant it. If the military—a branch of the government—had killed their friend, who did they turn to? The sheriff's department? Their parents? He felt suddenly powerless.

"Everyone," said Sam. "The press, the TV stations. Stevie Fly. The more people know what happened, the safer we are."

Van listened thoughtfully and nodded. That made sense. In the distance he heard the buzz of a helicopter. "Get in," he said to Stacy. "I'm going to turn my lights off. I don't want them spotting us. Everyone keep it down."

He shut off the truck's headlights, took a moment for his eyes to get used to the dark, and then began driving carefully through the desert toward Trinity.

O       O

The man Private Emil Washington had guessed—correctly, as it turned out—was CIA, was Agent Randal Kent, and he had assumed control. In ordinary circumstances this would have been a deeply unpopular decision, since neither Army, nor Air Force, nor Atomic Energy Authority were good at being told what to do by outside authorities. But in this case you could almost smell their relief through the smoky desert air. Trinity had become a hot potato that no one wanted in their laps.

Kent knew as much, and was fine with it. If anything, it made his job a little easier, gave him room to focus on the moment-to-moment operations. He would worry about the long-term fallout later. Right now he needed to get a tight grip on what was happening. Containment—of personnel, of information, of classified material elements—was his top priority.

He considered the now quiet sky over the runway.

"Do you believe this Andrew Lopez boy?" he asked. "That no one else got away?"

"No reason to think otherwise at this time, sir," said his adjutant.

Kent frowned at that. "And we have human remains for the kids he said died?"

"Just the one so far," said his adjutant. "A Charles Carter, according to his driver's license. High school student."

"The one shot by one of your men," said Kent bitterly toward an older man in uniform—Waltham, the base commander.

"He wasn't ordered to shoot," said Waltham. "He acted on impulse."

"I'm sure that will be a huge comfort to the boy's family." Kent turned his attention back to his adjutant. "Make sure it doesn't happen again. Deaths lead to questions. Can't keep things quiet if everyone is looking for answers. What about the others?"

"Not yet located, sir."

"Double the search efforts," said Kent. "I want to know who saw what, and I want anyone still alive in custody."

"Can't arrest the entire town," said Waltham.

Kent gave him a swift look but didn't argue the point.

"Everyone saw," Waltham pressed. "By morning it will be in every newspaper and radio report. TV people will be here if they aren't already. Something came down. What do we say?"

Kent nodded again, collecting his thoughts. When he began to speak it was clearly a memo to be taken down word for word.

"Tonight's atomic test was an unbridled success and, as a result, our country is safer from the threat of Communism, etc., etc. But for reasons that are currently under investigation the blast had the unintended consequence of initiating an unplanned de-orbiting sequence of one of our non-essential satellites. Due to the sensitive nature of these programs, nothing more can be said at this time. Everyone is safe, nothing to fear. Sightings of any space debris should be treated as potentially dangerous and reported immediately. You know the rest."

"You think they'll buy that?" said Waltham, bristling very slightly at Kent's confidence.

"That was a lot of debris."

"It was a big satellite," said Kent matter-of-factly. "Keep saying it till there's no room in their heads for an alternative, till anyone who says otherwise sounds like a kook. Say it till it becomes true by sheer force of repetition. That's how it works."

Waltham almost took a step back, impressed by Kent's forcefulness, his certainty, but managed to hold his ground and simply nod. As he did so, a jeep pulled up. A sergeant jumped out.

"What is it?" Waltham demanded.

The sergeant hesitated a second, his eyes on the CIA man. He had bad news and wasn't sure who he had to tell.

"Go ahead," said Waltham. "Agent Kent is in charge of cleanup and containment."

"Getting reports of a vehicle leaving the base by the south gate," said the sergeant. "A red pickup."

Kent processed this. "So the Lopez boy lied," he said. There was no trace of emotion in his voice, but his adjutant looked down anyway, and Waltham grew watchful. "Find them and bring them in. Fast."

O    O

Three miles away the agent called Skylark, binoculars in hand, watched from the ridge as a battered Ford pickup made its cautious way back into town.

O    O

After the pre-test rush, Monty's diner had been virtually deserted as everyone sought better vantages from which to view the explosion. Now only old George Singer was left to eat a slice of peach pie and listen to Monty's philosophiz-ing. The latter saw the pickup rumbling into the parking lot and checked the clock over the counter.

"Guess I'd better be gearing up for the after party," he remarked, getting to his feet.

The door blasted open and Monty's busboy, waiter, and some-time cook Red Hauser barreled in with several other teenagers. "Hey, we need to use the phone," said Red.

"The hell you do," said Monty affronted. "You need to learn some manners."

"It's urgent!"

"I'm sure it is," said Monty, languidly. "But you ought to remember who owns this establishment and who you work for."

"It really is important, Monty," said Stacy Nicholson.

Monty peered at her. He had always liked Stacy, even though some folks thought she was full of herself, wanting to go away to university and be a nurse or some such. She was pretty and polite, and that was mostly good enough for Monty. Now she looked unkempt, her hair wild and her face smeared with dirt, her eyes red-rimmed as if she might have been crying.

"What's going on?" he asked.

"The army took Andy and killed Chuck Carter."

Monty stared at them. "What? That can't be right . . ."

"Something fell out of the fucking sky, man!" said Sam, the skinny would-be soldier.

"You'll mind your language or I'll bar you for a year."

"He's right," said Red. "Something blew up and crashed."

"That was the bomb!" said Monty. "Of course it blew up."

Red shook his head. "It brought something else down, Knocked it right out of the sky."

"Again?" said George Singer.

There was a second stunned silence. Monty gave George a dismissive look, but Stacy took a seat beside him. "What do you mean, Mr. Singer?"

"Those A-bomb blasts knock stuff down sometimes," he said, eyes on his pie. He chewed thoughtfully.

"Like when?" said Sam, cautiously skeptical.

"Back in '45," said George. "I was living in New Mexico when they did the first tests . . ."

"That's baloney," said Monty. "George, you keep out of this."

"Hold it." Van stepped up. He looked even more beat up that the rest, and he was standing with Dylan who looked like he might be drugged, his face was so pale and blank. Those two generally couldn't be within 20 feet of each other without getting into it. "You lived in New Mexico in 1945?" he asked.

George nodded emphatically. "Up by the missile range with the white sand," he said. He pivoted on his chair and gave Van a long stare. "You know where I mean."

Van nodded. "I do," he said. Everyone else had gone quiet.

"Sure you do," said George. "You and your brother and your dad, your mom, too, back in those days. You lived right up there."

Van looked stunned. "You knew my dad?"

So far as Monty was aware, George and Van had never spoken except to exchange neighborly greetings, and even Monty hadn't known that George had grown up out of state.

"Not well," said George, "but yes. I moved a long time back. Way before you guys came here. You don't remember me, I guess."

"I'm sorry, sir," said Van. "I don't."

"That's OK. No reason you should. I doubt Monty here would give me the time of day if I didn't pay him for his pie."

"Can we get that phone?" Red cut in.

"Hold it," said Van, who was staring at old George like he was in a trance. "I wanna hear this."

"Not much to hear," said George. "Unless, of course, this all feels kinda familiar to you."

Van blinked. "This?"

"Explosions and things falling to earth that weren't supposed to be there. You remember? Your daddy sure as hell remembers."

Van stared. A loaded hush descended on the diner. Stacy instinctively grabbed his hand and squeezed it.

"I don't know what you mean," said Van, though for some reason Monty didn't believe him.

"Sure, you do," George said calmly. "Some folks said it was a plane that crashed after the blast, but it wasn't. Folks went out to the wreckage to see. Some of them never came back. Those who did . . ."

He tilted his head to one side and made a face that said that those people weren't quite right. Van stared fixedly at him.

"They closed the site down, bought up the land, and closed the ranches," George continued. "The cattle were dying anyway. Then they moved the test site down here and started over. Only they made it bigger this time. Keep people away from whatever they're doing, and whatever they have."

"What do they have?" Sam asked in a whisper. He was spellbound.

"I think you know," said George with a thin smile. "I think we all know."

Monty licked his lips. This was probably the longest he had been silent in his own diner in years. "And if they know we know?" he said.

"They?" said Sam.

"The military," said Monty. "The government. Whoever. You said they killed the Carter boy."

"And took Andy," said Red.

"Then they're gonna come looking," said Monty. "I don't want to get disappeared. I don't want to come back like Danny Lopez." Van shot him a quick look. "No offense," Monty continued quickly, palms half raised. "I say we shut the lights off and close up shop for the night."

"No way," said Van. "I have to find Andy."

Monty shook his head. "If they have him, he's gone," he said. "Nothing you can do."

"I don't believe that," said Van, jaw set.

"They already killed one of your pals," Monty shot back. "You want to be next?"

"It wasn't like that," said Stacy.

Everyone looked at her. She was looking down, her voice quiet, her eyes fixed on the counter.

"How do you mean?" asked Dylan. He matched her tone and, just for a second, her eyes flicked up to his.

"They didn't come after us to kill us," she said. "It didn't feel that way. It was . . . almost an accident. One soldier. A bad judgment call. It wasn't like he had been ordered to kill us."

"Makes no difference," said Monty, reasserting control. "They'll be after you now. You've seen too much."

"Wait till they see what's in the truck," said Sam.

It took a second for the remark to register and then everyone looked at him. Red sighed and looked away, as if Sam had given up a secret they had sworn to keep. Then he shrugged. "Whatever came down, there's a piece of it lodged in the back of Van's pickup."

George raised his eyebrows, then laid down his fork and got to his feet. He pulled a billfold from his pocket, slapped money on the counter, and made for the door.

"Wait!" said Van. "I want to know more about . . ."

"I know nothing," said George, walking out. "I saw nothing. I heard nothing."

And then he was heading out into the night.

"Nice going," said Red to Sam.

"What?" Sam sputtered back.

"Can you two shut up for a minute," said Van. "I need to think."

"I still think we should call the cops," said Dylan. "They're not allowed to do this."

Van held up his hand before Sam could weigh in. "There's a piece of this . . . *thing* in the truck?" he said.

"Big piece," said Red. "Like, the size of a basketball. I guess it wasn't burning or your truck would be toast."

"It looks light." said Sam. "But it's stuck right in, like nails thrown by a tornado or something."

"What's it look like?" asked Monty.

"Metal," said Sam, "but weird. Curved like part of a bell or something, but thin. When you press it, it changes shape, but then pops right back to the way it was."

"You touched it?" Monty practically shouted.

Startled, Sam put up his hands, to show that he meant no harm.

"I've never seen anything like it," said Red.

"OK," said Van, thoughtful, planning.

"You're gonna trade it for Andy," said Stacy.

She said it matter-of-factly, like it was obvious. Van held her eyes, and she nodded fractionally like she thought it was a good idea.

"This is nuts," said Sam.

And then the lights went out.

# CHAPTER TWELVE

**M**onty always left the back door of the diner unlocked until he closed up for the night. The agent known as Skylark had known this for years, but never assumed the knowledge would be useful until now. But watching and storing up information, whether it seemed valuable or not, was a vital part of what he did. You never knew when something ordinary, something to which most people would pay little mind, might turn out to be precious when times became desperate. If you were running, it paid to know where the roads went, where the phones were, which stores would be closed, which doors would be open. Doubly so if you were hunting.

So Skylark had slipped into the back of the diner right after the kids had arrived. From inside the kitchen, just to the left of the pass-through, he had heard much of what they had said, including the part about what was embedded in the bed of the Lopez family truck. That changed things in an instant.

Skylark's hand had gone to his gun, then stopped. He saw the fuse box on the wall in the corner and the knives by the sink. He selected one, then opened the panel and killed the lights.

*Divide and conquer,* he thought.

As expected, Monty came back first. The darkness was not complete but there was nowhere to hide. In the dining room the kids were jabbering away loud enough to cover all but the loudest of sounds.

Monty felt his way through the grayness toward the fuse box, only seeing Skylark when he moved. Startled, he put a hand to his chest.

"Jesus!" he muttered. "I didn't hear you come in. What are you doing back here? You should come through . . ."

"Sorry, Monty," said Skylark.

He moved with sudden and improbable speed, so that Monty barely even had time to register the surprise as one hand clamped over his mouth and the other thrust the blade home. Skylark had chosen a long, slim knife with enough of a point that it required only purpose and precision. It went into Monty's chest just to the right of the sternum and sank up to the handle. Monty's eyes went wide, then blank, though the moment between seemed to last an age.

Skylark held him to the wall for a second, then lowered him softly to the kitchen floor, leaving the knife in place.

*Less blood that way.*

He checked his hands and face for spray or smearing, waiting for his heart to return to something like its normal rhythm. He could feel the sweat breaking out on his face and knew it was more than exertion. For all his certainty of purpose, he felt the horror of what he had done even as he tried to think of Monty not as a man he had known, but more like a chess piece that had gotten in his way. There was a damp towel by the sink. It smelled faintly musty, but he used it to mop his brow, closing his eyes briefly at the coolness on his skin.

He looked at his hands. The tremor was minimal and stabilizing. He hadn't killed a man in years.

*At all costs.*

O      O

"I say we should go now," said Red. They were still sitting in the darkened dining room.

"Go where?" Sam countered. He had picked up a steak knife and was fidgeting with it nervously. "There'll be soldiers all over town."

"If they're looking for us," said Dylan.

"They're looking for us," Sam insisted. "Trust me."

"I can't stay here," said Van, getting to his feet. "I have to find my brother. If what's in the truck is so precious to them, I'll use it to get him back."

"You think they'll do you a straight swap and then let you drive away?" said Sam. "That's not how the army works."

"It's what I've got," said Van with finality. "No one needs to come with me."

"I'll come," said Stacy.

"Me too."

It was Dylan. Van gazed at him, amazed.

"They can't get away with this," said Dylan by way of explanation. "We may not have got along in the past . . ."

"Understatement of the year," Sam cut in.

"But they're not going to do to Andy what they did to Chuck. I'm in, if you'll have me."

Van held his eyes for a second, then nodded. "Thanks."

"I owe you," said Dylan. "You could have let me burn."

The others stared at them. They hadn't heard the full story of their escape.

"No," said Van. "I couldn't."

"I'm in too," said Red. "For Andy."

"Oh hell," said Sam derisively. "Fine. Me too. But it's a terrible idea."

"Hey, boys," said a voice from the darkness by the kitchen door. "Stacy. What's going on? Monty said you had some trouble."

They all turned, peering into the gloom at the uniformed man in the doorway.

"Hey, Sheriff Watts," said Dylan.

"Where's Monty?" said Red.

"Trying to fix the breaker," said Watts. "I'm gonna need to get your statements before you go anywhere."

"No time," said Van.

"Sure there is," said Watts smiling, and sitting at the end of their booth. "Just give me a minute to get some specifics down and then you can be on your way."

Van stayed standing, but Red sat down again, whipped out a lighter and lit the ancient votive candle that sat with the ketchup and mustard. Monty had set a bunch of them out a year or so ago in the vague hope of generating a more intimate evening atmosphere, but the idea hadn't caught on, and most of the candles had never been lit. The flame blossomed, then settled, giving the area immediately around the table a thin amber glow.

Watts got his note book out. "You want to put that down?" he said to Sam. "You're making everyone nervous."

Sam seemed to remember the steak knife in his hand and laid it carefully on the table.

"I gotta go," said Van. "You guys can wait but . . ."

"I said I'd come," said Stacy.

"We all did," said Red.

"Yeah but—" Van began.

"There's a warrant out for your truck and its passengers," said Watts, "so I suggest you stay here before you get into worse trouble."

There was a tense silence.

"You cut yourself," said Stacy.

Watts frowned, puzzled, then glanced down to where she was looking. In the glow of the candle flame his right-hand cuff was dark and shiny with blood.

"No," he said. "I just . . ."

"Where's Monty?" said Red, getting up again and moving quickly to the pass-through. He stuck his head through and raised his voice. "Monty? You OK?"

He hesitated, gasped and turned quickly back to the table, his face a mask of panic. Something flashed between them, a ripple of fear and some collective impulse to self-protection, as when a prairie dog spots a hawk and barks its alarm. Something also flashed through Watts's eyes, but that something was very different.

Sam snatched up the steak knife and, without a second's hesitation, stabbed the sheriff's hand to the table before it could reach for his gun.

"Go!" he bellowed.

They scattered, driven as much by horror at what Sam had done than a clear grasp of what Red had seen.

Momentarily pinned to the table, Watts roared, then used his left hand to ease the blade out of his hand, grimacing in pain as it came free. He snatched up a napkin to staunch the bleeding even as he fumbled for his side arm.

The pistol came out and he pivoted after them, loosing off three quick rounds into the darkness. A window shattered, but he had no idea if he'd hit anyone. He blundered after them through the kitchen, almost tripping over Monty's body, but they were already out the back door.

Or most of them were. As the sheriff hesitated, his mind racing, he caught the sound of movement back in the dining room. A chair shifting. A little gasping breath that might have been a sob. One of them was still inside.

He moved back as quietly as he could, pistol raised, thinking fast. The only reason one of them would have stayed was that they hadn't had time to go by him. That meant it would be the one sitting by the window with her back to the door.

*Stacy.*

Watts smiled bleakly to himself. The Lopez boy would no more leave her than he would abandon his brother.

Even as the idea occurred to him, however, he heard the engine of the pickup outside. He edged out into the dining room, his ears straining to locate the sound of the girl. It was too dark to see under the tables, but he'd find her eventually. He took another step, and then, without warning, the blackness was replaced by the dazzling glare of headlights flooding in through the diner's plate glass windows.

Watts froze, dazzled, turning the gun toward the truck and firing off a round just as the pickup crashed through the glass. It bucked as it bludgeoned its way into the building, catching him on the hip and sending him sprawling. The room spun and he felt the shout of pain in his right leg as he crashed to the ground, but then the truck was reversing away and the diner was plunged into darkness again. He heard confused voices and caught the flurry of movement as the girl emerged from behind the juke box and made a dash for the shattered window and the parking lot beyond.

Watts raised his hand to shoot, but the gun had been jolted free and had landed in the rubble by the counter. He scrambled for it, despite the protestations of his thigh, but he was off balance and fell clumsily on top of it. He fumbled, then grasped it by the handle and fought to get up, but slipped on a shard of glass. Eventually he sat up ready to shoot, but by then the truck was no more than a glimmer of tail lights and a screech of tires. And by the time he was on his feet and sighting down the barrel, it was gone.

# CHAPTER THIRTEEN

Stevie Fly rushed to sit back down at his console, adjusted his chair, and spoke into the microphone, eager to share the contents of a dispatch he held in his hands.

"So that's confirmed, cats and kittens. Trinity is officially on total lockdown. No one in or out without express permission as the military perform an emergency clean-up of what is being called *classified material*." He put the last two words in inverted commas. "Now you know I want to hear all about your experiences from tonight, what went down, and what came down, out there in our vast desert. And we'll get to that, you bet we will. But first, there's something real heavy that you all need to know—and I want you to hear me loud and clear on this—and that is that these folks ain't playing. All roads in and out of town are blocked, and any attempt to go around them or bypass the check points is likely to be met with what they call extreme prejudice. So, sorry to all you atomic tourists. You ain't going home just yet. But don't fret. Old Stevie Fly is here to keep you company, and while I start digging, let's keep the sense of awe and mystery going with this one by the Majors, 'A Wonderful Dream.'"

Upbeat doo-wop sound flooded the airwaves. Stevie Fly sat back and stared out of the window into the dark sky over Trinity, all trace of languid cool gone from his face, his eyes dark and hunted.

O    O

The radio played loud out of the battery powered transistor duct-taped to the handlebars on Vince Reed's Harley. It was, he knew, futile to try and hear it over the hog's engine, but he liked the way it gave him a soundtrack, like he was the star of a movie people on the street were watching. He didn't care what it played. Vince had no interest in music of any kind, and he got annoyed when his Tunnel Snakes started bickering over what they liked and didn't.

"It's just noise," he had said many times, genuinely baffled. "Beach Boys or Elvis or whatever. Who cares?"

Not Vince. He mocked their dancing and sneered at their singing, and the more the others argued, the more he took pride in being immune to it all, as if liking something, anything, was a sign of vulnerability. So even though it annoyed him to hear Len go on about Brenda Lee, he kind of liked it because it proved why Vince was the boss.

Now, as the music blared thin and flat in the background, and their bikes roared along the highway heading up into the hills above Trinity, Vince took a slug from a bottle of whiskey and handed it back to Moe, who took it by feel and without slowing down. Billy and Len rode behind them, slightly staggered so that between the four of them they occupied both lanes of the highway. The road curved just enough that anyone coming in the opposite direction would get a hell of a scare before the bikes got out of the way. Every time that happened Moe would whoop and laugh like a maniac for a full two minutes.

Vince caught the flashing lights in his mirrors before he heard the siren.

*Cops.*

He ignored it till the car closed in on their tails and settled in, lights spinning, siren blaring and horn blaring insistently. Len gave him a look and he shrugged and pulled over. The others followed suit and the sheriff's department cruiser parked behind them. Vince thumbed the radio off but kept astride his bike, pushing the kick stand out and settling back like he was enjoying the evening. After the roar of the engines the silence of the night seemed almost surreal.

"What the hell, man?" Len demanded in a stage whisper.

"Shut up," said Vince. "And toss the bottle."

Len considered the near empty whiskey bottle he had stowed in his waist band, made a sour face, then tossed it lightly into a clump of brush. It clinked, but didn't sound like it had broken. He made a note of where it was for later.

"What are you boys doing up here at this time?"

It wasn't the sheriff. It was his deputy, the greenhorn, Reynolds.

"Just taking in the evening, deputy," said Vince languidly. "Town's too crowded."

"That's right," said Billy. "It's antsville back there."

"And you know this stretch of road is a 35 limit, right?" said Reynolds.

"Yes, sir, sure do," said Vince, unflappable.

"I clocked you at 50," said Reynolds. He had ambled up and circled around to Vince's front and now stood only a yard away.

"Fifty?" said Vince in studied bafflement. "That don't sound right. Sound right to you, Len?"

"Sure don't," said Len.

"Maybe your speedometer is broke," said Vince. "You should get one of those new radar thingies that tracks speed."

"They take two men to operate," said Reynolds, sidetracked. "We don't have the personnel."

"That's too bad," said Vince. "So it's just guesswork for you."

"I know how fast I was going," said Reynolds, getting hot under the collar. He'd had run ins with the Tunnel Snakes before. Their insolence made him nervous.

"Well gee, officer," said Vince, mock contrite, "we sure wouldn't break the speed limit on purpose. If we strayed above it back there, we sure are sorry. Won't happen again."

Reynold's lips pursed as he tried to decide whether to take the apology at face value. Then he frowned and sniffed the air. "You been drinking?" he demanded, coming a step closer.

"No sir," said Vince. "I just wiped down my chrome work. Vinegar and baking soda. You're probably smelling that."

"I don't think so," said Reynolds, his eyes level on Vince's.

Out of the corner of his eye, Vince saw Len stir, and stayed him with a gesture. There was no need for this to escalate.

"Get off the bike, please sir," said Reynolds.

Vince tensed. "What for?" he asked.

"Just do as I say."

Vince dismounted slowly, kicking his right leg high and wide. In the process he caught Len's watchful eye and sensed that he was just waiting for the nod. Len carried an assortment of knives in his pockets and had a baseball bat lashed to the side of his bike.

But then the silence was filled by an approaching vehicle, a big, throaty engine, laboring at speed. It built fast and zoomed past doing at least double Reynolds's precious speed limit. It was the Lopez boys' beat-up pickup, looking even more battered than usual but still hauling the mail.

Reynolds spun around to see it go, and at the same moment the radio in his car crackled to life. He hustled back toward it, momentarily forgetting Vince and his gang.

"Son of a . . . !" he spluttered, waving away the plume of dust from the speeding truck.

He snatched the radio handset from the open door of his patrol car and snapped, "Reynolds."

There was a pop and Sheriff Watts's voice came over, staticky and flustered.

"Putting out an APB on the Lopez boys, last seen heading west from Monty's diner. Looks to have been some kind altercation there. One fatality."

"I'm looking at them right now!" Reynolds exclaimed. "Fatality? Who's dead?"

"Monty," said Watts. "I got there too late. He said Van Lopez stabbed him. Where are you?"

"Out on route 17, two miles east of town, heading toward the high school."

"Hold them till I get there," said Watts.

Reynolds faltered and turned his back on the bikers so they couldn't see his face. He lowered his voice.

"Negative, Sheriff. I don't actually have them with me. They just drove by. You want me to go after them?"

There was a fractional pause, then Watts's voice came back. It sounded careful.

"No," he said. "Not yet. Let me talk to them first. I'll send instructions when I know exactly where they are."

"You sure?" said Reynolds. "If they're dangerous . . ."

"I'm on it. Stand by, deputy. I'll let you know when I need you."

"OK," said Reynolds. "Copy that. If you're sure . . ."

But Watts was gone.

Reynolds thought for a moment, unsettled, and not just by the news that the Lopez kid—who had never seemed to be any real trouble—had killed Monty Sanderson. Something felt off, though he had no idea what. Maybe it was the test and what the radio folk were saying about an accident. A downed plane or something. It was turning into a strange night.

"OK," he said, half to himself, as he turned back to deal with the bikers.

In the same instant he heard the bellow of their engines, and winced away from the dust and rocks kicked up as they remounted the road and peeled off into the night.

"Hey!" he bellowed after them. "Hey! I wasn't done!"

O　　O

Red was still rattled from seeing Monty's stricken corpse, Dylan was brooding in grim silence, and Sam, whose leg had been hit by shattered glass when Watts had shot at them, was pale and clammy. His ragged jeans were soaked with blood just above the knee. Stacy forced herself to look closely.

"I need supplies," she pronounced. "Alcohol, bandages and antiseptic. There's too much blood for me to see how bad the injury is."

"I need a doctor," said Sam weakly.

"Where are we going to find one?" demanded Red. "They're looking for us."

"We should go to the school," said Stacy flatly.

"What?" Sam protested. "Why?"

"Can't go to a hospital without them finding us," said Stacy with a level of composure that Van found amazing. "I have a key to the nurse's office at school, and the place will be deserted. If we can get in . . ."

"We can get in," said Red, focusing. "We can jimmy the locker room window behind the gym."

"Does that still work?" asked Dylan.

"Trust me," said Red. "You think old Powell's gotten to it yet?"

Dylan smirked in spite of himself. Ray Powell was Trinity High's famously lazy janitor. "Not a chance," he said.

"Go," said Stacy to Van. She took Sam's bandana and tied it tight on his leg in an attempt to stop the bleeding. "Red, you ride up front. I'll stay back here with Sam."

Van drove like the wind, barely even registering the moment that he sped by the Tunnel Snakes, but he saw the lights of the deputy's car and gripped the wheel a little tighter. If Watts was a killer, who knew about Reynolds?

It made no sense, any of it. Why would Watts kill Monty Sanderson, for God's sake? And what had happened out at the base? Were those things connected? Instinctively he felt that they were, though he couldn't see how. And then there was the lingering question about what had happened back in New Mexico when he was only a year old—what had happened and what part his own father had played in it. He kept reaching for the memory, but he couldn't grasp it, and the images kept sliding into what he had seen at the quarry and what had happened earlier that night.

And then there was the hunk of strange metal embedded in the pickup's bed. He hadn't had time to examine it as they had sped away from the diner, had only been able to glance and see it was there. It had seemed to pulse faintly with light, though whether that was just a reflection of something else or an energy within the material itself, he couldn't say.

He focused on driving, conscious that Sam might be losing blood all the time.

"I know where Coach Hardy keeps his gun," said Red.

"What?" said Van, jolted out of himself. "Why does he have a gun at school?"

Red shrugged. "Thinks he's a cowboy. Or a soldier. Some macho bullshit thing. Still, might be useful."

Van said nothing. If they were tangling with the U.S. military he doubted one pistol would make much difference.

"What the hell?" Red leaned forward and stared out into the darkness. Ahead they could see the school, its floodlights lit and the parking lot packed with cars. "Shit."

"Fucking A-bomb," muttered Van. "They opened the bleachers to watch the explosion. Can't believe I forgot."

"What should we do?"

He let the truck slow down as it pulled onto the school grounds, and turned back to look at Stacy through the rear window. He pointed at the cars and made a quizzical face.

"Park at the front," she shouted. "Everyone is out at the stadium. Find somewhere out of sight. Watts knows what you drive."

Van eased the pickup off the lot proper and down an access track into a stand of trees. He glanced at Red. "You think you can get in through the locker rooms without being seen?"

"Count on it," said Red. He glanced around, then spoke softer. "I didn't much like Monty, truth be told. He gave me a job, and I was grateful for that, I was just the help. Or worse. Sometimes, the stuff he'd say . . ." He went quiet for a long moment and his knuckles balled. "Once in a while he'd be decent, like he had just remembered I was a person, you know? But usually . . . I don't know. I always kind of thought I'd set him straight one day. He probably wouldn't have listened. Wouldn't have heard," he said carefully, as if that was different. He looked out of the window. "Haven't been back here since I left," he said with a rueful smile, then caught himself and frowned thoughtfully. "I didn't much like Monty," he concluded. "But I didn't want him dead."

Van sat very still, not sure what to say. In the end he just nodded, but by then Stacy had jumped down from the back of the truck and was pulling his door open.

"Give me a hand with Sam," she said, then turned to Red. "We'll wait at the front doors."

"Give me two minutes," said Red.

He jumped down, all trace of his reflective mood gone as he broke into a powerful run. Van remembered the athlete he had been, remembered cheering him on as he had scored touchdown after touchdown, feeding on the love of the crowd. And the hate.

Sam didn't look as bad as Van had feared, though his leg was a mess, dark and wet. Sam was keeping his weight off it, one arm thrown around Stacy's shoulders. Van relieved her, though Sam was so sleight she probably could have managed just fine by herself.

He didn't see Red till the doors thunked open and there he was, grinning. "Good old Ray," he said softly. "Never found a job he couldn't dodge."

Van and Dylan manhandled Sam inside, Stacy one step ahead and moving with purpose.

"Better keep the lights off," said Red. "But I found this." He snapped on a rubber-coated flashlight and directed it down the darkened halls. "Where's the nurse's station?"

"Follow me," said Stacy.

They moved as quickly as they could, Sam half-hopping clumsily, the noise of their footfalls echoing through the empty school. It felt uncanny, as if the place shouldn't exist at all outside class time. Van's feet knew which way to go, but his eyes insisted that everything was strange and unfamiliar.

"In here," said Stacy. "Get in and close the door." She snapped the light on.

The nurse's office was a box with a desk and a couple of chairs, one of which could be reclined flat. It was made of thinly padded metal and looked like an instrument of torture. Bookshelves lined the walls over cupboards of Band-Aids, boxes of cotton balls, syringes, and stoppered glass bottles. A cartoon poster warning against headlice was stuck up over a stainless steel sink. There were no windows.

Stacy snapped the light on before pulling the cupboard doors open and rummaging through the contents, while Red and Van maneuvered Sam onto the reclining chair. Dylan kept moving around, chewing his fingernails, trying to stay out of the way.

"Get his legs up," Stacy said, as she studied labels and boxes of sterile swabs. "And his pants down."

"Hey, now!" Sam protested.

"Do as she says," Van remarked.

"I'm feeling better," said Sam.

"No doubt," said Red, leaning on him with one hand and yanking his belt open with the other.

"Come on!" Sam protested vainly.

"Gotta be able to see the damage," said Stacy.

"So long as you can't see anything else."

Stacy had found a hook-like needle and was threading it with one eye closed. "Get me a wet towel."

Van obliged, running the tap till it was warm. Sam still winced and gasped at the contact, but Van sponged the blood away, revealing a ragged cut some two inches long.

"Looks deep," he said.

Stacy appeared at his elbow with a pair of tweezers.

"Oh hell no," said Sam thinly. He squirmed, but Red and Van leaned on him.

"Gotta see if there's glass in there," said Stacy.

Sam fought and yelped as soon as she touched the wound, but she gave him a stern look.

"You need to be still and quiet," she said with such forcefulness that he nodded meekly.

"Sorry," he whispered.

She repositioned herself so the overhead light cast no shadow on her work area, and leaned in with the tweezers.

O     O

"You think the Lopez boys are here?" asked Len.

"You heard the cop's radio," said Billy. "And that sure as shit was their truck."

"Oh, we know their truck all right," Vince said musingly.

Len grinned. "Good thing they came to school, huh?" He made a flicking motion with one hand and his switchblade snapped into place.

"Why's that, Len?"

"Coz we're gonna teach 'em a lesson," said Len.

Moe giggled maniacally but Vince just nodded.

"That we are," he said.

# CHAPTER FOURTEEN

Once Sam had calmed down Stacy told Van, Dylan, and Red to step outside.

"I don't want my first act as a surgeon to be a spectator sport," she said. "You guys can keep watch."

Van and Red shrugged and went outside, and Dylan followed a step or two behind, separated from them by his own thoughts. Stacy seemed on top of things, and though Sam had given them imploring looks, he didn't seem to be in serious danger. She had already contained most of the bleeding and had pronounced herself satisfied that nothing crucial had been severed.

In the hallway between the nurse's office and the coach's—where Red thought he could get hold of a gun—Trinity High's athletic legacy was celebrated in dimly lit team photos and trophy cases. Van paused at those for

1961, scanning the smiling faces till he saw Red gazing back at him.

"Hell of a team," he observed. "And you were the best man on it."

Red shrugged and looked away. "And the one who cost us the championship," he said. Dylan took a breath and looked away. "That's the story, right?"

Van was going to contradict him but met his friend's eyes and shrugged. "I guess."

"You know how many times I've heard people tell the story of how I got thrown out of that final game for attacking the ref? Dozens. Maybe hundreds. It's become a Trinity legend. The day Red Hauser decked ref Scott Baylard, who was just doing his job, calling 'em as he saw 'em. The day the game turned savage. The day Trinity's star receiver saw red. That's what they say. Like it's a headline, or a punchline. Because 'Red' is what they call me, and because I'm Black. Hilarious, right? This shit writes itself. They tell it and everyone asks about the final score, and whether I ever played again, and who won the division after we blew it. But you know what they never ask? They never ask what that umpire called me right before I knocked him on his ass."

Van's eyebrows went up, but he just stared, ashamed that he was one of those who had never asked. Dylan turned back to them, his mouth half open in the question that never emerged. At last he tipped his head in acknowledgment and looked down. The gloom of the hallway made them feel miles apart. Red fiddled with the flashlight but kept its beam on the floor, tracing a tight little circle.

The door to the nurse's office opened and Stacy stuck her head out.

"OK," she said. "You can come back in."

"How is he?" asked Van, glad of something to say.

"Fine," said Stacy. "There was a piece of glass in there, but I got it out, sterilized him and closed it up."

"Wow," said Van, impressed.

"It was nothing," said Stacy.

"Where's the glass?" asked Red with a ghoulish grin.

Stacy nodded at the counter. A fragment smaller than a penny nestled on a fold of bloody paper towel.

"That's it?" Red exclaimed derisively. "My uncle passed a kidney stone bigger than that."

"Funny," said Sam. He looked abashed, but some of the color was coming back into his cheeks.

"You really OK?" asked Van.

Sam nodded. "Your girlfriend will make one hell of a doctor."

Stacy looked down but Van just nodded. "You bet your ass," he said.

"So now what?" asked Red.

"We could just hide out here," Sam suggested.

Van shook his head. He had been half-zoned out, one eye on Stacy, who was flicking through various medical textbooks from the bookcase, but he came back as if slapped.

"No," he said. "I have to go to them."

"Them?" said Red.

"The military," Van clarified. "The government. Whoever has Andy. I have something they want and they have something—someone—I want."

"And what makes you think," Sam said, "that when they realize that you have something they want they won't just take it?"

"Maybe leave you bleeding in a ditch," Red concluded.

Van shook his head. "I don't believe they'd do that."

"They did it to Chuck," said Dylan flatly.

"That was different," said Van. "It was a mistake. They wouldn't deliberately kill American kids."

"A mistake?" Dylan repeated, some of the old fire flashing back into his eyes.

"I mean it was one soldier who freaked out," Van said, flustered. "It was a moment of panic. That's what Stacy said—right, Stace? It wasn't like someone made a command decision. No one gave the order to kill him. They wouldn't deliberately kill their own people, no matter what they were trying to keep secret."

"What happened to *it ain't like in the movies?*," said Sam. "We're not always the good guys."

"I'm not saying we are!" Van protested. "But I don't think we're giving orders to kill our own people. Right, Stace? Help me out here."

He turned to her but she looked somber.

"The film gets contaminated," said Stacy. "By the radiation in the corn husks."

"This again?" said Dylan.

"The government issued warnings to the film manufacturers," said Stacy.

"And?" said Dylan. "This is just Stevie Fly crap."

"The corn is contaminated by the A-bomb tests," said Stacy, spelling it out. "Not just around here. All the way east across the country. It gets into the crops and stays there, strong enough to ruin the film."

"So?" said Van.

Stacy had grown more somber as she spoke, as if she was bearing some terrible truth on her shoulders.

"It means the radiation is strong enough to be dangerous," she said. "Lethal, even. And they know. The government knows, but they keep doing it, and while they'll warn the film companies because they can see the results, they don't warn those who can't."

"Like who?" asked Red leaning in.

"Like people who eat those contaminated crops," she said. "People who drink milk from cows that eat contaminated feed."

Van was almost relieved. "It's safe enough," he said, waving the concern away.

"Is it, Van?" Stacy shot back, looking fully at him now so that he could see her eyes were brimming. "You should tell your mom that."

Van stared.

"Wait," said Dylan. "What are you saying?"

"I'm saying that the most common radioactive element produced by atomic bomb tests like the one we saw tonight is Iodine 131," she replied, flicking open one of the textbooks and shunting it across the desk toward him.

"Which does what?" Van replied.

Stacy closed her eyes for a second and a single tear squeezed out. When she spoke it was in a voice that was weary, drained.

"It affects the thyroid," she said.

"Thyroid?" Dylan cut in. "My mom had thyroid cancer."

"Yes," said Stacy so quietly they could barely hear her. "I know." She gave him a sad, sympathetic smile. "I'm sorry," she said, then looked at Van, waiting.

"What?" said Van.

Stacy took another long breath as if bracing herself, then said, "It's not just about cancer. Thyroid conditions can take other forms. Weight gain, fatigue . . ." She hesitated, then added, "Birth defects."

Van looked at her, his eyes suddenly as glassy as hers. "What are you saying?"

"I can't be sure," she said, "but I think your mom has hypothyroidism, and it's why your baby sister didn't survive."

"And you think this came from the bomb tests?" said Dylan, fighting to get his brain around it. "My mom? And the government knew but said nothing?"

"And kept doing the tests," said Red. He seemed less surprised than the others. He nodded thoughtfully, as if this all made perfect sense and merely confirmed a view of his country he had always suspected was true.

"Maybe they don't know," Van tried, clutching at straws.

"Of course they know! You think they didn't study what happened after Hiroshima and Nagasaki? Whatever Trinity thinks, nuclear weapons aren't just a fireworks display. You think the government doesn't know how terrible they are? How long their effects last? That's *why* they want them! That's why we're locked into a race with the Russians to make more and better bombs! You don't think they know? They are spending millions on this stuff *because* they know!"

"And what about us?" asked Van. "Our families, our lives . . ."

"Collateral damage."

Stacy wiped her eyes. "All of which is to say," she put in, forcing the conversation back to where it began, "that if you go to them and expect them to deal fairly with you over Andy . . ."

"You're crazy," said Red.

"If what's stuck in the back of your truck is important to them . . ." said Dylan.

"And it is," Sam interjected.

"Then they will take it from you. And if you get in the way, there is no power on earth that can protect you from them."

"And if the government is prepared to hide stuff about radiation, imagine what they'll do to keep something like this secret!" said Sam.

"You don't need to imagine," said Dylan. "You saw what the soldiers did to Chuck and what Watts did to Monty."

A weighted silence settled on the room like snow, and then Red shook his head slowly. "So Watts is some kind of government agent? Not sure that tracks."

Sam frowned, thinking. "You're right," he said. "If he was working with the Feds he could have taken us in. Killing Monty was . . ."

"Unnecessary," said Red.

"Cold," said Dylan.

"He wanted us, or what we have, bad enough to kill Monty," said Sam. "But that's not the way to get it if you're a cop, or a Fed. That's, like, the way a thug or a spy would do it.

"Sheriff Watts? A spy?" said Stacy.

"Maybe. Like some kind of embedded operative," said Sam. "Planted in Trinity to monitor the atomic tests. Then something else happens. Something comes down. We want it. The Russians want it. And maybe Watts is their guy on the scene trying to get it for them . . ."

"There's something else," said Van, homing in on the elephant in the room, the thing they had all been talking around, too unsure or embarrassed to face it head on. He didn't want to be the one to say it, but he knew in his heart what he had seen, and he was sure he had seen it or something very like it, a couple of weeks earlier over the quarry, the night he had gone shooting with his father.

*It looked at me*, he thought, picturing the dark object which had hovered soundlessly above him.

"What was it that crashed down tonight?" he heard himself say.

"Not part of the A-bomb test," said Red.

"Not some minor satellite knocked out of orbit by the blast," said Dylan.

"Then what?" said Van, forcing the issue, needing to hear it.

The silence crept back in like fog, then Sam shrugged.

"Fine," he said. "You all are too chicken to say it, then I will. It's a God-damned, honest-to-God UFO, and you all know it."

# CHAPTER FIFTEEN

The stadium floodlights were on, but the school itself looked quiet as the grave, which was all to the good. Vince shut his bike down and did his best John Wayne amble up to the front doors, though he held back, letting Len try them as if he were some flunky preparing the way for a grand vizier or pharaoh.

"Open," said Len, with a wolfish grin. "That means they're here."

Vince nodded, a slight smile forming in the corner of his mouth. "Find them."

Len ducked inside, followed by Moe and Billy running, snickering, after him, like the Wicked Witch's flying monkeys, but armed with knives and bats. Vince followed at half speed, savoring the night air, the dark, the scent of ozone or something else he couldn't put

214

his finger on. It felt good, dramatic, like something was coming.

He was inside the dim lobby with the doors closed behind him before a solitary car nosed its way slowly into the parking lot, its headlights off. Sheriff Watts, a fleck of blood just beneath his right eye, had watched him all the way inside before stopping the vehicle, getting awkwardly out and closing the door softly. He scanned the lot, eyes narrowed. There was no sign of the Lopez boys' truck. He could drive around the school's perimeter, but he didn't want to be seen by the reveling idiots still at the stadium. He spat, noticing the taste of blood, and moved to the back of the car, favoring his left leg and grimacing between steps, one hand on the handle of the hunting knife he wore on his belt beside the pistol. There was a pump-action shotgun in the trunk as well as a hunting rifle with a scope. He got the shotgun out, checked the breach, and moved unevenly, but with rather more purpose than Vince, toward the school.

O        O

"You OK to walk?" asked Van as Sam emerged from the nurse's office.

"My uncle was," said Red. "You know, after his kidney stone."

"I'm fine," Sam said pointedly. Red grinned at him.

"Just take it easy," said Stacy. "I worked hard on those stitches."

"Oh," said a figure stepping out into the lobby from behind a bank of lockers. "I think you're gonna get some more practice."

In the low light it took Van a second to place the voice, and by then there were others. It was Vince and, as usual, he was leading a group of Tunnel Snakes. Len, wide-eyed and sporting a shit-eating-grin, was slapping a baseball bat into his open palm menacingly.

"What do you want with us?" said Red.

"Don't nobody want *you*, Hauser," said Moe. "Thought you'd have figured that out by now."

"We want the Lopez runt," said Billy.

"But we're fine going to town on you idiots as well," said Moe.

"Looking forward to it," said Len.

He clearly meant it. Van knew it wouldn't take much for him to break whatever leash Vince had on him.

"If you mean my brother," Van said, "he ain't here."

"Where is he?" demanded Moe, holding a knife away from his body so its blade glittered faintly in the dim light of the hallway.

"Where you can't get him," sneered Sam.

It was the wrong tone to take.

"Is that right," said Len, stepping up and jabbing with the baseball bat. It caught Sam hard in the gut and he doubled up, the air knocked right out of him.

Red moved fast, stepping in and grabbing the barrel of the bat before the other boy could swing it. They wrestled with it for a second, and then Moe was going to Len's aid, knife in hand.

216

Van took a long stride and cold-cocked him from the side, one hard, driving punch that hit him square in the cheek and set him crashing into the wall. Red came up with the bat and swung it in a wide arc to keep the others back, but Moe wouldn't be down long, and his buddies were all armed.

Red glanced over his shoulder. "Run," he said.

Sam and Dylan went first, heading back deeper into the school. Stacy looked at Van, then ran after them. Van thought fast. If Red stood there alone, covering their retreat, they'd kill him for sure, bat or no bat. He got hold of Red's shoulder and pulled him into a reluctant run.

They were through the double doors at the end of the hallway before their pursuers—Len back up on his feet—started after them, screaming their vengeful fury. They sounded crazed, like a pack of wild animals, and Van knew that whatever the Tunnel Snakes had claimed to want from Andy, what they really wanted was an excuse. They had one now. Their blood was up.

*If we can't find a way out of here without tangling with them . . .*

He wouldn't let the thought finish. He had other things to do.

The corridor ran down past the science classrooms toward the gym. Those rooms didn't have exit doors, but if they could make it past the principal's office there was a back door that opened onto a tree-lined quad, one side of which contained an arched exit out to the teachers' parking lot.

*Not ideal*, he thought. The hallway dog-legged indirectly a couple of times around the cafeteria, and once out they'd have to trek halfway around the school to get back to the truck. *A long time to stay ahead of these maniacs . . .*

O    O

Something similar had occurred to Vince.

"They're going out the back," he said. "Len and Moe, go around and catch them as they come out. We'll chase 'em right to you."

Moe had looked too furious to speak and his cheek might well be fractured, but he liked that. He gave his little hyena chuckle and sprinted off, Len trotting after him back to the front entrance.

"Keep the noise up," Vince added to Billy, watching them go. "Don't let 'em know we split up."

Billy nodded, ever the eager and obedient follower. The knife in his fist was cleaver-like and almost as heavy as a hatchet. He started to call out in a loud, high-pitched voice: "Here, kitty kitty!" He drummed his hands on the doors for emphasis and then shouted it again. "Here, kitty kitty!"

Behind them the front door snapped and Vince turned irritably.

"What are you doing here?" he snapped. "I said get around back or they'll get out!"

"Evening, boys," said the figure by the front entrance. There was a soft glow coming through the glass and it silhouetted the figure so that his face was impossible to see, but Vince was pretty sure it wasn't Len or Moe.

"Who's there?" he demanded.

The figure took a couple of steps toward him but didn't speak. Billy glanced at Vince and did what he thought duty required.

"Are you fucking deaf?" he demanded, walking toward the newcomer. "You heard the man. He asked who . . ." His voice tailed off as the stranger came a little closer. "Sheriff Watts! What are you doing here?"

"I have business here. And you are in my way."

Vince couldn't see what happened next. There was a sudden movement, and a thunking sound with wet edges, and then Billy was crumpling, issuing a long wordless gasp. Watts stepped over the body and Vince saw the dripping knife in his hand.

"What the fuck?" he muttered, but Watts kept coming, walking almost casually, one hand reaching for his holster.

Vince ran at him, bellowing like a charging bull, head down, switchblade poised.

The shot blew a hole in his rib cage just below the shoulder. It didn't knock him back like gun shots in the movies did, but it stopped him cold, dropping him to the linoleum. He lay there, unable to move, screaming soundlessly mostly at the pain, but also at the sheer horror of the thing. All his tough guy cool left him, and he felt suddenly like a lost child. He could feel the blood pooling beneath him, slick and warm under his hands. So much blood. He wondered at it, amazed that it could all be coming from his body, and uncertain how much more he still had in him. The puzzlement, vague and dreamy despite the agony in his side, was his last thought. Seconds later, when Sheriff Watts stooped to look into his face, Vince Reed's eyes were blank.

O    O

"Was that a gun?" asked Stacy. She was breathless from running and her eyes were wild, but she had stopped to process the sound.

"Sounded like it," said Van.

"Who are they shooting at?" asked Sam.

"Just trying to scare us," said Red.

"It's working."

"Keep running," said Van. "Through here and we're out."

He rounded the corner by the principal's office. It felt like it had taken an age to get this far, but their pursuers didn't seem as close behind them as they had been. Suddenly that made Van anxious. His eyes fell on the external door, hoping it wasn't locked.

There was light around the jamb, faint but unmistakable. The door wasn't just unlocked. It was slightly ajar.

Again the anxiety mounted in his throat and he swallowed, but Dylan was already blundering past him.

"Wait!" Van said, but the other boy had already shouldered the door wide open.

There was a confusion of movement and someone pulled Dylan and turned him back around to face Van and the others. Moe Taylor, his face dark and swollen where Van had hit him, loomed over Dylan's shoulder, one hand clamped around his chin and holding his head back, the other holding a knife to his throat.

"Just give me a reason," he snarled.

It wasn't a threat. It was a request, and it was loaded with eagerness, hunger.

Van raised his hands in a calming gesture. Dylan had grown very still. Len pushed his way into the hallway from outside so that they had their prey surrounded.

"Now," he said, "where were we? Oh yeah, you were gonna be fed to the Tunnel Snakes."

"The fuck that's supposed to mean?" demanded Red.

"You want my buddy to cut his fucking head off?" Len demanded.

Dylan moaned, and Red backed off.

"Let him go," said Stacy.

Len beamed. "Is that something you think is gonna happen, you prissy little bitch?" he said. Van flinched but Len raised his knife and pointed it at him. "Feeling brave, Lopez?" he demanded. "Let's see how that works out for you."

"Gut him, Lenny," said Moe, his eyes blazing.

"When we're all here," said Len, enjoying himself. "Speak of the devil." He looked past them. "Hey Vince, look what we found . . ."

But it wasn't Vince. It was Sheriff Watts, and he had abandoned any attempt at stealth. The shotgun roared, lighting the hallway like an electrical storm, splashing momentary color like blood. Len rocked back and Van felt a fine spray on the side of his face. In the enclosed space the sound was deafening and for a moment Van felt vague, stunned. Then he saw Moe Taylor release Dylan and fly at Watts, knife held high. Van ducked away, pulling Stacy with him. And then there was another shot and a cry of animal pain as Moe, torn half apart, collapsed on top of the sheriff, knife hand still alive enough to stab and slash as the last of Moe's furious, tragic purpose drove the steel into Watts.

"Go!" bellowed Van at the others.

He fought for the door, slipping on the wetness under foot, but pulling Stacy with him. Dylan was already out and retching. Red almost lifted Sam bodily through the hall and shoved him into a clumsy, stumbling run across the quad toward the arch.

Another whine of agony and despair curled out from the school behind them, and they knew that Moe Taylor was finally dead. It was too much to hope that he had taken the murderous sheriff with him.

Van led the long dash to where he had parked the truck on the tree-shrouded access road. The screen of vegetation was thick enough that for most of their run, even as they got clear of the school buildings, he couldn't see it and a nagging doubt began to fester in his mind.

*I won't be able to find it or, worse, I'll get there and it'll be gone.*

He looked anxiously about, trying to recall a particular buckthorn or beech tree that looked familiar. It wasn't till he saw the cinder track itself, arrowing back into the scrubby woods, that he knew he was in the right spot.

"I need a break," said Sam.

Even with Dylan and Red shouldering most of his weight, he had lagged a good 50 yards behind.

"We're here," said Van.

He had turned to face them, the pale shadows of the school buildings at their back, so he saw the flash of Watts's gun before he heard the blast. The sheriff had switched to his pistol, and Van heard the air fizz as the bullet sped by.

"Come on!" he shouted.

Sam looked stricken. He hadn't been hit, but he knew the odds of him making it to the truck were slim. He muttered something to Red and Dylan but they both shook their heads.

"Fuck that," said Red, lifting Sam off the ground and redoubling his speed, Dylan stumbling alongside him. Their faces were set, grim, determined to keep going even though they knew they might feel bullets ripping into them at any moment.

Van knew what he had to do, though it felt wrong. He couldn't wait. The smartest thing to do, the best thing for them, was for him to run hard as he could for the truck and bring it out to where they could get in.

He sprinted down the path to the pickup, barely glancing at the strange shard of metal pulsing with phosphorescence in the truck bed. He yanked the door open and jammed the key into the ignition.

"Come on, come on," he wished aloud as he turned the key.

The engine turned over, sputtered, and fired. Van gave it some gas and shunted into reverse, taking the brake off and turning in his seat as the pickup jerked backwards along the trail. He could barely see anything out of the back, but kept it straight based mostly on memory, until he broke the tree line and the sky overhead opened up. Stacy had to dodge the tailgate, then pulled the passenger door open and clambered in before he'd come to a full stop.

"They here?" he said, squinting around.

"Almost," she replied. "Get it turned around."

Van twisted the steering wheel and stayed in reverse, swinging the nose around and putting it in first gear, ready to go.

"Tell me when," he said, eyes front.

Stacy had pivoted in her seat. She was murmuring wordless encouragement. Van felt the truck rock as the others started clambering into the back.

"Hold on," said Stacy, her face pressed to the cracked rear window.

"OK!" yelled someone from outside. Red, Van thought.

"Go!" said Stacy.

In the same instant he heard another blast from Watts's pistol and the pop of the truck's big rear window shattering. Van and Stacy ducked low, then turned to see the hole punched in the glass and the spiderweb of cracks that made the rest of the window almost opaque. Van threw an elbow, clearing most of it so he could see, and floored the accelerator, changing gears almost immediately and sending the truck speeding for the road. He glanced at Stacy, then performed the briefest of checks to make sure he hadn't been hit.

"Everyone OK?" he shouted.

Stacy nodded, and Red raised a fist, thumbs up.

"OK, then," said Van, as the truck turned hard on the road, skidding slightly. He gave it as much gas as it could handle.

"Sheriff Watts," Stacy said, horror struck. "Back in the diner I thought it might have all been some horrible misunderstanding, but he . . ."

"Try not to think about it," said Van.

"I'm trying." She took a deep breath. "Where are we going?"

Van snapped the radio on.

"Music? Really?"

"I want to hear what Stevie Fly knows."

He twisted the radio knob and Stevie's smoke-and-syrup voice came on mid-sentence. ". . . but those crazy army cats have established a second quarantine area not out at the base but up in the mountains west of town on the 56, so y'all need to keep your distance from there. What I'm being told—and this is coming through official channels, dig—is that roadblocks have been established on all access points around Baldy Lookout. They're being pretty tight-lipped about what they're doing so far from the test site, but y'all saw the same thing I did. Whatever *nonessential satellite* fell from orbit," and here he leaned into the microphone and gave the key word a lilting tone that said he didn't believe a word of the official release, "scattered debris all over the edge of the base, and came down right there on Baldy Mountain. Again, let's be clear, folks. These guys aren't playing around. There's troops and trucks and armored cars and God alone knows what else, so take it from your old pal Stevie and stay the heck away. You don't want to be on the wrong side of this one. Now let's spin a tune or two while I chase down some more info. And if you've got anything to share, Trinity, you know my lines are always open. Here's Patsy Cline, and like a lot of us in Trinity tonight, she's falling to pieces . . ."

Van turned the radio down and looked at Stacy.

"Well, I guess we know where to go," he said. He thought for a moment and felt something settle into the pit of his stomach like dread. "But I need to make a pit stop on the way," he added.

Stacy continued to stare at him, one eyebrow arched quizzically, but he just stared fixedly ahead into the Nevada night.

"You think it's what you saw in the quarry," she said. "The thing that came down."

For a moment he said nothing, then he nodded. "I'm sure of it."

# CHAPTER SIXTEEN

His name was Robert—Bobby to those who thought they knew him and considered themselves his friends, not that there were many of them. And they were wrong. None of them knew him, though he supposed they'd be figuring that out soon enough. Mostly he was just known as Sheriff Watts, the person he was encapsulated within his title, the job he did for the county at the ass-end of the great failed experiment that was the United States of Capitalism.

Bobby was what his mother had called him. She *had* known him, truly and deeply, had known him and loved him. But she had been gone a long time now, and no one had loved him since.

He thought this now as he drove after the Lopez truck, though he wasn't sure why. He didn't feel sorry for himself.

He had never had much time for love—in either sense of that phrase—and considered the national obsession with it to be just another sign of a narcissistic and decadent culture. It was also a blind, a myth endlessly pumped out through the movies and the TV and the music on the radio, designed to distract the mole-like people from how badly they were being screwed by the politicos and the corporations, all the hearts and flowers little more than a big pink cloud obscuring their pay checks and their miserable and meaningless existences.

His mother had understood that. It was she who had first talked to him about the alternatives to the American way, its greed and self-interest masquerading as individualism, its empty religion, its fascination with the shiny and vapid, its groundlessness. Her father had spoken proudly of the great European revolutions that had turned out the kings and the tsars and enabled the pursuit of true equality in the name of a common humanity. Watts's grandfather had seen it happen, and his mother had recounted it with wonder and admiration.

It had made an impression, though these were ideas he had learned to keep to himself, particularly after he had run headlong into the thuggery of the school playgrounds of his youth. In those days they had moved around a lot, trailing after his military father from base to base, seeing up close the machinery of U.S. empire building thinly veiled as peace-keeping. He had learned to be quiet, furtive even, keeping his innermost thoughts to himself. That habit had become something closer and deeper when his asshole father had dumped them for a younger woman, trading his mother in like she was an old car.

*More selfish consumerism . . .*

Watts had had a front row seat to her collapse into alcoholism, bankruptcy, and destitution. That was when he saw it most clearly, the failure of the American system, because when she started to fall, there was nothing to stop her. Two months after her death he had made his first trip to Moscow. Four years after that he had been made a foreign agent of the Russian security services, and now carried the rank of major in the KGB. He had done his entire service in the American Southwest, moving from New Mexico to Nevada along with the nuclear tests, keeping his head down and his eyes open, sending his weekly reports even when there was nothing to say, being a good citizen of the world and a comrade of the Soviet Union. All those years had led him to this point, to this night.

And it was all unraveling.

He hadn't liked killing Monty, though the old blowhard had been one of those little monuments to all that was wrong with America, a type who you could find in any small town anywhere in the country. Watts had taken no pleasure in the act, but he had committed it without remorse and felt no trace of guilt.

The Tunnel Snakes had had it coming too, though—being younger—they were less personally responsible for the valueless, posturing bullies which they had become. Still, he would be lying if he said he hadn't relished giving them the ugly ends they had deserved many times over. He felt no guilt about them either, and if he felt anything at all it was closer to exhilaration, to pleasure. Finally, after years of standing on the sidelines and watching the corruption and moral bankruptcy of the country he lived in, he was truly involved, engaged directly, and making a difference. What he had to do was messy and unpleasant, but Bobby Watts's world was making a little more sense.

*For you, Mom,* he thought vaguely. *I'm doing it for you.*

It was as good a cause as any. Men had done far worse for far less.

But he had lost sight of the Lopez truck and was now driving blindly, guessing at where they might be going, and feeling the situation slipping steadily from his grasp. His thigh ached where the Lopez truck had hit him, his hand was rigid around where the Jenkins boy had stabbed him, and he had a series of gashes on his chest and right arm from the fight in the school. Those last were superficial, if painful, but there was a deeper incision on the left side of his belly, which was bleeding steadily. He groaned, half closing his eyes, till the sound became a roar of pain and frustration.

Sooner or later he would run headlong into the full might of the U.S. military, and that could only end one way. He had to do something that might defer that collision for as long as possible. The image of his mother's face came into his mind again. She looked as she had before times got bad, when she was still smiling, still loving, still herself. The image gave him an idea. His mother had, perhaps, one last gift for him, one that might be all he needed to save his mission.

He hit the brakes and spun the steering wheel, the cruiser's headlights sending the desert scrub leaping in patches of strobing amber light. He turned the car around and sent it speeding not after where he thought the Lopez boy was going, but toward what would give him the bargaining chip he needed.

He smiled grimly, imagining the phone call he hoped to make before the night was out.

"I have it," he would say, "and, as a result, as a *direct* result, the world will change."

O      O

Van Lopez slowed the truck diagonally across from the stationary blue Econoline and returned Stacy's expectant stare. In the back the boys were peering around, demanding what they were doing.

"This is your house," she said.

"Yes."

"Why . . . ?"

"My father has weapons," said Van.

"I thought you said that trying to fight the army was absurd," she countered.

He looked quickly away, annoyed at himself for trying so stupid a ruse. He focused on guiding the truck down the side of the house and around the back where it wouldn't be visible from the street.

"Come with me," he said.

He didn't wait for her to follow, but got out, feeling in his pocket for his keys.

"Dude, what the hell?" said Red.

"Yeah," said Sam. "What're we stopping for?"

"Just wait here."

"Seriously?" asked Dylan.

"Or you can go," said Van. "For real. This isn't your fight. It could get bad. It probably will. It ain't your fight . . ."

"Things already got bad," said Dylan.

"We'll wait," said Red.

"We will?" said Sam. He looked at the others who gave him hard stares. "Fine. We'll wait."

Van gave them frank looks and nodded gratefully. "Be right back," he said.

He opened the front door cautiously, peering around the jamb. "Pops?" he said. "You there? I brought someone to meet you." Silence for a moment, then the distinctive snap of a shotgun being racked. "Pops. It's me. Van."

He stepped inside, hands up.

His father was sitting in the kitchen. The shotgun in his unsteady hands was trained on the door. His face was sweaty and tight, his eyes haunted.

"It's OK, Pops." Van edged into the room. "It's me."

Danny nodded slowly but didn't lower his weapon.

"Who else?" he said at last.

"Friend from school. Stacy Nicholson. You remember Stacy?"

Danny's face clouded with uncertainty.

"Hi Mr. Lopez," said Stacy leaning around the door.

Van moved to stop her but Stacy's impulse had been right. Danny gazed at her for a moment, then smiled distantly. The barrel of the shotgun lowered as if he had forgotten about it, and Van took another step inside.

"Close the door behind you," said Danny. "They're watching the house."

"Yeah?" said Van.

Danny nodded to the window and Van recalled the blue van parked down the block.

*But that was just Pops being Pops.*

"What's going on?" Van said, affecting a casual tone and forcing himself not to look at the shotgun. The TV was on in the corner, its black and white screen fuzzy and flickering, the sound turned so low it was inaudible. "Pretty wild night, huh?"

Danny considered this as if it was some great truth and nodded unnaturally slowly. "Pretty wild," he repeated.

"You OK, Pops?" said Van, genuinely alarmed by his father's manner. "You didn't go out, right?"

His father shook his head with the same slow certainty.

"But you heard?" Van pressed. "About the test and everything."

He winced at the inadequacy of his own words, but he didn't know what else to say. Danny said nothing but he cocked his head slightly, a faraway look on his face. Stacy gave Van a wary glance.

"Where's Andy?" Danny asked suddenly.

The abrupt shift in direction caught Van off guard. He stared, knowing he should have planned what to say.

There were no beer cans in the living room, no tequila bottles, but his father looked out of it, dazed almost. On the drive over Van had thought vaguely that he would be able to talk to his father without having to refer to Andy, but he now saw how unlikely that was. His father sensed his hesitation and his look sharpened somehow, shed its dreamy quality and came into focus before Van had a chance to respond.

"They have him?" said Danny.

Van fumbled for words. "They?" he said, stalling.

Danny got to his feet. For a moment he rocked unsteadily, then became still as stone. "They have him," he said with finality, reading Van's face. "Where?"

Van sighed, defeated. "Not sure," he said. "Maybe at the base, but I think they've moved everything that counts into the hills."

"Baldy Lookout?" said Danny, one eye flashing to the muted TV.

Van nodded.

"So we go there."

"No, Pops," said Van, stepping forward and taking him by the arm. "I got this. You stay here."

"No," said his father, shaking him off. "He is my son. This began with me. It ends with me."

Van frowned, mouth half open but no words coming.

"What do you mean, it started with you?" said Stacy.

Van shot her a look, sure she had broken some kind of spell, that his father would clam up or worse, but Danny smiled wistfully.

"Van knows," he said. "Don't you?"

Van stared at him, then shook his head, fast and tight, like he didn't want to talk about it. Danny stared at him. "It's OK," he said. "I think it's time."

"I don't remember," said Van, a note of defiance in his voice.

"Sure you do," said Danny. "You remember in your sleep. Have done since you were two years old. In dreams. In nightmares. You wake up and you forget, but I see it in your face sometimes like a shadow. You remember."

"Riding a horse," said Stacy. "Right? That's what you draw. Riding through the desert and a light in the sky, something that comes down."

She looked at him, piecing it together. Van shook his head, feeling tears coming to his eyes, but he said nothing.

"Same as tonight," Stacy said, the realization dawning and leaving her breathless. "Oh my God. This happened before, in New Mexico, and you both saw it!"

"Fire in the sky," said Van, speaking as dreamily as his father had done moments earlier. "We were going to investigate on horseback. The two of us together."

"I was out checking the fences," said Danny. "You were only a year old. Your mom was working, so I had you with me in a sling like the way my mother carried me when I was small. I thought it was a plane that had been brought down by the blast."

"It wasn't?" said Stacy. She sounded tense, as if she was afraid to hear the answer, though she already knew what it was.

235

Danny shook his head sadly, as if taking pity on her, on all of them. "It was not," he said. "We saw what it was. And they have been watching us ever since."

"The military?" Stacy clarified.

"The government," said Danny, shrugging vaguely as if the precise term escaped him and didn't matter.

"So all these years . . ." she began, but couldn't finish the thought, though Van knew what she was thinking.

*All this time when everyone thought you were crazy, when they shunned you, all this time as your family fell apart, your life, all this time you were right . . .*

It tore Van open from the inside, because he had thought they—everyone else—were right. He closed his eyes for a moment, hanging his head, and when he looked again he was amazed to see that Stacy had gone to his father and thrown her arms around him. Danny stood quite still, but he tipped his head slightly into her hair, his eyes on his son, that sad smile still fixed on his lips.

"I'm sorry, Pops," said Van.

Danny's smile widened, but a single tear ran down his cheek. He nodded in acknowledgment, but said nothing.

Stacy turned quickly to Van. "We need to go."

"Andy," said Danny, all business now. "What makes you think you can get him back?"

Van smiled grimly. "I have something they want. Come on. I'll show you."

"Hold on," said Danny. He turned, opened the door to the basement, and descended the stairs.

Stacy turned to Van. "What is he . . . ?"

Van grinned ruefully, "He's gonna come back with enough fire power to stop an armored division."

"I thought you said . . ."

"I did, but this is how my dad deals with stress. And apart from the military, we have Watts on our tail. It would be good to even the playing field a bit. Don't worry about Pops. He won't do anything stupid. His guns are like a security blanket. I don't think he'd actually shoot someone, even if they were trying to kill him."

"Even if he thought they were going to kill Andy? Or you?"

Van paused to consider that. "He'll be careful," he said. "And thanks. For the way you treated him. Not many people around here . . ."

She kissed him then, quickly as if to shut him up, then slowly, intensely, until Danny came clomping up the stairs and she broke away.

Van gazed at her.

Danny stared at them. He had three pistols in his belt, a carbine over his shoulder, and the shotgun in the crook of one arm. In his free hand was an envelope. He held it out to Van.

"What's that?"

"It's Andy's. Figured you should know who you're looking for."

He thrust it into Van's hands. Van had to fight back his irritation. They had things to do. Then he took in what had been roughly scribbled on the envelope in black magic marker.

It read, "Van's college fund."

It was full of money. Bills of various denominations. Some crisp and new, some ragged, soft, and worn thin as the finest silk. Van stared.

"What is this?" he said stupidly.

"He's been collecting it," said his father. "I put in when I had extra, but it's mostly him."

Van gaped at him. "Why?"

"So you can go to—"

"I know. But why?"

Danny smiled a little sadly. "So you can leave," he said at last. "And because you're his brother."

For a long, speechless moment Van just stood there. Then he nodded.

"So." Danny turned toward the door. "We going or what?"

Once outside at the back of the house, they stood around the truck. Sam, Red, and Dylan stared blank-faced at Danny.

"He's coming with us," said Van flatly. "In fact, maybe you guys should take off. It's my brother they have . . ."

"My son," said Danny.

"My friend," Red cut in.

"And mine," said Sam.

"I kind of hate him," said Dylan, shrugging, "but I mostly hate all you idiots, and I'm still coming."

Red started to chuckle, and then the three of them were laughing hard. Even Van grinned. "OK," he said. "Truck's getting crowded. Pops, you want to bring your bike?"

He nodded to the ancient but carefully maintained Norton Dominator. It was gun-metal grey and powerful looking.

"Cool," said Sam. "How 'bout I take that and you ride in the truck?"

Danny managed a smile and shook his head, ready to say "no," but as Sam got up, Danny's eyes fell on the hunk of metal, which had fused to the truck bed. A remnant of the dreamy look from before clouded his face. Wordlessly, as if his feet were moving by themselves, he stepped up to the truck and clambered up over the tail gate.

"Oh yeah," said Sam. "There's this. Weird, huh?"

Danny settled into a crouch, staring at it.

"Does this mean I can take the bike?" asked Sam.

Without taking his eyes off the iridescent metal, Danny pulled a ring of keys from his pocket and extended them to Sam. He took them, grinning like Christmas had come early, and leapt down. Even as Sam climbed onto the bike, turned the engine over and whooped in delight at its guttural power, Danny's eyes never left the metal fragment.

"Pretty strange, right?" said Red. "When you push it, it kind of pops back into shape . . ."

"Don't touch it," Danny snapped. Red pulled his hand away as if the metal was hot, as Danny turned to Van. "You brought this here?"

"It's what will get Andy back," Van answered.

"They will know you have it," said Danny, his eyes furtive again. "They will have tracked you . . ."

239

He moved quickly to the side of the house and looked back into the street. His gaze found the blue Econoline van parked down the block in the dark.

"No," he murmured.

"It's fine, Pops," Van began, but before he could finish the sentence, the van doors burst open and men spilled out.

They wore suits, and earpieces, and they brandished pistols.

Van leapt into the pickup and turned the ignition. In a second he had the engine humming, but over the top of it was a droning sound which was getting louder by the second: a helicopter. Suddenly there was a splash of hard white light from above, and a megaphone was blaring: stop what they were doing and come out with their hands up.

"Split up!" shouted Van. "Meet at the wash in 15." As Sam roared off on the Norton, Red and Dylan vaulted out of the back of the truck and scattered, Stacy slid sideways out of the passenger door. Van scrabbled to reach her, but she was out and running, doing what she could to buy him time. With a stab of wild panic as the truck surged forward, he prayed that decision wouldn't get her killed.

# CHAPTER SEVENTEEN

t was a nice neighborhood. Quiet. Watts liked that. He checked his mirror and wiped a smear of blood from his cheek with the moist corner of his handkerchief, pausing to consider the result. He was wearing his uniform. Some of the starch had come out of it, and there was a dirty patch on the right side where he had fallen, but it wasn't too bad if he kept his jacket closed over the wound in his stomach. He got out of the car and forced himself to walk slowly up to the front door and ring the bell. A light came on upstairs, and he heard muffled voices. His right hand slipped to his holster and unfastened the flap.

A net curtain in the front window twitched and then, a moment later, the front door opened and Hank Sweet looked out. He looked annoyed, though that quickly shifted into something less certain.

"Sheriff Watts," he said. "Is there a problem? It's pretty late."

"I'm sorry, sir," said Watts. "But do you know where your son is?"

Hank's face puckered with bafflement and a hint of anxiety. "I don't," he said. "Not in any trouble, I hope. He's out with his friends. I know it's late but the tests are like Mardi Gras, am I right? I figure that so long as they aren't doing real damage or drinking, where's the harm?"

"Is your wife home, sir?" said Watts, still managing a genial professionalism despite the pain in his gut.

"She's upstairs, but she's in bed. What's this all about, Bobby?" Hank asked.

In a single movement Watts drew the pistol and pointed it squarely in his face.

"Get her," he said.

O        O

On the other side of town, Red Hauser ran, weaving around trash cans and parked cars, nipping down dirt tracks and the alleys behind stores, head down and running hard as he hadn't since the day he decked the referee. Dylan was in good shape, but he would have a hard time staying with him.

"Follow me," said Red.

The suggestion sent a rush of confused feelings across Dylan's face. Somewhere among them was resentment.

"It's all about the route," said Red. "Trust me. Or not. Your call."

Then he was running again.

After them came men in suits and shoes unsuited to running. They wore earpieces and brandished handguns, and though they were fit and savvy, they didn't know the town like Red Hauser. Red juked and dodged at near full speed, rounding post boxes and trees with efficient grace and making an open dash from the north side of Eighth Street to the hardware store on Twelfth. He turned without slowing, and saw Dylan. The white kid was strong and quick, but he wasn't trained for this flat-out endurance stuff. Still, he had done as he was told and was doing his best to follow.

*Trust? Probably more like desperation, but whatever . . .*

Red paused behind the ice cream parlor on Meadow Street then hopped the fence into the yard next door. He couldn't be sure whether or not his pursuers had seen him.

There had been a lot of shouting at first, but once they had settled into the chase, everyone had gone quiet, and Red wasn't sure where they all were. He knew where he was though. This was what the white kids called "the Rook." Dylan wouldn't know his way around. Red slunk over to a shed with a trash can against it, and used the can as a step up onto the shed roof. He lay flat, listening, and soon enough came the sound of a hesitant, stumbling run.

"Goddamned Hauser," muttered a voice.

Red grinned bleakly to himself, then leaned out over the roof's edge.

"Hey," he whispered.

Dylan jumped visibly, then gazed up, stunned and afraid.

"Give me your hand," said Red.

Dylan looked around desperately, as if wondering if he would be better throwing himself on the mercy of the agents, then reached for Red's hand. Red hauled him up, the shed roof creaking. It wasn't built to bear this much weight.

"Fucking thing's gonna fall down," Dylan hissed.

"No way, man," said Red. "Come this way and stay low."

He led the way in something like a crawl, clambering deftly from the shed to the eaves of the adjoining house. Red had never been great with heights but he gritted his teeth and made his way—quick as he dared—over the gables, and reached into a tree overhanging the roof. Carefully he transferred his weight onto one of the branches.

"The hell you doing?" Dylan gasped.

"They're looking for us at eye level," said Red with a casualness he didn't feel. "They won't think to look up here. Also—check it out."

He nodded to where the tree spread a long branch away from the house till it almost touched a metal gantry some 20 feet high: a signal platform, below which was the pale gleam of railroad tracks. Again he paused, but his indecision ended with the low buzz of an approaching helicopter. He swallowed his fear, reached out one hand, then the other, got hold of a branch and tested it. It moved a little, but felt sturdy enough. He swung across, heart in his mouth and breath held, feeling for purchase with his feet, then did it again, and again, till he had gone out along the branch as far as he dared. Now the signal tower was only a few feet away, almost close enough to touch. Almost.

"D'you even know where we are?" Dylan said in a hushed voice. It wasn't a real question. He was stalling because he didn't want to do what Red clearly had in mind.

"The wash is a hundred yards that way," said Red. He pointed beyond the tracks to a ragged stand of trees. "Those guys following us? They don't know that, so they won't go this way. If you head back to the street, you'll walk right into them." He let the statement hang in the air for a second till he saw the truth of it register in Dylan's mind, then he added, "See you on the other side."

And then he half jumped, half fell onto the gantry, landing poised, legs bent and arms spread. There was a dull metallic clang, and then he was shuffling along the walkway past the oversized signal lamps, and turning laboriously in order to navigate a rusted metal ladder. Behind him he heard approaching road vehicles. Dylan would have to decide whether to follow or be caught in a tree like a raccoon. He glanced back just long enough to see the searchlight from the chopper raking the roofs of the town, and to see Dylan jump from the branch.

The sound of trucks was getting louder, and Red thought he could hear raised voices. He descended as quickly as he dared, dropping the last few feet and stumbling before breaking into a run, relieved to be back on the ground.

He pushed through the dry, scratchy bushes, and then there was one of the most beautiful sights he had ever seen: the Lopez family truck, escorted by Sam Jenkins on a motorbike. He vaulted into the back and turned back in time to see Dylan, wide-eyed, busting through the undergrowth.

"Come on!" Red called, his arm extended.

Dylan ran, put one foot on the tailgate and reached out. Red grasped it and, for a split second, their eyes met. Again the rush of uneasy feeling in the Sweet kid's face, this time mixed with something like shame. Red grasped his hand and dragged him into the truck, saying nothing.

"Hold on!" called Van from the cab.

Van sent the pickup bursting through the thin hedge at the top, up the embankment and down into the wash. The headlights swung up and down wildly, and then they were sliding hard to the right and roaring along the creek bed. In their wake, its headlight like a great white eye swaying back and forth behind them, was Sam on Danny's Norton. He was riding closer, swinging to the left as if wanting to come alongside. Van pulled right to give him room and turned to see the skinny kid grinning at him, his face all joy and victory.

"They couldn't get the truck over the embankment!" he crowed. "We're home free. Woo!"

Van grinned back at him, but even as he did so he caught movement in the corner of his eye and turned. Fifty yards ahead something big and boxy was blundering over the embankment.

"What the hell is that?" he gasped.

It was an ugly, blunt object of a vehicle. In the pickup's lights Van saw that it was fully tracked, with a square nose and a hatch on top, where a soldier in a helmet sat training a large machine gun on them.

"Fuck!" shouted Sam, equal parts dismayed and impressed. "That's an M113! We better stop."

That was clear. The armored personnel carrier had slid out in front of them, almost entirely blocking the wash. Overhead a helicopter banked hard and yawed sideways, a searchlight stabbing down to earth and dazzling the dust and sand of the desert floor.

Van slowed the truck and glanced at the others. Danny was cradling his carbine, but he knew better than to start shooting. The carrier was basically a tank for transporting soldiers. Nothing they had in the pickup would make a dent in it.

Sam slowed the motorcycle. Straddling the big machine he looked even smaller and thinner than usual.

"Think you can make it up the other bank?" he said, his voice lower now that he didn't have to fight to be heard over the Norton's engine.

Van glanced to where Sam had looked. It was steep and overgrown with brush, but unless there was a boulder they couldn't see, he figured the truck could handle it. Even so, he frowned.

"Don't think they're gonna let us go," he said.

"Leave that to me," said Sam.

"Wait—what?"

Stacy leaned across. "Don't be a hero, Sam. It's not worth it."

For a split second he seemed to consider that seriously. "Then what is?" he asked.

"Seriously," said Stacy earnestly. "Don't."

"Hey," he replied, smiling. "I come from a long line of military idiots. It's in my blood."

He turned and looked hard at Van. "Ready?"

Before Van could respond, Sam was revving the bike and moving across the blunt nose of the great olive-colored vehicle, which came to a hard stop. "Go!" he shouted.

Van punched it, and the F100 jumped forward, across the wash and up the bank, crashing through the shrubs and jolting hard onto the railroad tracks on the other side. For a second it juddered to a halt, straining, but he pushed it till the wheels spun, and suddenly the truck was rocking unevenly over the rails and on into the darkness.

Stacy turned back to where Sam was blocking the armored personnel carrier from coming after them. The back of the M1113 had opened, and soldiers were spilling out, rifles at the ready. The carrier made a surging feint forward, but Sam held his ground, staring them down. Suddenly the night was torn apart by a yellow-white flash and the thunderous crackle of machine gun fire.

"No!" screamed Stacy, but the pickup was hurtling away, and no matter how hard she strained to see, the wash fell behind them, screened by the thin bushes beside the railroad tracks. "Sam!" she called, but he didn't come after them, and as she gazed backwards through the shattered rear window of the truck, past the stunned faces of Red, Dylan, and Danny, the night gathered behind them, somber and empty.

The blackness lasted only a moment before the beam of the helicopter's light reached for them like a great white hand, groping in the dark. The chopper swung out in pursuit.

"Kill your lights!" shouted Red, "and take that right up ahead!"

He pointed, and Van obeyed, bringing the pickup around hard and barreling along a treelined track. "I can't see!" he protested.

"Just go straight!" Red responded, leaning in from the truck bed through the broken window. "In about five hundred yards you're gonna see a white painted stone. Take a left there."

Van swallowed and leaned forward in the seat. Beside him, Stacy was sobbing quietly. He was almost glad that he was responsible for the driving. The focus it took, speeding dangerously through the dark, crowded everything else out of his head.

"There!" shouted Red. "Turn now!"

Van did so, a blind, reckless maneuver during which he held his breath and braced himself for impact with God knew what. It didn't come, though his limited view of the path ahead got still tighter and darker. They were moving through the closest thing to a forest this part of the county had to offer.

"Where's that chopper?" he shouted, not looking back.

Red looked around.

"Behind us," said Dylan. "It's going in circles over there. I think we lost it."

He said it without joy or triumph. The helicopter wasn't the only thing they had lost.

○      ○

Agent Randal Kent peered into the darkness outside the chopper's searchlight and cursed.

"Where the hell are they?" he called over the roar of the rotors.

The pilot shook his head. "Must have gone dark and moved under the tree canopy.

"*Tree canopy?*" Kent shot back. "It's fucking *Nevada!*"

"Yes sir, but there are some dense trees over there," the co-pilot volunteered, pointing.

"Near the crash site? Great, they're heading in the one direction we don't want them going and we can't see them!"

"There are checkpoints all around the perimeter," said the copilot confidently. "They can't get in."

"I wouldn't be so sure," Kent replied. "It's not exactly the Berlin Wall."

"You think they'll try?"

"Have you not been paying attention?" Kent shouted back, face and voice hard. "Of course they are going to try. Do I have to explain to you again the level of security we are supposed to be enforcing here, the consequences if their stories get out? Get over there. Now."

The two pilots exchanged the smallest of looks, and then the helicopter abandoned its slow circling, picking up speed as it veered off toward the foothills, leaving Trinity behind.

○      ○

No one in the pickup was speaking. They had driven in a despairing silence for at least five miles but they could see next to nothing without the truck's lights on, and Van had had to lower their speed to a crawl as they came out of the woods and climbed a slow rise where the vegetation gave way to jagged rocks and sunbaked dirt. They had caught the sound of the helicopter flying overhead to the west but they had lost its lights in the trees. Privately, Van figured that the agents on board would be waiting for them at the base, and in his heart of hearts he thought the idea of trading the fragment of metal for his brother was futile. He just didn't know what else to do. The military and whoever was pulling their strings held all the cards.

"Over this ridge we're gonna join the road that heads out to the base," said Red. "I used to hike up here. My bet is that . . ."

"They'll be waiting for us," said Van, stopping the truck.

"Pretty much," Red agreed.

"Anyone have any better ideas?" asked Dylan.

"Better than just asking the people who killed Chuck and Sam for my brother back?" Van snapped bitterly.

No one spoke. Dylan looked down, his lips pursed.

"We keep going," said Danny. It was the first thing he had said since leaving the house.

Van muttered to himself, but his father cut him off. "What did you say?"

The tension deepened, became uncomfortably private.

"I said it was a waste of time," Van replied, defiant. "In case you hadn't noticed, we're up against the U.S. military.

You ought to know better than all of us that if they want something kept quiet, they're gonna make sure it's kept quiet. No one gets in the way. Ordinary people—U.S. citizens—kids. They wind up silenced, even dead. They have armored cars and helicopters and soldiers. What are we supposed to do against that? We have nothing."

"Us," said Stacy.

"What?" Van asked.

"We have us," she qualified, taking his hand.

"And what if that's not enough?" Van asked. Stacy smiled weakly and shrugged.

"It's all we have," said Danny. "It has to be enough."

For a long moment Van looked at his father then, by way of answer, he set the truck rolling forward toward the ridge.

# CHAPTER EIGHTEEN

The guarded barricade was codenamed Checkpoint India. If they'd had time to set up a truly functional perimeter, it would have been strung with concertina wire and monitored by watchtowers, but for this hasty deployment the military were relying on the famously rugged Nevada landscape to provide most of the obstacles and were blocking the roads with a pivoting single beam gate. It might have been almost comically inadequate but for the trucks, armored cars, APCs, and tanks that were dotted along the roads every few hundred yards, each one with armed infantry support. Here by the gate, a couple of open-topped trucks had been equipped with powerful searchlights that moved hard-edged pools of brilliance over the landscape, and a little way off sat the business end of the U.S. army: a single but imposing Walker Bulldog tank.

At the sound of an approaching engine, they swung hurriedly into action, scouring the terrain till they saw the red pickup coming over the rise. Soldiers moved into position, the guards on the gate suddenly alert as they readied their weapons. A couple of hundred yards over to the right, the tank—its commander watching from his hatch—rotated its turret, bringing its massive 76mm canon to bear on the advancing Ford.

Like a sentient thing knowing its peril, the truck slowed. A hand stuck out of the cab and waved a white tee shirt as a flag of surrender or truce.

One of the officers on the barricade gave the order to hold their fire and then nodded at four troops, who trained their rifles on the pickup, scuttling forward in crablike half-crouches. The officer approached the truck, side arm drawn but held by his side, his posture upright, projecting an air of command.

"This road is closed!" one of the troops barked. "Turn your vehicle around and withdraw from the area immediately!"

But the vehicle didn't withdraw. Instead, the driver's side door opened and a man—actually little more than a boy—got out. He had his hands raised over his head, but the soldiers were on high alert and started yelling at him to get down on the ground.

He didn't, standing tall and seeming to take a long, steadying breath, hands still up.

The officer raised one hand to his men and kept walking, supremely confident, until he was close enough to the teenager who had been driving the truck. There was a girl on the passenger side and three other men in the back, though only one of them looked old enough to merit the term.

"Not a good night for curiosity," said the officer, the hint of a smile just audible beneath the steel of his resolve.

"Not being curious, sir." The driver was a tall, good-looking kid with dark hair and eyes. He was possibly Latino, as was the older man in the back. "You have my brother, and I'd like him back."

"Is that right?" said the officer, the amusement in his voice clear this time, but with enough edge to show that it could quickly turn to irritation.

"Yes, sir," said the kid. "Andy Lopez."

"That you or him?"

"That's him. I'm Van Lopez."

"And what makes you think we have your brother?" asked the officer, his eyes wandering over the watchful faces in the truck. He could see their tension and anxiety like smoke, but he sensed no hostility from them.

The girl got out of the passenger side. "You took him at the base," she said. "When the ship came down."

"The what?"

He feigned ignorance, but there had been the merest fraction of a delay before his response, and he knew he had given something away.

"The ship, sir," said Van Lopez, eyes level. "The UFO or whatever you want to call it. My brother saw it come down." He hesitated and then, as if reading the officer's rapid calculation in his face, added, "We all did."

The officer looked into the night for a second, thinking. "Is that right?" he said.

"Yes, sir," said Van, unflinching.

"So you've come to turn yourselves in."

"No, sir, like I said, we've come to get my brother and take him home."

This time the officer's amusement was unavoidable. He glanced at the armed men, then back to the searchlights and the brute force of the solitary tank. "I don't think that's going to happen, do you?"

"Actually, sir, yes, I do."

"I don't think you have the firepower."

"Didn't come to fight, sir," said Van. "Came to trade. Have your men look in the back of my truck and you'll see . . ."

The officer took a step toward the back of the truck, shadowed by the cautious infantry, but there was a sudden crack, loud, coming from somewhere out there in the dark. For a second the officer thought it had been the pickup backfiring, but as he turned around, he saw that the tank commander was slumped over the Bulldog's turret. He spun around, raising his weapon, as two more quick shots came out of the night. In the brilliance of the hastily focused searchlights he caught the crimson spray as one, then another of his troops dropped, dead before they hit the ground. He had maybe a second to register the panicked horror of the kids in the truck to know that whatever was happening, it wasn't them. Then the first of the searchlights went out. He moved for cover behind the truck, but he felt the bullet tear through his side moments before another shattered the second searchlight, and the desert was suddenly plunged into darkness.

○      ○

Van shrank away from the gunfire, bracing himself for impact as the troops around him fell. Dylan and Red vaulted out of the truck bed, and, together with Stacy, they bolted across the check point and into the night.

"Find Andy!" he bellowed after them, then ducked down low as another shot came from the town side of the road. Van heard no shout of pain, no stumbling fall to suggest they had been hit, and he pivoted on his heel, scouring the now lightless desert for the shooter. He heard the repeated snap of a rifle being reloaded but couldn't home in on the location. His father was kneeling in the Ford's bed, his carbine ready.

Without the great searchlights, the blackness became impenetrable only a few yards away, and the voice, when it came, was surprisingly, alarmingly close.

"Drop it," it said simply.

It was Sheriff Watts, but he wasn't alone, and though he was holding a powerful looking rifle with a scope, it wasn't pointed at them.

"Mom!" Van yelped. He took a half step toward her, but Watts tightened his grip on her neck and pressed the muzzle of the rifle to her chin. Gray duct tape covered her mouth and bound her wrists together, and she looked pale with fear, her eyes wide and bloodshot.

"Come any closer and I'll blow her fucking head off," said Watts.

He sounded different, his studied professional calm worn ragged as his blood-soaked shirt. There was no doubting his willingness to kill again. Van raised his hands once more and grew still. Danny hadn't moved, and his carbine was now aimed right at Watts.

"I said, *drop it!*" Watts screamed. Even under the dust and blood, Van could see that his face was flushed and his eyes bulging with something close to madness. "Put it down," he added after a pause, eerily quiet and reasonable now. "If you make me wait another second, I swear by every dumb-ass value you idiots hold dear that I will paint the ground with her brains. You hear me?"

Van saw the struggle in his father's eyes, the furious indecision, then he snapped the carbine down to his side like a soldier on parade.

"Better," said Watts. "Now get out," he said to Danny. "Leave the gun."

Cautiously, his eyes never leaving the blanched face of his ex-wife, Danny climbed out and down.

"Soldiers will be here in a second," Danny said as he moved. He half turned to where the tank sat, now invisible in the brooding gloom.

"Then we had better make it quick," Watts replied.

"Sheriff," Van tried, stalling, "I'm sure we can talk this through. There's obviously been some misunderstanding..."

"Don't call me that," said Watts bitterly. "Do I look like I'm here to protect and serve?"

"O . . . K . . . ?" said Van. "So what do you want?"

"I want the damn truck!" he fired back, spitting with exasperation. "Haven't you even figured that out yet, you fucking rube? I want what's in the back of your shitty pick up."

"Fine," said Van, making calming gestures with his hands. "You can have the truck."

"Walk over there," Watts snapped, motioning with one elbow. "Both of you."

Father and son exchanged glances, then did as they were told, sidling onto the passenger side and walking a few yards till he told them to stop. Van thought he could hear muffled movement from the direction of the Bulldog. Their commander was dead, but the rest of the tank crew were still alive, and they were going to do something.

"Give me the keys," snapped Watts, forcing Tammy Sweet to her knees. She looked weak, struggling to breathe through the tape. "Toss them over."

Van patted his pockets showily. Somewhere in the darkness toward town he could hear the steady purr of an engine getting closer. Elsewhere there were other noises, the drone of a chopper and distant shouted orders; word of what had happened at the checkpoint was spreading along the perimeter. He shrugged apologetically, showing his empty hands.

"The keys!" Watts demanded, but Van cut him off.

"I don't have them! They're in the truck."

Watts nodded as if in some private dialogue with himself, then raised the rifle at Van. In the same instant the engine of the tank roared to life and its lights came on. It was at least two hundred yards away, but it began to move immediately, spinning uncannily as one set of tracks turned and the others stayed still. The Bulldog turned to face them and rolled forward, its headlamps dazzling in the darkness. A head was poking out of one of the lower hatches, and the turret rotated a few degrees as it prepared to fire its machine gun.

Instinctively Watts moved behind Van's mother and redirected his rifle at her.

"Mom!" Van yelled, close to despair. As the tank got close, he could feel its hesitation. The surviving crew members weren't used to making command decisions. If they had a sniper they might still take Watts out, but Van knew in his gut that whatever the circumstances they weren't about to spray a group of civilians with machine gun fire.

"Get out of the tank!" Watts shouted. "Get out, or her death is on you!"

There was a long, uncertain moment, then—over the noise of the engine—Van heard the squeak and clang of a hatch being thrown open. Men began to climb out, and though Van understood their impossible predicament, his heart sank. He thought suddenly about Chuck and Sam, about his lost baby sister, and he knew like a stone settling into his gut that Watts had no intention of leaving them alive. That just wasn't how the world worked. He'd take what he wanted, lying to get it, then he'd kill them all.

"Turn the engine off!" Watts yelled as the last of the tank crew clambered out. One hesitated, vanished for a second, and then the noise dropped as he shut the Bulldog down.

Van blinked and turned. The noise had dropped, but not gone away. There were other sounds, one of them another engine coming from the direction of the town. He had noted it before though it had been distant at the time, but it now sounded a lot closer. For a second, Watts was too pleased by his victory to notice, and his attention stayed on the silent tank.

"The pride of the American military," he sneered. He raised the rifle again, his finger curling around the trigger and only then did he register the swelling growl of the engine Van had been listening to. It suddenly grew dramatically louder as if the sound had been screened by obstacles or terrain, and Van saw the uncertainty register in Watts's face.

"What the—?" he began, but by the time he turned there was only a single headlamp appearing suddenly out of the scrubby trees of the track they had ridden in on. It seemed to leap over a sudden rise, getting big as the engine grew loud. It was like a great mechanical horse bringing a knight into battle.

Watts swung around to face it, trying to find the rider with his rifle, but he was half blinded by the headlight, and his shot was wild. Then the Norton clipped him and sent him spinning. He sprawled headlong in the dust. Van rushed forward, grabbing for the rifle, as the bike slid to a halt. Only then did Van see past the headlamp to the driver's face. He gaped in amazement.

"Sam!" Relief rushed through him. "We thought you were dead!"

"They only fired warning shots! Just warning shots!"

"I can't believe it!" Van said, blinking and shaking his head.

"I think this hero thing really is in my blood," said Sam. "But I'm having some serious second thoughts about joining the Army."

Van hugged him quick and hard, but broke away before Sam could complete the embrace. In another second Van was kneeling beside his mother, tearing at the tape around her mouth.

She took a series of long, gasping breaths made all the harder by her persistent, alternative whisperings of "Sorry" and "Thank you."

"Shh," said Van, folding her in his arms. "It's OK." The phrase gave him pause as everything Stacy had said swirled in the back of his mind. "How are you feeling?"

Her face flooded with confusion as she sensed that he was asking about more than her abduction, but she managed a wan smile. "Better now," she said.

"How is Hank?"

The question had come from Danny, and for a moment she didn't know how to respond. She fought to find the words. They began as a sob, but she pushed through. "He's OK, I think," she managed. "Sheriff Watts hit him with his gun, then tied him up and gagged him, but I think he'll be OK. He was conscious when we left."

Danny nodded. "That's good," he said with such simple honesty that the tears broke from her eyes.

"I'm sorry, Danny," she began. "For everything . . ."

But he shook his head and cut in. "Speaking of the Army," he said and turned east to where a cluster of headlamps was bumping its way along the road toward them. "We should get out of here." He glanced at Watts who hadn't moved since being hit by the bike. "Leave him for them."

Van nodded his agreement, but took the sheriff's rifle and the holstered pistol, rolling him roughly as he tore it free. For a second he stood over the man who had tried to kill his friends, his family, the pistol held loosely in his hand.

"Come on, Van," said Danny meaningfully. "Time to go."

Van met his eyes, nodded curtly and tossed the guns into the back of the truck.

"Come on, Van's Mom," said Sam, grinning and patting the Norton's seat behind him. "You're with me."

"You are enjoying yourself way too much," Van muttered to him. He helped Tammy onto the bike.

"Let's go!" shouted Danny from the pickup. He had already raised the barrier gate. The lights of the approaching convoy were getting very close.

Van ran, leapt in beside his father and turned the key. Keeping the truck's lights off, he drove through the barricade, leaning forward to make out the road ahead.

# CHAPTER NINETEEN

Dylan, Red, and Stacy had been running at half speed, hunched over against stray bullets, their hands out in front of them, because of the low light. They stumbled constantly on the uneven ground, and Dylan had already fallen hard once. Only Red, who had clearly maintained his old football training, seemed comfortable, and while the others looked close to beaten, he had barely broken a sweat, his long legs striding ahead like a 1500-meter pace-setter poised to crank it up for the final lap.

"Hold it!" Stacy exclaimed at last. She bent double and wheezed. "Can't keep up. Maybe you go ahead and we'll follow."

"No way," said Dylan. "We gotta stick together. Maybe just tell Jim Brown here to cool it."

Red's face split into a grin at being compared to one of his heroes. "Can do," he said, smiling at Dylan who, recognizing the moment for what it was, grinned back. "Y'all know where we're going?"

"Mostly away from the men with guns," Stacy said.

"Right. But I meant . . ."

"I used to come out here with my old man," said Dylan. "It wasn't all closed off then. I think there are some campgrounds a little further, and some storage buildings, maybe a barracks. There's a good chance it'll be crawling with more men with the guns," Dylan conceded, "but it's as good a place as any for them to be holding Andy."

"If he's under guard in some concrete bunker we won't be getting him out," said Red.

"True," said Stacy. "But maybe they just shut him in somewhere and the guards are doing other stuff. It's a busy night."

"OK," Red conceded. "So we press on and see what we can see."

"At the fork, bear left," said Dylan.

"Yeah?" said Red. "You remember it that well?"

"Honestly, no. More hunch than memory."

"Okay," said Red. "Left it is. You ready?"

Stacy straightened up. "Absolutely not."

"But we're gonna do it anyway?" asked Dylan.

"Oh, hell yes," she replied.

Red nodded, then began to jog.

"Ugh, I knew there was a reason I didn't hang out with you guys," said Dylan, following.

They ran for another 10 minutes, getting off of the road once and taking cover among the boulders and sun-blasted trees when a truck loaded with troops came barreling out of the dark and sped past them. They held their positions, crouching in the momentary red glow of the truck's tail lights, and then they were out and running again.

"Came from over yonder," said Red.

"Yonder?" Dylan echoed dryly. "Dude, you get to be Jim Brown 'cause you're . . ."

"Brown?" Red finished for him.

"I was gonna say *crazy strong and fast*, ok? But that means you can't also be John Wayne. If any of us are gonna be cowboys, it's me."

"Leaving me to be . . . ?" Stacy began, then changed her mind. "No, don't answer that. You'll only get it wrong and then I'll have to kick your asses."

"None of this changes that the trucks came from over there," said Red. "And if my eyes haven't stopped working entirely I think I can see . . ."

"A light," said Dylan. "And those are tents. And trucks."

"You think Andy might be . . . ?"

"Over yonder?" Dylan took a wide stance as if he just got off a horse. "Reckon he might."

Stacy shook her head and led the way, keeping low and quiet.

The light was a battery lantern mounted on a pole amidst a cluster of tents with a couple of lean-tos and a pair of silent, stationary trucks like the one that had sped past them. There was no sign of life anywhere in the camp.

Stacy held up her hand to stop the others from following after her, and then she inched closer to the first khaki tent. She moved slowly and noiselessly, picking her way across the uneven ground as if she was in a mine field.

Dylan crouched behind a rock a few yards away, his breath held. Red had drawn a folding pocketknife, though he knew exactly how much use that would be if the camp turned out to be guarded. He watched as Stacy crept up to the first tent, stooped at the entrance and, with almost impossible slowness, pulled the canvas flap back an inch. She hesitated, then opened it wider, turned back to them and shook her head. The tension which had been in her every movement evaporated, and they knew the tent was empty.

She moved on to the next, and the next, then—her posture more relaxed now—inspected the sheds, ending with an exaggerated shrug, hands upraised.

*Deserted.*

Red and Dylan stood up and came to join her.

"So if he's not here, now what?" said Red.

"I don't know what else there is in this direction," Dylan replied, "but if we're basically wandering the desert at random, we'll be caught before we find him, assuming he's out here to be found."

"As opposed to . . . ?" Stacy asked.

"Assuming he's still alive," said Dylan, speaking quickly and holding up a hand before she could interrupt, "they'll have taken him somewhere more secure."

"Then there's nothing we can do," said Red.

Stacy turned to say something stern to him, but leapt half out of her shoes.

A horn had blared. One of the parked trucks. It shattered the tranquil night, stuttered into silence, then blared again.

"What the hell?" Dylan said. He was turning to run, but Stacy caught hold of him.

"Wait," she said. She ran lightly over to the truck, peered inside, then turned back to them, her face lit with a smile as bright as a headlamp. She yanked the driver's side door open.

The cab wasn't fully separated from the rear section. Through the partition they could make out a pale shape. Red stared for a long second before realizing it was a foot wearing a dusty Chuck Taylor sneaker.

"You have got to be kidding me," he said.

Andy was gagged and his hands cuffed behind his back and anchored to a ring in the truck bed by a chain, but he had been able to wiggle his leg into the cab to stab at the horn. By the time Red made it over there, Stacy had removed his gag. He rolled and spat.

"Let me guess," said Red, "you talked too much."

"What the hell kept you idiots?" Andy fired back.

"You have no idea," said Stacy.

"Can you get me out or what?" said Andy, squirming so he could see the padlock on the end of his chain.

"I'll get a rock," said Red.

"That's the master escape plan?" said Andy in disbelief. "*I'll get a rock?*"

"What am I?" Red asked. "A safe breaker?"

Dylan cocked his head, listening. "Be quick," he said. "I hear a chopper coming."

○     ○

As the terrain got worse Van decided they couldn't risk driving without their lights on. Even with them, he could see dangerously little.

"I don't know what we're looking for," he said. "Wait. The road splits."

"Go right," said Danny.

He spoke with such certainty that Van gave him an inquiring look. Danny shook his head. "Just a feeling," he said.

"Better than nothing," said Van, pulling the truck to the right. He checked his cracked mirror. Sam was still behind them astride the Norton, Tammy hunched down behind him, her arms around his waist.

It was all very strange. He almost grinned at the thought, but suddenly he imagined that he could see the world as his mother was doing right now, peering around Sam's body to see the road ahead, except that—almost immediately—it wasn't a motorcycle beneath him but a horse, plodding its way across the New Mexico landscape as the sky burned . . .

"You OK?" said Danny.

"Yeah," said Van. "Just remembering stuff. I wish . . ." he hesitated, trying to frame the apology and not knowing how to phrase something so big in words.

"Forget it," said Danny. "Not the crash. The other stuff. You were just a kid."

"I should have trusted you."

"I didn't even trust myself."

Van said nothing, staring hard at the road ahead. It was little more than a track now and curved, following a crescent-shaped ridge that dropped off sharply on the right-hand side. They were high up, and the headlights revealed nothing of the long drop beside them: some kind of steep-sided valley or gorge of the type that ran like cracks through the mountains all over the state. Under the wheels the gravel popped and spat, and Van hunched forward, studying the path ahead, feeling the peril in the darkness on his right like heat from a fire.

Suddenly he saw the lurch of the motorcycle's solitary headlamp as the bike veered to the left and vanished. Van hesitated, then realized too late what had happened.

Out of the blackness came one of the great searchlight trucks.

*Watts.*

It crunched into the pickup's near side taillight, slamming it forward and to the right. Van fought to control the skid, but the power shoving them forward was too great. He braked, and twisted the steering wheel hard, but he couldn't stop it. The Ford tipped to the passenger side, wavered for a moment, and plummeted into the gorge.

○　　○

Sam watched in horror as the searchlight truck he had only narrowly avoided roared past him and slammed into the back of Van's pickup. He watched the little truck fight to hold its ground, but it was no contest. The sheer bulk and power of the military vehicle drove it across the road to the lip of the precipice. It teetered there for a moment, as if the laws of gravity had been momentarily suspended, and there was a kind of silence, as if all sound—including Sam's wail of protest and despair—had been sucked out of the air.

Then it fell.

Sam brought the bike to a halt and got off quickly, throwing his arms around Tammy Sweet who was weeping, fighting to get past him, moaning the names of her son and her one-time husband. He was so focused on her that he almost forgot that the searchlight truck had a driver, until he saw him jump down from the cab, and stagger clumsily around to the cliff. He was, it seemed, unarmed, and Sam's first impulse was to release Tammy so he could charge the sheriff, knock him flying over the edge. But by the time he freed himself from Tammy, Watts had started to clamber down the ravine and out of sight.

Sam ran to the front of the searchlight truck, scanning the ground for rocks he might drop on the sheriff, his bloodlust high and raging for vengeance, but when he got there, he froze, spellbound. There was Van's prized F100, lying on its side, its nose badly crumpled by the fall, and its tail somehow twisted, but the drop hadn't been as vertical as Sam had assumed, and it had only fallen about 20 feet. It had caught on an escarpment that was little more than a craggy ledge some 70 or 80 feet above the desert floor. As he watched, it seesawed unsteadily. One false move and it would go crashing the rest of the way down.

And that mattered, because he was pretty sure he saw movement in the cab. Sure enough, as he watched the driver's side door thudded, once, twice, then popped open and Van's arm pushed it, creaking, wide. If Van and his dad could get out before the pickup fell the rest of the way, they might still make it.

But there were other surprises. Because the pickup wasn't the only wreckage in the ravine. Some 20 yards further along the ledge there was something else, large and strange and flickering with uncanny light. Something, Sam knew instantly, not of this world.

# CHAPTER TWENTY

**I**t was not a flying saucer like you saw in the comic books or in the movies. In fact it had no clear aerodynamic properties at all. At first glance it looked almost egg-shaped, but on closer scrutiny in the thin starlight, Sam thought it bulged at one end, like a pear or an avocado. It was larger than the ruined pickup, but not by much, and a portion of one end—though whether that was the front or the back, he had no idea—was partly embedded in the cliffside. He had the impression that the section that was still intact had been part of something considerably bigger, something that had mostly disintegrated in the blast, leaving only this core, like the pit at the heart of a peach.

A dark and inconsistent trail led backward across the desert floor below, as if the craft had hit the ground and bounced up and into the cliff wall. In places fire flickered, as if its propulsion system, or the friction of impact had set the scattering of shrubbery ablaze. Sam stared, momentarily forgetting Watts in his astonishment, scanning the smooth, pulsating surface of the object's surface for signs of that propulsion system, though he saw no jets, no nacelles, no hint of how it might fly. There was an irregular opening at one end—the source of some of the flickering light—though at this distance it was impossible to tell if that was crash damage . . .

*Or a door.*

Sam realized that his breath was held when Tammy came stumbling up beside him, saw the thing, and—feeling its strange power—stood there, speechless.

It was the sight of Watts, crawling spider-like toward the truck, that brought Sam to his senses. "Van!" he called. "Look out! He's coming!"

Though he couldn't see Van's face, Sam knew from the way his body tensed, then quickened that he had heard the warning. The sheriff half turned, his right hand going to his waist, and when it came back into view, something long and metallic glittered in his hands.

"He has a knife!" Sam shouted, though he felt like a spectator yelling warnings at the defenseless hero in a movie.

But Van didn't come around to meet Watts. Rather he fought his way across the cab and dragged the passenger door open. It groaned and shrieked as the misshapen panel snagged on the frame, but he got it open and was soon fighting to get his father out. Sam stared, powerless, as Van tugged at the slumped and seemingly lifeless figure.

Watts made for the tailgate, knife at the ready. It occurred to Sam that he might not be able to see where Van was, though he would surely hear him struggling to get Danny out.

*He's going for the piece of wreckage*, Sam thought, though why the sheriff was still obsessed with that when the rest of the craft was right there, he couldn't say. It was only when Watts stood up, and Sam saw the pistol in his hand that he remembered there were guns in the back of the truck.

O     O

Van heard the click of the pistol being cocked. Watts was going to delay his investigation of the craft, and whatever salvage operation he was aiming to complete, until he had dealt with them. It almost didn't matter to Van, who remained focused on getting his father out. Danny's head was bleeding from where he had hit it on the dash as the pickup went over the edge, and his eyes looked unfocused, but he was still alive. Van felt the truck pivot as Watts moved in the back, and with his hands laced under his father's arms, he made one last pull, leaning back and using every muscle in his body.

Danny finally started to slide free, but then Van felt the shadow of Watts looming over them, and heard the deafening thunder of the first pistol shot. It would have gone through Danny's heart, but the action of dragging him out meant that the bullet went in lower down on his chest and a few inches to the right. His father's eyes went wide but his mouth just gaped, no sound emerging.

Watts resighted along the barrel, but as Danny's body came free from the cab, the pickup's balance point shifted, and the whole thing rocked forward. Watts stumbled, and his next shot went through the roof of the cab. He swore, lost his balance and fell forward, and then the truck was sliding inextricably over the edge.

Van, still holding his father around the chest, rolled hard, and the pickup slid past them. Watts cried out, rage mixed with fear, as he went with it, over and down. There was enough silence before the impact that Van knew the truck had fallen clean. It hit the desert floor and exploded.

Van barely noticed. His attention was on his father, now lying on his back, one hand clamped to the hole in his chest, his eyes rolling as if searching the sky. The gunshot wound was bleeding heavily, spreading under his slick fingers like a poison flower, soaking his shirt and the waist band of his pants.

"Pops," said Van quietly. "Hey, Pops. Come on. Stay with me."

His father's eyes stopped roaming and his brows tightened as his gaze found his son and focused. There was a moment of confusion. "Van?"

"Yeah, Pops. It's me."

"No," said Danny. "Van's a little boy. I carry him right here." He patted the awful, sopping hole in his torso. "We ride together . . ."

"No, Pops." Van's eyes brimmed. "It's me. All grown up."

He almost choked on the phrase, but somehow it helped. His father's clouded brow cleared suddenly, and he smiled as if someone new had walked into his field of vision. "Hey, Van," he said.

"Hey, Pops," Van managed. He was aware of movement behind him, people climbing down the steep slope toward them, but he didn't turn around.

"Got myself shot," said Danny vaguely.

"Yeah," said Van, taking his hand and pressing it to the wound. "We gotta keep the pressure on that. You'll be OK."

His father smiled sadly at the lie but he didn't argue the point. Instead, he tipped his head back, twisting slightly, though that must have hurt considerably, looking along the ledge to the strange pear-shaped craft half wedged into the cliff side. Its erratic, pulsing lights lit his face like holiness.

"Take me to it," he whispered.

"You need to stay where you are . . ." Van sputtered, fighting back the tears, but his father shook his head minutely.

"Please," he breathed. "I have to see."

Van opened his mouth to argue, but he couldn't speak without sobbing, so he slid his fingers under his father's body, right hand under his thighs, left under his shoulders, and tried to sit up.

"Let me help," said Sam, skittering down the rock face. He moved quickly, recklessly, and took hold of Danny's feet.

Van met his mother's eyes as she half-slid down. They looked haunted, distraught. He adjusted his grip and, with

Sam's help, lifted him. He wasn't nearly as heavy as Van had expected.

Tammy hovered, hands to her mouth. "Be careful," she said, as Van inched backwards along the ledge.

There was a rattle of stones, and Van saw other people climbing down toward them. Not the army or the CIA or whatever. Red and Dylan. Stacy. Then . . .

"Andy!" Van gasped.

"I'm OK," said his brother, waving his concern away. "What happened?"

Van tried to speak but the words wouldn't come.

"Watts," said Sam. Then, in a lower voice, "He's hit."

Andy didn't ask for details or clarification, but he scrambled down and ran toward them.

"Is that . . . ?" said Dylan, staring at the strange craft with the inconstant glow.

Sam just looked at him, and Dylan's eyes went round.

"Is it safe?" he asked.

"How the hell would I know?" said Sam, not stopping.

They had reached the curious, rounded hull of the ship now. They set Danny down, and Sam stepped back so that Andy and Tammy could get to him.

"Let me see his wound," said Stacy, easing her way through, but Van couldn't look at her. He knew.

She knelt beside him but, while she would not speak the terror and despair she felt when she saw the hole in his chest, Danny could read it in her face.

"It's OK," he said, soothing her as if she was the one who had been hurt. "It's OK now." And, as if in explanation, he looked at the crashed vessel whose side was partly open so that they could see inside. The shifting, phosphorescent light played over his face more clearly now, and he smiled. "You see it, right?" he said. "You all see it?"

"Yeah," said Andy through his tears.

"I see it," said Tammy, taking his free hand and squeezing it.

"We all see it, Pops," said Van.

"Good," said Danny, so quietly that only those right next to him heard it.

He smiled once more then his eyelids fluttered and closed.

"Pops?" said Van. "Pops?"

The light from the ruined craft flickered across his father's face like a blessing. Stacy put her arm around Van, and then he knew for certain, and turned to her, burying his face in her neck.

O      O

They were like that when the helicopter came overhead, splashing the site with brilliant light, when the soldiers started spilling down the ridge with their guns drawn, shouting commands. They did not move. They were like statues around a grave.

# CHAPTER TWENTY - ONE

Agent Kent sat back and considered Van. The room was empty except for a featureless table with a running reel-to-reel tape recorder, two chairs, and an overhead light that buzzed faintly. It was one of several interview rooms on the base, and Kent had used all of them on this strange and busy night.

He had one mission: to find out what these kids knew—specifically—and what they had seen. So far, any real information on that score had been thin on the ground, but whether that meant they didn't know more, hadn't seen more than what had been paraded across the night sky for the whole town to behold, he didn't know. What would happen after he learned what they knew, he didn't know. Orders would come down from higher up. Some hard decisions would be made. He thanked God it wouldn't be him making them. And that was tomorrow's problem. First, he had to find out what they knew.

"Let's try this again," he said. "Walk me through what you saw after your truck went over the edge."

"After my father died, you mean?" Van asked, an edge of defiance in his tone.

"Exactly."

"What, no *sorry for your loss*?" Van said.

Kent leaned forward and took a steadying breath. "You have our condolences on the death of your father."

"*Our*, meaning . . . ?"

"The military. The CIA. The United States government."

"I'm glad you can speak for them all," said Van dryly. "He could have used some of that support over the last, I don't know, 16 years or so."

Kent said nothing. He knew there was nothing to say.

He had been surprised that the Lopez boys were so calm about their father's death. He had understood them to be a close family, in spite of their father's reputation for paranoia and antisocial behavior, but while they had shown some considerable belligerence—especially the younger boy, whose every other word had been an expletive—neither showed what Kent thought of as grief. Maybe they hadn't actually liked him all that much after all and were glad he was dead, however much it suited their sense of adolescent rebellion to rail at the establishment for its part in his demise.

The others had been no help. Even the mother had sat there in a near catatonic state muttering her answers so quietly he could barely hear her, though he put that down to the trauma of her abduction by the Watts traitor, coupled with the death of her ex-husband. But even though she had somehow seen nothing, she had been a picnic compared to the teenagers. The Negro boy they called "Red" Hauser had stared him down and talked about their infringement of his civil rights. Sam Jenkins had continued to repeat his name in answer to every question, like he was a POW in a movie, though each time he added "no rank, no serial number and never gonna have one," whatever that was supposed to mean. Stacy Nicholson had leaned into a long invective about government concealment of the consequences of nuclear testing, a stream of medical stats and government reports about something called Iodine 131, and local instances of thyroid conditions and cancers. That was fine. If all she knew or cared about was the radiation poisoning, he could cross her off the list. Dylan Sweet had ranted about the death of Chuck Carter, who had been shot by that idiot private. There had been real grief there mixed in with the outrage about the needlessness of the boy's death, as if all they had done was a little harmless trespassing. He said nothing about what they had seen on the base, and, no matter how much Kent pushed him, he couldn't get the kid away from his anger. All that fury and sorrow masked what, if anything, the boy knew. But at least the passion made sense. The Lopez boys, by contrast, were unreadably blank, and that made Kent suspicious.

Van Lopez was the heart of the thing. Kent sensed that much. He probably knew more than the others, but he was saying even less. He had requested a note pad at the start of the interview, and Kent had got one for him from a supply closet, thinking that maybe the boy was a bit slow and might give up more in pictures than he could put into words. That impression hadn't lasted. Lopez had started sketching immediately and with total absorption, but it was just scribbles, a mass of meaningless pencil strokes. When he filled one page with blackness, he went on to the next, and the next. Each was slightly different, some more deeply shaded, or hinting at some deep pattern, but it was all still nonsense. Each finished sheet went under the pad, and he started on another, avoiding Kent's eyes even when answering his questions.

Or not answering. Kent still didn't know what they had seen and was beginning to wonder if they knew anything at all, even though they had all been found mere yards from the wreckage of what was being referred to officially as a non-essential satellite. It had been a tense and difficult night, full of strangeness and horrors big and small, but there was something else that Kent couldn't put his finger on: a hazy quality around the memories of all who had been involved. Not just the kids. His own men should have been bouncing off the walls at what they had seen tonight, but there was a fogginess about the way they conducted themselves, and twice Kent had had to remind people of things that should have been branded into their minds for eternity. It wasn't that their memories were blank. It was more that their minds seemed to move around or past key events and images.

*Moved around, or were moved around by something else?*

That was the question. He'd ask soldiers and agents to report on what they had seen, and they'd get a vague, hunted look in their eyes. When he prompted them, they'd remember, and be surprised both by what they recalled and the fact that it had slipped their minds, but a few minutes later it seemed to be gone again.

*Slipped their minds*, thought Kent, wondering about the phrase. It felt right, like the thing forgotten had a life of its own, an intelligence. It had been caught unexpectedly, briefly caged in someone's head, but it had keys, maps, tunnels, and when the guards weren't looking, it found its way out . . .

Even he had felt it, a sudden uncertainty about what he was doing there, what he was asking them about, as if he wasn't sure himself. Like he had forgotten what he was doing, what he had seen. It made no sense. Each time it happened he'd concentrate, and it would eventually swim back into focus, mostly. But a few minutes later he would feel that cloudy vagueness settling back into his head, and he'd have to rethink, to force himself to remember. Kent rubbed his face, pushing these preposterous ideas out of his mind in order to focus on the task at hand. If nothing else, it made sense that these kids might not know anything at all, or if they had known something, they had subsequently forgotten it. Still, he had to be sure. He stared at Van Lopez, opting for the direct approach.

"Was there anything else with you on the ridge close to the truck?"

"Stones," said Van, eyes on his paper. "Boulders. Some bushes."

"I mean other than features of the landscape," said Kent with studied patience.

"Like trash or something? Coke cans or whatever? I don't think so."

"Anything larger?" said Kent, moving around the subject like a man defusing a bomb. "Anything unusual?"

"Thought I saw some cushion buckwheat," said Van, scratching away with his pencil.

"Some what?" Kent replied, his curiosity piqued.

"Kind of wildflower," said Van. "Don't usually see them in this part of the state."

Kent sat back again. "Are you fucking with me?" he asked.

The boy shook his head very slowly, eyes still down. "Just working on my drawing," he said at last. "Mind if I take it with me?"

Kent just shrugged and looked away. This was going nowhere.

There was a knock at the door and an aide poked his head in.

"There's a call for you, sir," said the aide.

"Who is it?" Kent snapped.

"Someone from something called..." the aide checked a note, "the Maynard Consortium?"

The name hung between them for a moment, then Kent gritted his teeth and nodded resignedly.

"I'll be right there," he said.

O    O

Van and Andy sat with their mother in the back of the army transport truck, with Stacy, Dylan, and Red in the row in front of them. Sam had pointedly taken a seat up front and stared in stony silence at the unit commander throughout the journey, till Van started to feel a little sorry for the soldier, who clearly had no idea what was going on. No one spoke as they rode back into town, but there was a shared sense of looking at the familiar buildings—the school, Monty's diner, even their own houses—as if they were seeing them for the first time. It wasn't just that those places were now marked by memories that would always be bound to trauma and sadness. It was as if the people they were had been changed in some profound way, as if they had crossed into adulthood not as ordinary humans did, but like some insects, who change their entire form and means of perception, emerging from their chrysalises as unrecognizable shapes. They had new senses now and the world looked, smelled, and tasted different. It was, if nothing else, so much bigger than they had assumed, so much stranger than they had been taught.

To fill the silence, the driver clicked on the radio and in between the ballads and the doo-wop, there was Stevie Fly, languid and cool as ever, telling them "the whole skinny" on tales of a downed satellite, the murders of local restaurateur Monty Sanderson and the gang known as the Tunnel Snakes at the hands of ("and I swear by all that's holy this is what we're being told") an honest to God Soviet agent the whole town had known as Sheriff Bobby Watts, the accidental death of a high school kid called Chuck Carter, and the incredible actions of Trinity's least probable hero,

Danny Lopez, and a number of local kids. He began listing their names, but Sam Jenkins reached over and turned it off. When the driver protested, Sam gave him his practiced *whatchyagonnadoaboutit?* stare.

The rest of them said nothing, though they exchanged loaded looks at that part about the satellite. Red smirked to himself and stared out of the window. Back near the base they had passed a heavy-duty mobile crane and its crew speeding back up to the cliff. No one thought they were looking to recover the Lopez truck. But they had all given the same story to agent Kent and his team, which is to say that they had all said nothing.

Back home, Van dumped a dozen sheets of note paper all covered in scribbled pencil onto the kitchen table and his brother stood over him with a quizzical look on his face.

"Pops told me about the money," he said.

"What money?" said Andy.

"My college fund," said Van.

"Oh. Right. Yeah. It won't get you all the way there but . . ."

"I'll find the rest. Thank you."

"Of course," said Andy with a shrug, as if nothing could be less important.

"I'll do the same for you when it's your turn," said Van.

"Not sure I'm the college type," said Andy.

"Are you the get-the-hell-out-of-Trinity-type?"

"Oh hell, yes."

"Then, like I said," Van concluded, "I'll do the same for you."

Andy put a hand on his shoulder, then leaned over and began pushing the sheets of pencil sketch around. At first it was casual, then it became earnest, frantic even, his hands sweeping the pages around, lining up their edges until a larger pattern began to emerge out of the fragments. When it was done, and the tabletop was entirely covered in a great gray and black rectangle, he became suddenly still, then climbed onto a chair so he could look down on the whole. His eyes seemed to struggle to make sense of what he was seeing, but then they adjusted, and he saw.

Taken as a whole, the picture was a stylized and heavily shaded sketch of a dark, cave-like hollow, but too smooth in its lines to be a rock formation. Metal, then. But strange metal. It was sleek and shadowed, and there were points of light, some of which might have been controls. For all the lights, however, the overwhelming sense of the thing was its darkness, which spilled out like a pool. At its deepest, in the very heart of the image, was . . . something else. A form, not quite human and not quite insect.

Andy tipped his head in wonder, gazing into the creature's eyes. "I remember," he whispered in awe. "It had sort of slipped from my mind—how is that possible?"

"I don't know."

"But now I see it and I remember."

Van remembered too, the way the being had locked eyes with theirs, the way his father had sighed and smiled when he saw it, as if he had known it all his life but had somehow forgotten . . .

"I don't know what it is," said Van, "and I don't know why it was up there, or why it came down, but I *felt* it somehow. Like it touched our minds, touched Pops. It knew who we were. I'm pretty sure I saw it the night you got beat up by the Tunnel Snakes. Over the quarry, and even then I felt sort of connected to it. I don't know why or how, but it reached him, Pops I mean, and . . ." He sought for the words, knowing they would sound stupid and inadequate, and finally he said, "He died happy because of it."

Andy listened then nodded his slow agreement.

○        ○

The funerals were separate, but they came together by a kind of social osmosis, fanned in part by Stevie Fly, Trinity's unofficial one-man chamber of commerce. They gathered in the town square to share a moment of silence, make speeches, talk about civic pride and the place of the dead in the thoughts of the living. Some of it was hollow and posturing, as such things often are, and some of it was real and heartfelt. The mayor spoke. Some friends and family members of the deceased offered a few words, even managing to paint Vince Reed and his boys as misguided angels cut off before they could get their lives on track, while Jim Reynolds—now acting sheriff—stood by, his hat in his hands and his eyes down. But it was Red's speech about Danny Lopez that drew the media coverage.

He read from a letter that Andy had found while going through his father's things. In it, Danny apologized for what he hadn't gotten right, for his failure to be the father he wanted to be, though he had tried to keep his boys safe and secure. He said that he regretted that he had let fear control his life, that there was so much to say and do in the world that he had missed out on, and that they should not.

"There is danger and strangeness in the world," Red said, looking up from the paper in his hands, "but there is also wonder and mystery that is so much bigger than ourselves. We are all connected in ways we cannot begin to understand. Your tribes, your differences, they mean nothing. Do not let your lives be controlled by your fear of things you don't know, or people you don't understand."

Red let that thought hang in the hot Nevada air and, for the briefest of moments, it was like everyone knew he was right, knew that they had misjudged Danny, and a whole lot of other people, Red included, and that they ought to do better, to be better.

The briefest of moments.

The death of Sheriff Robert—Bobby—Watts and the truth of who he was and what he had been doing, though somewhat shrouded in mystery, had caused a ripple of baffled horror through the community. It wasn't just that they had known him, it was that as the head of local law enforcement he represented what many thought of as the official version of "us." That he should turn out to be "them," the enemy of all things they took to be synonymous with American values was, for many, like finding a tiger in your kitchen. It was more than surprising. It upended their sense of how the world worked, maybe even what the world was.

It didn't last, of course. Some folks may have briefly had a heart-to-heart with their core assumptions, but for most the example of Sheriff Watts merely confirmed old beliefs: that the enemy were everywhere and had to be guarded against, that patriotic Americans needed to dig in, to seize what they took to be normal and fuse it at the molecular level with what they took to be right. That didn't coincide with the lessons from Danny's letter, and you knew which would win out in a place like Trinity: on one hand, confident moral superiority and a clear sense of who was in and who was out—on the other, the riskiness of expanding minds, including those who had been pushed out, all for the gossamer possibility of hope.

It was, I suppose, the way of things.

Not for everyone, though. Sam Jenkins managed to flunk his army physical by smoking four packs of cigarettes on the day of the test, a dodge that diverted the worst of his family's disappointment. Sam came out of the recruiting office dancing, waving the proof of his "physical incapacity" over his head like a check for a million dollars, but the perceived failure hung over the family home like a storm cloud. A year after graduating from high school, Sam left Trinity and headed east. I got postcards from Philadelphia, Washington, D.C., and New York. Over the next few years, I saw similar postcards pinned up on the wall over the counter in Monty's diner—which was renamed Hauser's and featured Red's more adventurous menu which was known to occasionally bring foodie tourists all the way from Vegas. We went there the day of the funeral, we didn't know where else to go, and Red made us another round of his incredible barbecue sandwich. The diner was a tricky business, as Monty had no family and had made no will. In the end, Red became the manager and head cook, and Hank Sweet helped to pull together a consortium of local lenders to shoulder most of the costs. It worked well for a time, but it was only four years before Red sold his stake in the diner and moved on, completing his great grandparents' journey to California, so that their decades in Nevada looked, from the view of a larger history, like a kind of rest stop.

Dylan stayed in Trinity. Eventually, he got a job working for his dad's firm and was, I guess, good at it.

Andy and I went out for a burger with him the summer after my first year of college, and we talked mostly about our time in high school; hearing stories that we knew so well being told from the other side, the Sweater side, made us realize how different and yet how similar we all really were. But when I tried to reminisce about that one great, terrible night together, when we had witnessed something impossible fall from the sky, his face glazed over.

"That was the night the sheriff killed all those people, right?" he said vaguely, like he was recalling something he had read about in the newspaper.

Andy gave him an odd look. "You remember the truck crash on the cliff, right? The craft?"

"The craft?" Dylan repeated blankly. "Oh, you mean the stories about the satellite that came down, and all that malarky?"

He laughed as he said it, as if we were all kidding around. Like we knew it was all bull.

"No," said Andy, his eyes narrow with bewilderment and the beginnings of irritation. "It wasn't a satellite. You remember, right? You saw it!"

"Me?" he said, and something chased across his face, something uncertain and cautious. I couldn't decide if he genuinely didn't remember or if he just didn't want to.

"Yeah," Andy insisted. "You were there, man! How can you not . . . ?"

"It's OK," I said, putting a hand on his arm. "Leave it."

Andy stared at me, aghast, but then the waitress arrived with a tray of drinks and Dylan turned to her with something like relief. His face cleared, and it was as if the conversation we had been in the middle of had never happened.

I felt the opposite. I felt as if that day in the desert was going to shape my life. My memory of the moment is inconsistent, but it has never been as bad as Dylan's. I mark my calendar with a specific instruction for the last day of every month, and, even if I don't quite recall why, I go with Stacy and Andy—if he's around—and we get my old art folder out of the attic and lay out the pages I sketched in the interrogation rooms while it was all still fresh. Every month we look, and we remember. Every month we wrestle with the strangeness of having forgotten, and every month we make our appointment for 30 days in the future.

Because it's not just about remembering what happened, what we saw. It's about what that means, and about holding it consciously so that it doesn't become merely a shadow in my mind as it was for my father, an uncertain hollow that left him incomplete and fearful. It reminds me of the scale of the universe, its vast and staggering unknowableness, and it makes me want to make more memories all the time, hammering them out with action, with travel, with adventure, with passion and emotional risk. It makes me want to shun the persistent greyness that so many people slip into in the pursuit of normality. Memories have to be forged, and forging takes both effort and heat. We remember what is untypical, what is intense, earned, and charged with the joys and discoveries that make life worth living.

Pops's letter, the one Red Hauser read aloud at his funeral, ended with this: "Live your lives as I should have. Chase mystery. Embrace the unknown. Don't be afraid. That above all. Don't be afraid."

I thought of that a few weeks later as Stacy and I drove out of town for college, for California, and for the rest of our lives. The future was laid out in front of us like the long stretch of desert road under that wide blue sky. We knew things about that sky, things other people didn't, and though it scared me, it also filled me with excitement, with a sense of discovery and the thrill of possibility. It hummed through my body like the vibrations of our old truck. Stacy felt it, too. She turned and smiled, wide as the road, wide as the horizon itself, and I knew we were heading toward good things.

# THE END